W9-ATT-461

DANCE IN THE DARK

ALSO BY TERENCE FAHERTY

A SCOTT ELLIOTT MYSTERY

DANCE IN THE DARK

TERENCE FAHERTY

FIVE STAR
A part of Gale, Cengage Learning

GALE
CENGAGE Learning

Detroit • New York • San Francisco • New Haven, Conn • Waterville, Maine • London

GALE
CENGAGE Learning™

LIBRARY OF CONGRESS CATALOGING-IN-PUBLICATION DATA

Faherty, Terence.
  Dance in the dark : a Scott Elliott mystery / Terence Faherty.
  — 1st ed.
    p. cm.
  ISBN-13: 978-1-59414-957-3 (hardcover)
  ISBN-10: 1-59414-957-7 (hardcover)
  1. Elliott, Scott (Fictitious character)—Fiction. 2. Private investigators—California—Los Angeles—Fiction. 3. Runaways—Fiction. 4. Motion picture industry—Fiction. 5. Hollywood (Los Angeles, Calif.)—Fiction. 6. California—History—20th century—Fiction. I. Title.
  PS3556.A342D36 2011
  813'.54—dc22   2010051993

First Edition. First Printing: April 2011.
Published in 2011 in conjunction with Tekno Books and Ed Gorman.

Printed in the United States of America
1 2 3 4 5 6 7 15 14 13 12 11

For Jim Huang

ONE

"You used to be a nice guy pretending to be tough. Now you're the character you used to play at."

"Come again?" I said.

"You used to be a sweet guy, somebody who had to think about how to make a fist," Ella said, speaking slowly and using short words. "Now you're one of Paddy's hard cases. His last one. His life's work, as it's turned out."

"Let's leave Paddy out of this," I said. "He's got his own troubles."

I tried to say it lightly, but Ella still sprang from her chair and stalked to the window. From the strain across the shoulders of her pink cashmere sweater, I guessed that she had her palms pressed together.

When she didn't speak for a ten count, I said, "It happens, you know. Playing the same part too long. Duke Wayne was born in Iowa. But he's spent so much time in the saddle—"

"Shut up about the movies," Ella said. "I don't want to hear about the movies."

That was more comeback than I'd been after. It surprised me both because Ella and I didn't often tell each other to shut up, even after twenty years of marriage, and because we both owed a lot to the movies. Our professions, for starters. Ella was a successful screenwriter. I was a professional tough guy, an operative for an almost-defunct security company that had, in its glory days, milked the big studios like its private herd of

Holsteins. Prior to that and to an intervening stint in the Army, I'd had an even closer relationship to the motion picture industry. I'd been an actor, though that happy time was getting harder and harder to recall.

Ella and I even owed our being together to the movies. We'd met when Warner Bros. had hired Hollywood Security to save a movie from a scandal. Ella had been a Warners publicist then, and there'd been something between us from the get-go, "the old curling iron in the pants," as my boss, Patrick J. Maguire, once described love at first sight. I could still see Ella as she'd been then, a petite woman who carried herself like a showgirl, with under-the-radar blonde hair, a slightly cockeyed nose, and watercolor-blue eyes. I could never dance with her back then without fighting the urge to carry her off. Now, in 1969, after two decades of me and two kids, she was still that beautiful. I saw the few gray hairs, so far unretouched, in her now-short hair and the laugh lines around her eyes as mine, my life's work as I was Paddy's. My work and the kids'.

One of my fellow laborers briefly appeared in the doorway to the living room and then flitted away. It was our daughter Gabrielle, who was just old enough now to hate the nickname Gabby, which I couldn't stop calling her. She'd been on the edge of things ever since word had come about her brother being missing in action. Tall and skinny and, like me, dark-haired, she couldn't seem to settle down, didn't seem to want more contact than a fleeting hug. But she couldn't stray far from us, either. We'd been promised a follow-up call from a high-ranking friend at Fort Ord, and whenever the phone rang, Gabby was right there.

Her restlessness was something else she'd gotten from me. It was all I could do to sit there on the sofa and play punching bag for Ella. So far, she'd blamed me for letting Billy go to Vietnam and before that for letting him join the Army and before that for letting him play with my medal from World War II and before that for letting her name him after her brother, who'd been killed fighting in France. All of which was as unreasonable as it was understandable. I'd stood up under it—or at least sat still through it—because I knew what Ella was feeling and I couldn't do anything else for her. She wasn't interested in hugs, however fleeting. Wasn't interested in anything except the phone ringing.

Our living room had been redecorated about every other year we'd lived in our house in Doyle Heights. Ella liked to give work to aspiring set designers, which in Hollywood were as thick on the ground as would-be Natalie Woods. The last one who'd blown through had been into neon colors and severely modern pieces, the latter an old weakness of Ella's. As a result, the room we occupied was way too bright and spare for the scene we were playing in it. It was like doing Ibsen on the set of *Laugh-In*.

The one right note was the photo of Billy that sat on a coffee table shaped like the flight deck of the carrier *Enterprise*. It was his service portrait, so he wasn't grinning, as he was in almost every other photograph he'd ever had taken. Still, you could see he was thinking about it. He was that proud of his uniform, of himself. He was Ella's kid through and through in that picture, tow-headed and clear-eyed. He even had his mother's wandering nose, his courtesy of a collision with a second baseman.

In my Army days, most service portraits had been hand-tinted, which had given them a storybook quality that was somehow perfect for my romanticized, celebrated war. Billy's war was anything but romanticized. It came to us every night straight out of the television, without the benefit of editing or musical score or patriotic subtext. Billy's photo was in step with this modern take, being totally unretouched, his acne scars as clear as his promise.

I caught myself starting to think of the young man who'd sat for that portrait and yanked myself back, as I had every time my foot had strayed toward that pit. Ella seemed to read my mind—or my attempt to make my mind an unreadable blank. She turned on me, and I heard the bell for another round.

"I remember your telling me about a whole squad of men getting killed at Bastogne. You didn't cry a tear the night you told me. So I guess I shouldn't expect any for Billy."

I hadn't told her that story. Paddy had, and behind my back. I'd only admitted to its being true. I didn't point that out, though. I also didn't point out that this new offense exonerated Paddy of the charge of turning me into a thug. Ella and I had had that heart-to-heart about the war way back when I was supposedly still a sweet guy only pretending to be soul dead. I didn't even observe that Ella herself hadn't done any crying yet for Billy, that she'd been too angry to. I tried to say instead that it was too early to give up hope.

"We don't know—"

The phone cut me off. Gabby was in the doorway immediately. My impression was that she'd actually gotten there a beat before the first ring.

Ella picked up the phone almost as quickly. Her hello was a whisper compared to the tone she'd been using on me. A second later, her expression went from frightened anticipation to everyday annoyance. Gabby melted away.

"Can he call you later?" Ella asked, cutting off, I was sure, whatever the other party had been trying to say. She listened for a few more words and then held the phone out to me.

"It's Forrest Combs," she said, her palm almost over the receiver. "Get rid of him."

"Scotty," Combs said, before I quite got the phone to my ear. "What's wrong?"

"Family trouble," I said. "What can I do for you?"

"I've got family trouble, too, Scotty. The worst kind." He added after a pause, "Miranda's run away," Miranda being his daughter, who was a couple years older than Gabby. "She's been gone for four days. *Four days.* You've got to help me find her. I'm going out of my mind."

Combs sounded close to tears, reminding me of Ella's charge against me. Reminding me of it and convincing me that it was true, which did nothing for my bedside manner.

"Have you talked to the police?"

"This is Los Angeles. Runaway teenagers get as much attention here as stolen bicycles. Yes, I've spoken to them. All they did was fill out forms."

"Look, Forrest. I've got a lot going on right now. Maybe next week—"

"The trail's almost cold now, Scotty. Next week there'll be no trace of it. We have to act. Nothing else you have to do is as important as this."

I could have won that point, but only by telling Combs about my own family troubles. And even that wouldn't have carried the whole debate. Not from Combs's point of view.

He was crying plainly now. "You'll be saving at least one life, Scotty. Miranda's life may be in danger. I feel that, though I've no way to be sure. But I know I won't survive if I lose her. I won't want to survive."

I'd had that bluff used on me before, and I'd always been able to call it. But not on this particular day.

"I'll be right over," I said.

It was very quiet in the room when I hung up the phone. Ella seemed almost calm as she said, "You can't be thinking of leaving."

"I'm not doing Billy any good sitting here."

"You'd better ask Forrest—" She cut herself off. I wasn't sure how she would have ended that sentence, but I thought it might

11

have involved Combs renting me a room.

I wouldn't have asked her even if she hadn't walked out, balled fists unmoving at her sides. Gabby took her place.

"I'll call Mr. Combs and say I'm not coming," I told her.

"Don't do that," Gabby said. "You've got to go."

"Miranda will be okay," I said.

"Who cares about her? I'm worried about you and Mom, what'll happen if you stay. She'll keep beating on you, saying things she'll hate herself for saying. She almost just told you not to come back. She's breaking strands, Dad."

Gabby assumed I'd understand that cryptic closer, and I did. She was an aspiring poet with theories about almost everything—a trait she'd inherited from her mother—theories she loved to bounce off me. One of her best involved marriage, or really the bonds that hold married people together. They weren't the heavy chains of popular imagination, Gabby had once told me. They were tiny filaments built up over time. Individually, no one strand could hold two soap bubbles together, never mind two human beings. But collectively all the shared memories and intimacies and tiny acts of kindness were very strong. A marriage withered, in Gabby's view, when a couple stopped adding to their strands and began to pluck at the ones they had.

"Go now," she said.

"I'll call," I said. "Stay close to your mother."

"Right, Chief."

Two

Forrest Combs had once owned a very valuable piece of real estate, a house on Mulholland Drive, on the crest of the Santa Monica Mountains, high above the smog of Los Angeles. He'd picked it up when he'd hit Hollywood in the early forties, a young, blond Englishman imported to play the junior officer in one war film after another. Then the war had ended and films about it—especially films celebrating the British side of things—became less of a staple.

He'd still been on top of that mountain when I'd met him in 1948, but he'd already been struggling to hold on to his piece of the sky. That struggle carried him right through the fifties, through years of bit parts in movies and decent ones in television, followed by years of bits on TV and no movie work to speak of. Then, sometime in the early sixties, I'd spotted a for-sale sign in the yard of Combs's house. I hadn't stopped to ask about it or to commiserate. I'd seen similar signs on nearly every piece of Hollywood by then, movie studios included. Shortly afterward, the wedding anniversary card that Combs inevitably sent to Ella and me acquired a much less prestigious return address.

The address was in the valley that had once been a hazy backdrop for Combs's tennis court, the San Fernando Valley, LA's gigantic overflow basin. Now his lost mountaintop was background for his cookie-cutter ranch, one of about ten thousand almost identical homes in the valley. There were a few million more in the sprawling suburbs of our sprawling nation, and I wondered, as I parked my car on Combs's cracked concrete drive, if growing up in these faceless neighborhoods was what had caused the current crop of teenagers to place such a high value on individuality. And on being somewhere, anywhere, else.

Combs interrupted the sociology class by opening his front door and waving me inside. He was tall and thin with delicate, almost feminine features that went well with his yellow hair. He was the kind of man who looks boyish for decades and then all of a sudden doesn't anymore. Combs's crash had come about ten years back and had had a very specific cause: the death of his wife.

"Scotty, thank God," he said, still holding the door for me like a good butler. "You made great time."

That was a natural lead-in to a comment on the traffic, a subject we locals often used for small talk, our weather not being varied enough to hold our interest. I let the opening pass. I could see at a glance that Combs was in no shape for chitchat. His short-sleeved white shirt with the baby-blue windowpane plaid was into its second or maybe third day of continuous service, and he hadn't shaved recently. His breath, I noted as I stepped past him in the doorway, was high-test.

He wasn't making a secret of his drinking, either. "Can I get you anything, Scotty? A Gibson, perhaps? Or is it too early?"

"A little early," I said, though it wasn't particularly. I wouldn't take a drink for the same reason I wouldn't indulge the pressing memories of Billy. Because if I did, I'd be signing off for God knew how long.

The front room was furnished in pieces so nondescript they'd probably come with the house. There were two exceptions. One was either a very large drinks cart or a very small bar. It was made of wrought iron, and Combs might have picked it up at

14

John Barrymore's estate sale. While I found a seat, he crossed to the relic and poured scotch in a glass that had plenty of room for it, as it contained no ice. The scotch was drugstore quality, and the cigarette Combs lit to go with it was a Parliament, which, despite its name, was no more English than Una Merkel. It had been Dunhills or nothing for Combs once.

"What's wrong with Ella?" Combs asked. "She wasn't herself on the phone."

"Who is, these days?" I answered, knowing that would deflect what interest Combs had.

He caromed nicely. "It is a strange time. An ugly time. It's Vietnam. It's this damn war."

He studied my reaction, and I worked at not having one. I didn't exactly expect a painful question. Combs shouldn't have known that I had a son in that damn war. Still, I set my jaw.

Finally, he said, "No objections, Scotty? I'm a little surprised. You held your country's commission once, didn't you?"

"No," I said. "I was a corporal. All I held was a low draft number. Let's talk about Miranda."

"Miranda," Combs said and took a long drink. He'd been in a hurry on the phone. Now he wasn't. "When did you last see her?"

"It's been a few years," I said, thinking back to a chance meeting one afternoon at a crowded Hollywood Bowl. Combs had had his daughter in tow, and Ella and I had had the kids. Miranda had looked like a ten-year-old on stilts, still a kid compared to Billy but obviously not so next to Gabby. So she'd been around thirteen then and had to be sixteen or seventeen now.

"You wouldn't know her," Combs said. "Or maybe you would. You knew her mother."

He looked toward the other object in the room that didn't match the decor, a large oil painting of a gorgeous blonde,

Combs's late wife, Betty Ann. The brushwork of the portrait was first rate, but the pose leaned a little toward cheesecake. That is, Betty Ann leaned a little that way, leaned toward the viewer to display a line of cleavage as long as a presidential campaign. The pose reminded me that she'd been a burlesque star when I'd first met her. A headliner. I wondered if the painter had worked from one of her publicity stills.

The portrait took me back to the night Ella and I had caught her act at the old Avalon Theater. I'd gone there to break up Betty Ann's romance with Combs, at the request of the nervous producer of a picture Combs had just signed to do. Ella had tagged along to see that I didn't save Combs by throwing myself on the grenade, by which I mean bombshell. It wasn't that big a risk, Ella and I being only a day or so away from tying the knot. By the end of that case, we were safely married, and Combs and Betty Ann were on their way to the same chapel, a co-incidence Combs celebrated with his annual anniversary card to us.

He confirmed my guess about the painting. "I had that done after she passed. The artist worked from one of her old photographs. She wanted to be remembered that way. Not the way the cancer left her."

I thought of the photo of Billy in his uniform. Luckily, Combs kept talking.

"Miranda is her mother's daughter. Intelligent, independent, headstrong. And beautiful. So beautiful. I was a fool to think I could raise her by myself. She was only seven when Betty Ann died. Imagine what it would be like for you without Ella, Scotty."

I'd been doing my best not to imagine that. "How long has Miranda been missing? Four days, did you say?"

"Yes. She left for school as usual on Friday. Reseda High. The school called later that morning to ask where she was. I checked her room and found that her suitcase was gone. And her favorite clothes. She must have packed her bag and slipped it out the window so she could pick it up as she left."

"Your first reaction was that she'd run, not that something had happened to her?"

"Yes," Combs said to his half-empty glass. "You see, this isn't the first time it's happened. Miranda ran away last spring. That time I thought first of kidnappers and auto accidents. This time, I knew to check her closet."

"When last spring did she run off?"

"It was six months ago. In April."

"Where did she go that time?"

"I'm not sure who she stayed with. She never told me. I got her back through a call from a man named Ted LeRoy. You may have heard of him."

Combs made it sound like I'd be embarrassed to admit it. I might have been, once.

"I know LeRoy," I said. "I met him a few years ago on a job."

"A stag film maker," Combs said, his voice as prissy as it got. "He phoned me to say that a Miranda Combs had approached him for a job and that she'd claimed to be my daughter. And that she'd insisted on being billed under her real name. I gather that most of LeRoy's actresses try to avoid that.

"At first, I thought this LeRoy might be trying to shake me down. But he insisted that he only wanted to verify Miranda's story. And her age. She'd told LeRoy she was twenty-one, of course. When I told him she was really only seventeen, he couldn't have been more cooperative. He arranged for her to come to his studio and called me when she arrived. I expected a scene, but she came home meek as a kitten. We cried in each other's arms when we got back here. That ended the business, I thought."

I didn't. "How did she happen to go to LeRoy?"

"She'd heard about him from some school chum. That it was

17

an easy way to make money. And a start in pictures, of a sort."

Neither one of us was buying that. I conveyed my disbelief by staring at Combs like he hadn't answered me at all. He showed his by getting up to pace.

"You see the way we're living here, Scotty. I don't need to tell you what it's been like for us financially. We're not poor; I'm not saying that. I've gotten some steady work recently narrating educational films. But it's easy to feel poor in this town, where some people have so much. And if you were once among those lucky few, a normal, middle-class life can seem even more tawdry."

I cut in at that point in the waltz. "Miranda can't remember your glory days. They were gone before she was born."

"She remembers the house on Mulholland Drive that we suddenly had to give up. And there are such things as inherited memories. We don't pass them along in our genes but in our stories, our keepsakes, our attitudes. Don't tell me your children don't know you used to be an actor. They've probably heard so much about your old studio in the thirties—Fox?"

"Paramount."

"About Paramount that they think they were there themselves. Don't tell me you never let them stay up to watch the late show to catch you walking through some shot."

"Getting back to Miranda. So she resented not being rich. How does that get us to Ted LeRoy? Drive-ins pay their help better than he does."

"It wasn't the money, Scotty. It was me. It was the way I've overdone the genteel poverty act. Or perhaps I should say the noble sufferer act. It's ironic, really. You'll recall that you and I met because my romance with Betty Ann was imperiling a motion picture. The producer was afraid that even a breath of scandal would scare off the old British stars he needed to make his production work. I remember thinking how absurd and unfair that was. I don't anymore. Those actors were simply anxious to protect their good names. I understand that now. To preserve my reputation, I've turned down work I thought unsuitable. A good name is all I have left, and I've guarded it jealously."

"Miranda was going right after your good name when she approached LeRoy," I said, seeing daylight at last. "By insisting on being billed as your daughter. Why?"

"Who knows?" Combs waved his empty glass around like he was christening the room. "Teenage rebellion, probably. I only know we have to find her before it's too late. She failed to hurt me with LeRoy, and it frightens me to think what she might try this time. She might even hurt herself to get her name—and mine—in the papers. That's why I told you on the phone I feared for her life. Whether she's punishing me for being a failure or for not saving her mother or for something else doesn't really matter."

It mattered to me. "Let's talk about what that 'something else' might be. Have you ever hit Miranda?"

"Scotty! How could you think that?"

"Hang on, it gets a lot worse. Have you ever molested her?"

I wouldn't have thought to ask that question once. Or been able to ask it so point-blank. But, as Ella had observed, I was a hard case now. And I'd encountered that kind of abuse before, once involving another beautiful daughter of another movie name.

Combs considered throwing his glass or maybe throwing me. Then he said, "Never. Never once, in thought or deed."

"If I find her, I'm going to ask her the same questions. I won't bring her back if I don't like her answers."

"I wouldn't want you to," Combs said, smiling a wan smile. I was a good guy again. I was looking after Miranda, if only hypothetically. "Then you'll find her for me?"

"I'll try."

THREE

Combs gave me a few wallet-size photographs of Miranda and the names and addresses of a couple of her school "chums." I asked about a boyfriend, and he said Miranda didn't currently have one, sounding so puzzled about it that I took him at his word. We didn't talk money. We both understood that I was doing this job on the cuff, which meant I was also doing it on the sly, my boss having no patience with what lawyers called "pro bono" cases.

The photo confirmed that Miranda no longer had one foot on the child dock and the other in the adult canoe. She looked remarkably like her mother, as her mother had looked when I'd met her in 1948. The resemblance might have sent me on a tour of strip clubs around town on the theory that, having failed to cash in on her father's reputation, Miranda might be trying her mother's old route. I didn't start with that hunch: Miranda was underage, and the club owners had to be fastidious about age if they wanted to stay in business. As fastidious as one Ted LeRoy.

Still, Miranda's resemblance to her mother haunted me. If it hadn't been for her insistence on being billed as Miranda Combs when she'd gone to LeRoy, I would have bet that whatever demons she was trying to exorcise had more to do with her mother's past successes than her father's recent failures. If that had been the case, though, if she'd been following some genetic urge to take off her clothes in public or just

21

wallowing in Betty Ann's old shame, I would have expected her to insist on using her mother's stage name, Baker, not her father's.

I started to wonder if Combs had gotten that name business wrong somehow, and that decided me on a visit to Ted LeRoy. I had time for one, as it was still a little early for high school kids to be at home and receiving guests. I didn't think Miranda had gone back to LeRoy—he surely would have called Combs if she had—but it wouldn't hurt to verify what had happened six months back. And there was a slight chance that Miranda had given LeRoy the address or phone number of the place where she'd stayed when she'd run away the first time. In his eagerness to ambush her at LeRoy's studio, Combs might have forgotten to ask about that.

First, though, I had to call home. I pulled into a gas station that had a phone booth under its flying-horse sign. I was driving a '68 Dodge Charger that year, a big two-door with a wide stance and lines that narrowed at the waist. A "Coke-bottle shape," one article had called it, one written by a kid probably. A Jane Russell shape was more like it. I'd managed to get the sports suspension and the big V-8 without springing for the whole R/T package. That package came with racing stripes, the last thing you wanted on a car you planned to use on stakeouts or to tail people. Paddy thought the big, blue coupe with the black vinyl roof was too conspicuous even without the stripes, but he'd thought that about every car I'd ever owned. My kids thought the car was too young for me, Billy especially. He wanted me to give him the Dodge and get something else for myself, a used Rambler maybe.

I would have thought of Billy as I climbed out of the Charger even if I hadn't been planning to call about him. He'd borrowed the car on his last leave before going overseas and had brought it back with a long white scratch above the left wheel well. I ran my hand along that scratch now and decided that the call home could wait. I told myself that I was giving Ella more time to cool down, though I knew that wasn't true. I was giving myself more time, not to cool down but to breathe.

The San Fernando Valley boosters loved to brag about their movie and television studios. But somehow the guidebooks all overlooked the Ted LeRoy Studio, which was located under the flight pattern of the Hollywood-Burbank Airport. They might have missed LeRoy because his operation was modest to a fault. There was almost no signage on the outside of his ex-warehouse, no fancy gate manned by uniformed guards, no information booth with posted times for studio tours, though those tours would have been quite an attraction.

Combs had called LeRoy a stag film maker, but that wasn't strictly true. Stag films were as old as film itself and as popular at a certain class of all-male get-together as cracked ice. They were coarse—almost always involving filmed sex, some of it using prostitutes—and primitive, the products of an underground industry, not people you could track down, like LeRoy.

He made films featuring nudity, as opposed to sex, which kept him on the right side of the jailhouse door. Nudies, as the films were sometimes called, had been pioneered in the late fifties by Russ Meyer. In some respects, the whole decade, with its barely controlled breast fetish, had been foreplay for Meyer's films, though, as was often the case, the buildup had been better than the payoff.

Ted LeRoy was one of Meyer's most devoted imitators, a maker of what he called "adult comedies." Once in my hearing he'd likened them to the pictures Doris Day and Rock Hudson made together, except that "Doris pops a bra strap every other reel."

I'd had the chance to hear that bon mot when Paddy and I visited LeRoy in the early sixties in connection with the disappearance of an Oscar statuette that might have gone missing in the company of one of LeRoy's "actresses." The lead had turned out to be all dead end, but it'd been worth the drive to meet LeRoy, a man who was sure he'd hit on the formula for success. His kind of confidence had been rare in Hollywood in those days.

A quick glance around LeRoy's kingdom as I parked the Charger told me his confidence had been misplaced. The building needed paint and a new window pane or two. The only grass that wasn't dead was the hearty stuff pushing up through the cracks in the parking lot's asphalt.

Inside was a nearly completed set of a locker room. It was being painted by a guy who moved like he hoped the job would last him till retirement. He told me that LeRoy was in the editing room and pointed me toward a lean-to shed built against one of the inside walls. The room's door was closed. There was a movie poster tacked to it, advertising a film called *Valley Vixens*. The layout featured a cheerleader who made Miranda Combs look like Twiggy. Some wag had written across the young lady's chest, "Please use knockers." I did, my knuckles producing a disturbingly hollow sound.

Ted LeRoy was crouched over an editing machine so old it might have had Thomas Edison's initials on it somewhere. He looked over his shoulder, removed some bulletproof reading glasses, and switched off the machine.

When he swiveled on his tall stool to face me, I saw that he hadn't changed much. He was a small man with a big, square face and an almost bigger mouth, a mouth that opened and closed like a ventriloquist dummy's: in a flat line almost the width of his jaw. Above the mouth was a pencil-line mustache and above that a nose that had more red veins than I remembered, an accent picked up by the dull, dark eyes. His scalp was plainly visible through the worst comb-over this side of Zero

Mostel. I couldn't tell how he was dressing these days because he hadn't gotten around to it yet. He wore only a sleeveless undershirt and plaid shorts that might or might not have been a bathing suit.

It struck me that while LeRoy hadn't changed a lot physically, his expression was lacking its old spark. Then he brightened as he placed me.

"I never forget a face," he said proudly. "On names, I'm not so good. You're one of Paddy Maguire's boys, right? How is the old son of Erin?"

"Fine," I said.

"That's not what I hear," LeRoy said, and I remembered something else about him. He was quite the gossip. That was a common failing in Hollywood, maybe the most common, but LeRoy really stood out in the field. During my previous visit, he'd matched Paddy rumor for rumor for an hour, something few people could do.

For the moment, though, he held himself in check. "What can I do for you, Mr. ah . . ."

"Elliott. Scott Elliott."

"Right. In this town, even the errand boys rate stage names. Somebody lose another statuette?"

"No," I said, ignoring the "errand boy" crack. "A daughter."

I told him about Miranda Combs and started to remind him of their meeting, not stopping to think that this same guy had just placed me after a seven-year gap. He flagged me off a little testily.

"I remember the kid. Hell, it was only four or five months back."

"Six months."

"Okay, six. Time flies when you're getting old. You'll find out sooner than you think. So she ran off again, huh? Not so surprising. Something not right there. If you're thinking she came back to see me, you're not the brains of your outfit. She had no reason to. She knows I'd only call her old man. And I told her the last time I couldn't use her. She's built, sure, but like a real woman. I only use the ones built like fantasy women. Longshoreman's fantasies, if I can get them. Otherwise, I go poor house."

It looked to me like he'd already checked in. I didn't actually say that, but my poker face had had a hard day.

"Okay," LeRoy said, "so I'm not rolling in it. Jean Paul Getty wouldn't be doing so good either if he had my kind of competition. When I started in this business, I had a field to work in as wide as the Rose Bowl. Now it feels like I'm sharing a one-lane bowling alley. The big studios are easing my way a little more every year. Did you see *The Night They Raided Minsky's?*"

I nodded. The comedy he'd named was a tribute to old-time burlesque, released the year before. It had been the great Bert Lahr's last film, but I knew it resonated for LeRoy for an entirely different reason. The climax of the film had been a widescreen shot of Britt Ekland's bared breasts.

"That was our basic plot done with real actors and a real budget. How am I supposed to compete with that? Where's the Legion of Decency when you need them? Where's the damn Hays Office? That's one side of the squeeze play. The other's this pornography. It's worse than anything the old stag film perverts ever thought up, only at feature length with color photography and a soundtrack. Why aren't the cops shutting that down?"

"They do," I said.

LeRoy waved his glasses at me. "As quick as one film gets yanked, another opens. Pretty soon they won't even bother raiding them. And I'll tell you why. Mob money is financing that hard-core crap. It won't be long until mob money is paying off the cops and the judges. Then every town will have a porno palace. And don't get me started on that foreign stuff playing at the art houses. It's a failure of morality is what it is," LeRoy said in the summation I'd been hoping for. Then he added, "But I don't need to tell you about that."

"Pardon me?"

"I don't mean you personally, of course. I mean you professionally. I mean that company of yours, Hollywood, ah . . ."

"Security."

"Right. This new morality, aka no morality, is squeezing your racket harder than it is mine. How much has that boss of yours made over the years hushing things up when some star drove drunk or smoked a little weed or got caught with the cheerleading squad from Long Beach High? Plenty. But who's afraid of any of that in 1969? Hell, Bob Mitchum would have to roll his reefer on the corner of Hollywood and Vine to get picked up today. And then they'd probably let him off with a warning. That's why you scandal hounds are on welfare, in case you hadn't figured it out."

"Who said we were on welfare?" I asked.

"I hear things. And if you've got time to track down runaway heartbreakers, business can't be so good."

I was grateful for the shortcut back to the point. "You said something wasn't right about this heartbreaker coming to you back in April. What did you mean by that?"

"It was fishy, is all I meant. Her reason for coming wasn't right. Most of my walk-ins are excited. Eager, almost. They know this isn't MGM, but they figure it's a baby step that way. The Combs girl was grim about it. And she wanted to use her own name, wanted everybody to know who her daddy was. That wasn't kosher either. A motel clerk gets more right names than I do."

Confirming Miranda's insistence on using her own name took care of fifty percent of my reasons for being there. I took care of the other half by asking LeRoy if he had jotted down an address or phone number for Miranda.

"No," he said. "She wouldn't give me one. I remember because that's why we had to work it out for Combs to grab her here. I called him 'cause I was worried about the kid."

"He said you called to verify her age."

"Listen, there isn't a better judge of female age or cup size in Hollywood. Nobody's fooled me in either category since you were in short pants."

"Sorry. You got her back here how?"

"We cooked up a phony screen test—clothes on—and while she was busy with that Combs showed up as arranged. Wasn't the big blowup I expected. No name calling, no yelling. Natural underplayers, these Brits."

He should see Combs now, I thought. I was through with LeRoy and started to thank him for his time, but he wasn't through with me. Not if I was good for a little gossip.

"I heard Paddy's wife's not doing so well. Stroke, I heard." I waited him out, and he added. "A shame. I never met the lady, but I heard she had all the business sense in the family. I also heard Paddy had to move her to a second hospital. At the first hospital's request. He broke some furniture at Queen of Angels over them not being able to help the missus, I heard."

For a little guy in a hole-in-the-wall, LeRoy heard a lot. Too much, in fact. "You want me to tell Paddy you were asking for him?"

"Ah, that's okay. I'll send a card, maybe."

"Thanks for reminding me." I flipped a business card onto his workbench. "If you hear anything about Miranda Combs, give us a call."

FOUR

My approach to Miranda's school friends started badly, with an awkward interview at the home of a girlfriend named Cecile. Cecile's mother insisted on being present, which I understood, although her daughter wasn't exactly a temptress. She was as plain as a new broom handle, in fact, the kind of friend a beauty like Miranda often used for protective cover. And as a confidante, I hoped.

That turned out not to be the case. At least, Cecile hadn't heard anything about Miranda's plans that she cared to repeat in front of her chaperone. I tried to give her my number, in case her memory improved later, but the mother intercepted my card and squeezed it to death in a thin hand.

My second stop was only a block or two away. There, on an oil-stained driveway, I found a kid named Glenn Starkey. He was working on a car, a 1961 Ford Falcon. A transistor radio, perched on the car's curved roof, was playing music Gabby might have recognized. It sounded to me like Alvin and the Chipmunks, only more nasal.

Starkey's mother never came out to supervise, if she was even home. Still, I thought I'd drawn another bad hand. Starkey was an underfed kid with a lava-field complexion and sandy hair that curled over his ears. His nose, a dorsal fin in the Tony Bennett class, had used up most of his last growth spurt. Maybe his last two. He pointed it at me briefly, then stuck it back in the carburetor of the Falcon.

Luckily, he found my car a lot more interesting than he found me. While I delivered my opening spiel about Miranda being missing and her father being worried, Starkey stole glance after glance at the Charger. I might not have been the brains of my outfit, but I could spot an advantage when I had one. I asked Starkey if he wanted to check out the car.

He did, though he only gave the bodywork a quick once-over before popping the hood and sniffing at the engine. He looked like he might be planning to examine all four hundred and forty cubic inches individually, so I tapped him on the shoulder bone.

"About Miranda," I said.

"What's it sound like?"

"Too loud to talk over." I swung my keys back and forth under that nose. "Miranda's father says you and she go way back."

"Yeah," Starkey said. "Fourth grade."

Combs had told me that, also that Miranda and Starkey had split a bout of puppy love once. Miranda had gotten over it. Starkey maybe not.

"What's she like?"

I hadn't asked Combs that question because I didn't think his answer would be objective enough to be worth much. He'd volunteered that Miranda was intelligent, independent, headstrong, and beautiful, which made her sound like the heroine of a book. Or a play. She'd been named for a character from Shakespeare, after all, the idealized daughter from *The Tempest*.

"She's honest," Starkey said. "It hurts sometimes."

"Hurts you?"

"And Miranda. She thinks everybody is that honest. She believes things."

"What things?" I asked, thinking he meant the pickup lines her classmates used on her.

"Song lyrics," he said, surprising me. "Movies, TV." He waved a hand at the grainy valley air, suggesting that what he really meant was some invisible thing floating all around us. "She talks about San Francisco like it's Paris or maybe heaven. Like what they have up there is so much better than here."

"Is that where she went, Frisco?"

Starkey shrugged, and with the same motion seemed to draw back from me, without actually stepping away. I'd rushed things, evidently.

"You and Miranda dated, right?" I said, picking a topic that may or may not have been safer.

Starkey nodded.

"When?"

"Ninth grade," he said, sticking to his kid's way of measuring time.

"What happened?"

He shrugged again, which might have reflected his best thinking on the subject. My own thinking was his girlfriend had simply outgrown him. Once upon a time, it might have been possible for a knockout like Miranda Combs to end up with her childhood sweetheart, however scrawny. It might still be possible in some remote corner of the globe. But not where we stood. Not this close to the industry that had done so much to make looks the national currency.

"But you still want to protect her if you can," I said. "You think you're protecting her now by not talking to me."

An extension phone on the wall of the garage began to ring, and the sound was like a sap to the back of my skull. Starkey made no move to answer it, and after a few more rings, it stopped.

I swallowed hard and said, "If she's gotten herself into some kind of jam, your not talking to me or her father could be hurting her."

Miranda's childhood friend didn't dismiss the idea that she might be in trouble. He broke the tentative eye contact he'd been maintaining, gazing toward the southern horizon. Toward Miranda's lost mountain home, I thought, but I was a few degrees of the compass off.

"You know Topanga Canyon?" Starkey asked.

"Know it? A guy threw a shot at me up there once."

His eyes finally looked big enough to share the same face with his nose. "No kidding? What did you do?"

He seemed to be expecting me to say I'd caught the slug in my teeth. I might have obliged, just to move our budding friendship along. But the truth seemed a better way to go with this worshipper of honest Miranda.

"I hit the ground so hard I can still taste the dirt," I said. "What about Topanga Canyon?"

"Miranda talked about it. Just last week. She said it's a place where things are happening, like Haight-Ashbury."

"You sure she didn't say the town of Topanga? Or Topanga Beach?"

"I think she just said the canyon."

"How about boyfriends? Who was she seeing?"

"Nobody."

"How could that be? What was stopping her?"

"I dunno. I thought there might be somebody she was seeing behind her dad's back. But she wouldn't say. It was just a feeling I had. Probably nuts."

He looked at my car keys, which I was still dangling in my hand, signaling that he'd met his part of our unstated bargain. I tossed the keys to him.

"Fire her up," I said. "I'm going to borrow your phone."

To call J. Edgar Hoover about this latest lead, Starkey might have thought. Actually, it was to call home. When the garage extension's ringing had made me see stars, it had been because the sound had taken me back to the phone Ella had been willing to ring all morning. For a second, I'd been in our living room again, waiting with her. The reaction reminded me of the call I'd been afraid to make.

I marched up to the wall phone now like the tough guy I'd played too long. Ella answered the first ring, which told me the call from Fort Ord hadn't come in.

"It's me," I said.

There was a pause. It wasn't a silence exactly—Starkey was playing with the Charger's throttle linkage, making the engine growl—just the absence of a reply. Then Gabby came on the line, whispering. "No news, Dad. Did you find her yet?"

No doubt in her voice that I would, by and by.

"Not yet. I've got one more stop to make. Then I'll be home. Can you hold out till then?"

"Can do," she said.

FIVE

Topanga Canyon was as close to a hole-in-the-wall as you could find within a short drive of Los Angeles. A one-pipe drive, Gabby would have called it, based on her father's bad habit, not her own. Before I left Reseda, I filled an old briar, a long-ago gift from Ella. Its last embers were giving out as I approached the fifteen-hundred-foot crest of Topanga Canyon Boulevard.

I'd told Starkey that I'd been shot at in the canyon, but it had really happened on a lonely residential road west of the main drag. The boulevard, or Highway 27 as it was also known, was a popular route between the valley and the ocean, so it wasn't surprising that a high-school kid like Miranda Combs would know it. What was surprising was that anyone would consider the area another Haight-Ashbury, the neighborhood in San Francisco where the hippie movement had gotten its start. That was why I'd asked Starkey about the towns of Topanga and Topanga Beach. Neither of those places was exactly in with the in crowd, but at least they had people. Topanga Canyon had coyotes and pine trees.

Just south of the crest, in one of the road's horseshoe bends, I came to a knot of little shops that catered to the beach traffic. Two of the structures were old railroad cars set on concrete blocks, a boxcar and a caboose. How they'd found their way to the top of the cut was anybody's guess. A little way off from them in a stand of wind-sculpted junipers was an old frame house that had been painted mustard yellow. The house looked embarrassed about that or maybe about the stylized flowers in pinks and blues and greens painted here and there on its windows. A hand-lettered sign, hanging from the roof of a front porch where Ma and Pa Kettle had once rocked the evening away, identified the establishment as the Infinite Pad.

A single car was parked in front, an old Chevy Bel Air decked out with a lot of chrome accessories General Motors hadn't thought to offer. Interestingly, though there was no one inside the car, the engine was running. It might have been left on out of simple carelessness or because it was hard to start or for some other innocent reason. Then again, the car was parked with its front end facing the road.

I often stashed a gun, a worn forty-five automatic, in the glove compartment of the Dodge, but that was when I was working on a real case, not doing a favor for an old friend. I thought about getting the tire iron out of the trunk, told myself I was imagining things, and started inside.

Halfway through my third step, some glass broke and a woman screamed. If it had just been the glass, I would have gone back for the lug wrench and maybe the jack, too. The scream made it a whole different proposition.

I set off running, took the three front-porch steps in a bound, and yanked on the screen door. It made a sound like Bela Lugosi's coffin opening, and that froze the three people in the room beyond. Two of them could have been Glenn Starkey's brothers: mop heads that maybe weighed two-fifty as a pair, dressed in T-shirts and jeans. The one who'd twisted halfway around at the sound of the door held a knife. The other, who was facing me, held a girl.

She was a strawberry blonde with cockeyed, blue-lensed eyeglasses and a small mouth poised for another scream. She wore a smock shirt with flowing waist and sleeves that gave her the look of a storybook princess. A princess tied to a stake, as

35

her arms were being held at her sides.

The stake came to first, yelling, "Cut him, Bobby! Cut him!"

Bobby finished his turn and came for me, which was a mistake on a couple of counts. For starters, if he'd joined his friend and put the knife to the girl's throat, I would have been stymied but good. And, though he couldn't have known it, I'd been trained to handle a man with a knife by the US Army, with the occasional refresher course thrown in by the civilian population of Los Angeles.

When he thrust the blade at me, I sidestepped it and grabbed his forearm at the wrist and elbow, twisting them in opposite directions. The kid cried out, and the knife dropped. A little more pressure might have broken something, but I let him go, pushing him toward a rack of clothes. I kicked the bowie knife into a far corner and started for the noncombatants.

The second kid had learned from his earlier mistake. He waited until I was within a few steps of him and then shoved the girl at me hard. As I caught her, he bolted for the door, grabbing his partner as he passed.

The girl yelled after them: "Get 'em, Dad! Break their necks! Don't let them get away!"

The last instruction seemed a little optimistic, since the Chevy's doors were slamming at that moment. I waited until the sound of screaming tires had died and then said, "Dad?"

The girl, who was still in my arms, freed herself before answering. "If they think they'll run into you again, they won't come back. It gets lonely up here."

That kind of presence of mind I didn't run into every day. I gave her a closer look while she straightened her crazy glasses, shifted her smock, and checked the center part of her long, straight hair. Its reddish-blonde color was picked up by the freckles that covered her face and neck. They were standing out plainly against her skin, which was so white I decided her calm demeanor was an act of will.

To give my own nerves time to settle, I retrieved the knife, which had buried its tip in the molding at the foot of a dark staircase. For the first time, I noticed an onlooker to the fight, a woman standing on the stairway a few steps up from the bottom. She was a brunette, wearing very dark lipstick and eye shadow for two and standing about six feet tall in bare feet. Before I could say hello, she turned and climbed the stairs.

"Who was that?" I asked the redhead.

"Myrna."

"Guess you didn't really need me. She could have tossed those two out with one hand."

"If she'd felt like getting involved."

"What were they after?"

"Money. And whatever."

She pointed to a display case whose glass front had been kicked in. An ancient brass cash register sat on the counter above. Inside the case, covered with shattered glass, were strings of beads and other junk jewelry, incense burners, and a rack of brightly colored packets, a little bigger and a little flatter than chewing-gum packs. They held cigarette paper, five or six different brands.

"You roll your own?" I asked.

"Doesn't everybody?"

She went to sort out the rack of clothes Mack the Knife had landed on. In addition to those and the minor-league drug paraphernalia, the shop sold posters, some of which were displayed around the walls. Most were psychedelic imitations of the works of Peter Max, but old movie stars were represented in all their black-and-white splendor: the Marx Brothers, W.C. Fields, Mae West. Torrance Beaumont, the 1940s heartthrob who had delighted in ribbing me way back when, stared down from over the front door, his dark eyes as mocking as ever. He held a lit cigarette, maybe the very one that had touched off his fatal cancer.

I might have mentioned knowing Beaumont as a way of breaking the ice that still separated the shop girl and me, my saving her money and maybe her neck not having done the trick. But that kind of claim was a dime a dozen around Hollywood. So I said instead, "My name's Elliott. What's yours?"

I'd been watching for some additional reaction to her narrow escape, shaking or tears or the works. When it came, the reaction took the form of bad manners.

"It's Jill. If that's any of your business."

"Not Petunia or Petunia Seagull Sunrise?" I asked, having a little reaction of my own.

"Is it just Elliott or is it Joe Friday Flatfoot Elliott?" she asked back.

That explained why she hadn't been in any hurry to call the police. She thought a representative was already on the scene. I told her I wasn't a cop and never had been.

"Yeah, right. You just sleep in the same sty."

I handed her my card. She raised her glasses to read it, revealing blue eyes almost as pale as Ella's. And long lashes, golden at their tips.

"A private cop," she said, as though that was even lower on her social scale.

"An errand boy," I said. With a stage name. "I'm looking for a girl. A runaway."

Before she could slip the cheaters back down, I passed her one of Miranda's mug shots.

"Pretty," she said. "You just going door-to-door?"

"No. She told a friend she'd found Haight-Ashbury around here somewhere. You're as close as I've seen."

Jill laughed at the idea, the humor lending a little light to those pale eyes. It didn't last. "So she's pretty *and* naive. God help her. I don't recognize the face," she added, holding the photo out to me. "But we get a lot of Daddy's-little-girls passing through. Sometimes I think they hire buses."

That gave me an idea. "Would you mind posting that picture? You could tape it to the register. Somebody might recognize it."

"How many years am I dedicating to this?"

"A week?"

She didn't say yes, but she didn't tuck the photo into my breast pocket either. "I'm a runaway myself," she said. "From Little Canada, Minnesota. My parents must have forgotten to send you after me."

I felt bad about that, though it made no sense to. "Somebody sent me today," I said.

"Yeah, the great seagull in the sky. Okay, flatfoot. One week. I'll call you if I hear anything."

I'd handled the interview without a slip, so naturally I crossed feet on the way to the door. "If it's that lonely up here, you ought to get a gun."

"That's what the world needs," Jill replied, her blue glasses dropping into place like an out-to-lunch sign. "One more gun."

Six

It would have been nice to have hit Topanga and Topanga Beach on that same run, but I'd told Gabby it was one stop and home, so I headed home. She already had dinner going, her attempt to rush us into a normal, domestic evening. That plan was sabotaged by a call from Fort Ord. It was the caller we'd been expecting, a tame brigadier, but not the call. That is, he had no news for us. He told us to be patient. Things were more screwed up than usual, he said. He might be a day or two getting definite word. Maybe more.

At that point, I might have irritated Ella with some reminiscences of Army life that illustrated how hard it was to ever know exactly what was going on. I was saved from that faux pas by her refusal to listen to me. Or speak to me. Or share a bed with me, which I found out later in the evening.

That last discovery drove me into the arms of an old enemy, television. Gabby joined me in the downstairs den just as a late movie was starting, *Here Comes Mr. Jordan,* the Robert Montgomery classic about a prizefighter snatched up to heaven prematurely. It might seem a poor choice in the circumstances, but it wasn't, being one of the most successful renderings of Hollywood's favorite theme: even the most hopeless situation will turn out okay in the end. Or, as Mr. Jordan himself put it, "Nobody's ever really cheated." Gabby stuck with it until Montgomery and Evelyn Keyes got together for keeps. She teared up a little at that, kissed me, and went to bed.

I started the next day with a headache, having spent more time smoking than sleeping during the long night. Leaving Gabby to hold the fort again, I drove to the nearest post office substation and mailed one of Miranda's photographs to a detective agency in San Francisco, just in case she'd tired of local Haight-Ashburys and gone after the real thing. The agency was one that owed Hollywood Security a big favor, so I didn't have to worry about a bill landing on Paddy's desk. After that, I returned to Route 27, trying the shops and stores on the beach end first and then canvassing the little town halfway up the canyon. Neither effort got me anything.

Next, I drove into Hollywood proper and worked Sunset, showing Miranda's photo around and getting the usual head shaking along with the odd request for a phone number, sometimes Miranda's, sometimes my own. During a break for a burger at Shaw's, I toyed with the idea that she'd reversed the national trend and run away from the West Coast, perhaps to Little Canada, Minnesota, wherever that was.

I was tempted to follow her example. The old strip was the embodiment of the moral laxity Ted LeRoy saw everywhere. Once the home of sophisticated nightclubs, it was now as close to a red-light district as Hollywood had. Even Ciro's, the club I'd dreamt about in boot camp, was gone, its building converted to a place where teenagers deafened one other with electric guitars.

I checked in faithfully with the house all day long, getting my daughter every time. Ella was using her to filter me out. She was filtering everyone else out, too, as Gabby told me during my last call: "Mom's in the cone of silence, Dad."

Gabby used that reference—to a running gag from her

favorite television show, the spy spoof *Get Smart*—very seriously, so I took it that way, hurrying home.

I didn't stay there long. Gabby met me in the hydrangea-choked drive.

"Paddy called. He wants you to meet him at the nursing home. A job's come in, a big one. I didn't say a word about Billy."

I'd asked her not to, if Paddy should call. As I'd told Ella the day before, he already had plenty on his plate. Though the idea that we could keep the news about Billy from his honorary grandfather was a pretty hopeless one.

When I started inside, Gabby added, "He said right away."

I found Ella at her post in the living room. She didn't stomp off at my approach, not even when I sat down beside her, but she stiffened when I put my arm around her. It reminded me of the moment at my mother's viewing when I'd put my arms around my father in greeting and he'd all but turned to stone. It had been his way of telling me what he thought of my hanging on in California where I wasn't wanted or needed while my mother died slowly in Indiana.

I shook off the memory and said, "I'm going over to the nursing home to talk to Paddy. Do you want to ride along and visit Peggy?"

"No," Ella said.

"Do you want me to stay here?"

"No."

I squeezed her shoulder. "I'll be back."

I waited for the third no, more frightened than I'd been in the Infinite Pad with cold steel headed my way. The fatal word never came.

St. Anne's Home was in La Mirada, out east off the 101. Traffic was heavy, even heavier than usual, which made the home's wooded grounds seem even more like an oasis. I spotted Paddy sitting on his favorite bench under his favorite tree. He nodded to me as I got out of the Dodge and nodded again when I pointed to the nursing home's front door.

The plump, pink nun on duty at the front desk and I greeted each other by name. I wondered, as I always did, if she could still smell the place after years of working inside it. The wide hallway had its usual share of escapees in wheelchairs and on foot, several of whom also greeted me by name, a different name in each case.

Peggy Maguire was not one of the residents moving about, her stroke having left her paralyzed. I entered her room and sat down beside her bed, which seemed small to me by hospital standards. Not that she used that much of it. She'd always been tiny, and she was very tiny now, her wasted limbs having contracted almost to a fetal position.

She was covered by a sheet, which exposed only her head and the hand Paddy had lately been holding. Her mouth was slightly open, as were her dark eyes. Whether she knew me or even saw me, I couldn't tell. Since her stroke, she hadn't even been able to blink once for yes and twice for no.

Peggy had taken an interest in me back in the waning days of the thirties, when Paddy had brought me home, an especially wet-behind-the-ears contract player from the studio where he worked as a gate guard. She'd been thin and dark then, with only a hint left of the Irish good looks that had lasted her through a career in vaudeville as Paddy's partner.

Then I'd been drafted, and Peggy had become a faithful correspondent. In one of her chatty letters, she'd told me of Paddy's plan to strike out on his own as a private security specialist. He'd seen an opportunity in the breakdown of the understanding the movie studios had had with the local police. In exchange for regular cash donations, the cops had protected the stars from all but the very worst of their indiscretions. The studio heads had shoveled away faithfully until the war, when, perhaps to get back at their talent for setting up the Screen Actors Guild, they'd cut the payola off.

Nobody had been happy with the unpleasantness that followed, except defense attorneys and one Patrick J. Maguire. He'd observed the workings of the old system for years from the inside and he'd decided that a private firm could do the hushing up more efficiently than the police, since it would charge by the case rather than the week. The result was the Hollywood Security Agency, which had taken me aboard once my career as a soldier had gone the way of my career as an actor.

The shriveled woman whose hand I now held had been a second mother to me then. She'd taken to Ella, too, and had helped us raise our kids, while running the business side of the agency and keeping her very buoyant husband anchored to the ground. It was no wonder she'd been used up.

I was tempted to tell her about Billy, just for the relief of talking it over with someone. I didn't, because of the one chance in a million that she could hear and understand me. I wouldn't risk adding to her suffering, not even at those odds. Instead, I patted her close-clipped gray hair, only the tips of which still showed the old dark dye, and stood up, saying, "See you next time, Peg." Then I headed for Paddy's bench.

He was nursing the last of a double corona as I walked up, looking, as he often did, like he didn't have a care in the world. I'd never admired the talent more than I did at that moment. Not that Paddy didn't have his darker moods, as I well knew. The gossipy Ted LeRoy had been right, for example, when he'd said that Paddy had broken some furniture at Peggy's previous stop, though LeRoy had gotten the reason wrong. It hadn't been over the hospital's failure to cure her. At least, that hadn't been the catalyst. Peggy's wedding and engagement rings had been stolen, right off her hand, probably by a member of the staff. Paddy's redecorating had been his way of registering a complaint.

At the moment, though, he sat, homburg pushed well back on his head, like a man who had just enjoyed a benefit dinner in his honor. But I couldn't help noticing a few sour notes. As long as I'd known him, Paddy had been a well-fed citizen with a wide, florid face. His color was off now, and his gray suit needed both pressing and taking in. A subtler clue, one only a familiar would spot, was Paddy's tie. He usually wore neckwear colorful enough to embarrass a matador. Today's brown-and-blue number would have bored a Boston banker. It was hard to imagine him even owning a tie like that. I wondered if Peggy had bought it for him in hopes of reining in his fashion sense. If so, he'd waited too long to show his appreciation.

"How'd you find her, Scotty?" he asked. "She was more alert today, I thought."

I hoped not, for her sake, but I said he might be right. "What's this big job you've lined up?"

"Something worthy of our talents at last. I got a call this morning from Roland Hedison, the successful independent producer fellow. You're to see him bright and early tomorrow morning at his Zodiac Productions offices. As early as possible and as bright as you can make yourself."

Paddy's praise for Hedison was another sign, like his low-wattage necktie, of things not being right. Hedison was the producer of cheap horror films and other drive-in fodder. My boss wouldn't have touched his hat brim to him once.

"You won't be there?" I asked.

"No. I've a meeting with the doctors in the morning." He pointed to the nursing home with what was left of his cigar. Then he flicked the butt away. "You can handle it, I'm sure.

Feel free to discuss anything but the money end. I'll take care of that. I see a nice payday for us out of this."

Hollywood Security badly needed one, as LeRoy had suggested, though whether the cause of our hard times was the rise of a new immorality, as he'd theorized, or the fall of the old studio system was anybody's guess. What was certain was that we'd reached a crisis point. The firm no longer even had a roof over its collective head. The little building on Roe Street was still one of the agency's assets—almost its only asset besides Paddy's brass and my shoe leather—but that was only on paper. The entire building had been sublet to a telephone answering service called Jordan's Jingles. Even Paddy's plush office had been give over to the phone business. The service's owner, Mary Jordan, answered our old number for us and passed on messages as part of her lease. And she'd made Paddy a generous offer to buy the property, one that would have provided for Peggy's care for some time. So far, though, Paddy had resisted the temptation.

"If only . . . ," he said, his deep voice fading away like a distant surf.

I knew how he'd ended that sentence in his head. If only Peggy could tell us where she'd hidden her coffee can. She and Paddy had joked about that can for years, the legendary place where she stashed whatever money he didn't toss at the world. After her stroke, Paddy had looked everywhere for it. He'd checked every bank in California and in Maryland, where Peggy's family lived, without turning up a dime. He was haunted by the idea that the bankroll was out there somewhere, perhaps in a safe-deposit box in some whistle-stop town Peggy had passed through on her annual train trip to Baltimore. Ella didn't think the secret fund existed. She thought the lean sixties had used up whatever Peggy had socked away. I went back and forth between the two points of view.

"About this job," I said. "What exactly does Hedison want?"

I said it to change the subject, not because I thought Paddy might actually brief me for once.

True to form, he replied, "I'd rather preserve your tabula rasa quality, if that's the expression I mean. Your open mind. Let Mr. Hedison tell you about it himself. Then you and I can compare notes. And speaking of notes, I got a nice one from Billy the other day, asking after her nibs. He said he expected to be in the thick of things soon." He checked his vest pockets. "Damn. I meant to bring it with me."

"Next time," I said.

I thought I'd delivered the line as smoothly as Cronkite read the news, but Paddy's ear thought differently.

"What's wrong?" he asked.

I had to give up something then and quick. Luckily, I had a secret to spare.

"It's a little job I forgot to mention. Forrest Combs called me yesterday." I told Paddy all about the Miranda Combs mystery, watching him relax into boredom as I rambled on.

"Drop it," he said when I finally ran out of material. "Combs is too broke to pay you back for the ethyl your behemoth's been burning. There'll be time to look for missing children when we've finished with Zodiac Productions."

SEVEN

Hollywood is one of the most evocative place names known to man, up there with Rome and Cairo and Hong Kong, but in '69, the actual business district would have had a hard time winning a beauty contest against Des Moines. Greater Los Angeles was enjoying a building boom, its third or fourth since I'd hit town, but Hollywood proper was still making due with its prewar skyline, if you could call it that.

The town's architecture had stayed modest because the studios maintained most of their office space on their widely scattered lots. When they needed more, for bean counters, say, or ad men or brothers-in-law, they looked to LA or even New York. An exception to this pattern was Roland Hedison's Zodiac Productions, which had its headquarters within a stone's throw of Hollywood and Vine.

Hedison had no studio proper. He rented shooting space wherever it was cheapest. He liked to get a deal on his office space, too, I decided as I stood outside his building, four stories of gray-green tile, grouted with leftover smog and chipped at the edges, like the dinnerware at a greasy spoon. Running above the first-floor windows was a frieze depicting scenes from literature or maybe just from movies. A pair of Elizabethan lovers gazed at each other over the front door, probably Romeo and Juliet. They looked suspiciously like Norma Shearer and John Gilbert, who had played the famous balcony scene as part of *The Hollywood Revue of 1929,* only the ceramic duo was a little less stiff.

Zodiac Production's outer office was a genuine beehive, with four women of widely varying ages trying to answer what sounded like ten or twelve phones. While I waited for one of them to notice me, I examined the movie posters that decorated the walls. Their subject matter divided Hedison's oeuvre into three categories. The first featured bug-eyed monsters, the second motorcycle gangs, and the third kids with surfboards. One ambitious undertaking, an epic called *Malibu Mutant Mayhem,* blended all three genres. The poster nearest my spot by the door hung beneath an electric sign identifying it as the company's latest release. The title was *Die, Zombie, Die,* although the zombie pictured actually appeared to be doing the twist.

The senior member of the riot squad finally took pity on me. "Hollywood Security?"

I nodded. I would have offered my name next and maybe even ventured a smile, but she cut me off by raising a hand too large and round for the skinny arm that held it, the combination looking to me like a squash racquet, hinged. She used the same paddle to wave me through the maelstrom and into an office that was comparatively peaceful. There were only two phones in view and only one of those was in use.

The man who held it was Roland Hedison. I'd never actually met him, which was unusual. Not that I knew everyone in Hollywood or even every producer. That wasn't possible. The movie industry wasn't huge, but these days the turnover was tremendous. More and more, my life on the fringes of Hollywood was like living on the outskirts of an enchanted village, a good chunk of whose population was spirited away every night and replaced by total strangers.

Hedison, though, was far from a newcomer. He'd been around for ten years, at least. But until this moment, he'd stayed happily clear of Hollywood Security. I had to hand it to him for that.

The producer hung up the phone by flipping it toward its cradle, where it more or less came to rest. "Sorry about the nuthouse," he said. "We've got four different units shooting four different pictures right now. It's always crazy in the morning when they're calling in to report and complain. Have a seat."

I liked the way he'd said "we" when he'd spoken of four crews shooting four pictures. The average studio head would have used the first-person singular from long habit. The ones with a serious Sam Goldwyn complex would have implied they were filming the pictures single-handed.

I had a positive first impression of Hedison in general. For one thing, his office lacked the usual photos of the occupant kissing screen goddesses and shaking hands with presidents. Hedison's memorabilia all involved football. USC football, to be exact. The producer was a former Trojan and proud of it. I would have guessed the football part even without the visual aids. He was built like a linebacker and shook hands like a lineman.

He was less impressed with my grip. "You don't look so good, Elliott," he said after very visibly committing my name to memory. "Can I get you some coffee? Rough night last night?"

"Yes," I said to both questions. It had been another night in the den with too many memories and too little rest. But I let Hedison jump to the more conventional conclusion.

"Got to watch the booze. We can't put it away like we used to. Not at our age."

He was giving me all the breaks with that bit of camaraderie, since he'd barely cracked his forties.

"The trick," he added as though confiding a state secret, "is to think young without trying to act young."

I felt a strong desire to ask him about dressing young. He

was a walking example of what Ella had taken to calling the "Peter Lawford look," a relatively recent phenomenon in which middle-aged men affected the "mod" style popularized by British rock groups. Hedison's outbreaks were hair worn in a heavy swoop across his forehead, a flowered shirt very open at the collar, and a scarf of the same bright blue. On his big neck it looked like a streamer tangled around a tree trunk. But I decided not to needle him. I hadn't gotten my coffee yet and I didn't want the order canceled.

"I've got an advantage," Hedison was saying. "The kids I work with keep me young. People think Zodiac uses kids right out of school because they work cheap. It's really because they're in touch with our target audience, teenage America."

My coffee landed then, delivered by a recent escapee from teenage America. It was so good it revived my rosy feelings for Hedison. Even the belated arrival of his ego only ruffled me in a small way.

"That's what I'll be remembered for someday. Not for the pictures I made but for giving a lot of writers and directors their starts. Wait and see. I'm going to be mentioned in a lot of Academy Award acceptance speeches."

"You're a lock for mine," I said, toasting him with my Zodiac Productions mug.

Hedison took it just as friendly. "Okay, to work. I've got a problem, a big one potentially. I'm told Hollywood Security is the company to handle it. Like I said, I use a lot of young crews. I don't pay them much—I can't—but I give them experience. And freedom, a lot of freedom. My only rules are hit your deadlines, stay inside your budgets, and keep the teenyboppers in the seats. Ask anybody, that's the longest leash in the business."

Hedison's emphasis on leeway suggested the transition he seemed reluctant to make. "Somebody abusing that freedom?"

51

"Yes," he said. "Some bad egg on my best crew, the team that made our most recent release."

"*Die, Zombie, Die?*" I said, trying to sound as though I'd read all about it in *Variety*.

"Right. A good picture, too. Groundbreaking. I never thought those zombie movies from the forties fully exploited the potential of the concept."

"Let's talk about what your bad egg's been exploiting." My coffee was going fast and my patience with it. Unlike my boss, I didn't see any big payday coming from Zodiac Productions. If I had to be breaking strands with Ella, to borrow Gabby's haunting image, I preferred to be doing it by finding Miranda Combs.

"It's drugs, I'm afraid," the producer said. "Drug smuggling. If you consider marijuana a drug."

"I do keep mine in the medicine cabinet."

"Right, okay. I only said that because some people don't think pot's a big deal."

"And yet you're concerned."

"Yes. Most of that zombie picture was shot down in Mexico. I found a great location, an abandoned mission right on the coast. Crashing surf, a ruined chapel, even a cemetery. It had everything."

"Including access to grass."

"Exactly. I even furnished the smuggler, whoever he is, with transportation. An old bus for the cast and two panel trucks. I don't imagine it was hard getting the stuff over the border. Customs isn't much down there, and the trucks were crammed with cases of legitimate equipment. An extra packing case or two wouldn't have stuck out."

"Two packing cases? So this wasn't just for personal use."

"No."

"How did you find out about it? An anonymous tip?"

"How did you know?"

"Lucky guess." Anonymous tips were popular in Hollywood, where naming names was the only unforgivable sin. In the fifties, they'd flown back and forth like singing telegrams. "Go on," I said.

"It was a note, sent to me here."

"Got it handy?"

"No. I burned it."

"There's an interesting filing system."

"I was afraid to have it around. Anyway, it wasn't very detailed. All it said was that someone from the crew had brought in some pot and sold it off."

"Could one person do that without everybody else in the crew knowing?"

"Probably not. But these kids still operate by the code of the school yard. No tattling to the teacher. The others would look the other way."

"All but one."

Hedison shrugged. "Even that one didn't go to the police."

"When was this?"

"Six weeks ago. It doesn't take us long to get a picture in release once it's been shot."

"Or to reassign the crew," I said. "I take it there's been another trip to Mexico."

That was another guess but a reasonable one. The way Hedison had tried to dismiss the importance of marijuana told me he wouldn't have wasted my time and his money on any smuggling that was safely in the history books.

"Yes. They did some shooting down there last week for a project called *Duo-Glide Rider*. That's a motorcycle picture, only without the gangs this time. It's a road-trip thing, an Annette Funicello, Frankie Avalon comedy, only without Funicello and Avalon. But cute. You'd love the script."

I ignored the signpost for the scenic route. I was past banter-

53

ing with Hedison. He ran a hand through his hair, absentmindedly clearing it from his forehead and revealing an old, deep scar.

"How many *Zombie* alumni are we talking about?"

"Not that many. Most of our technical people are freelancers who come and go. They work for whatever independent is hiring at the moment. It happened that a lot of them went after *Die, Zombie, Die*. The people who stayed on were what you might call the creative nucleus."

"Why did you let this nucleus go back to Mexico?"

"Because it was all set up. Had been for months. I thought I'd gotten the word to them that I wouldn't put up with any more business on the side. I'm sure I did. I told them I didn't want to know who the smuggler was, but I expected it to stop."

"Only it didn't."

"No. Right after the crew got back, I got another anonymous note."

"Burn that one, too?"

"Yes. It wasn't hard to memorize either, though it was longer than the first one. It said more pot had come back with them. And this time my correspondent told me where it was going to be sold. You may have heard of a big rock concert they're holding this weekend at a place called Avenal. A British rock group, the Roads of Destiny, is headlining it. It's going to be another Woodstock, they tell me. The *Duo-Glide Rider* crew is going to be there. One of the warm-up acts, a band called the Proposition, has agreed to let us film their numbers and use them in the picture. My bad egg plans to sell the pot at the concert, which should be almost as easy as giving it away."

"Whose idea was it to film at the concert? Whoever arranged it is probably behind the smuggling."

Hedison shook his bangs back into place. "*I* arranged it, Elliott. I read about the concert plan and decided it would be the cheapest way anyone ever came up with to get ten thousand extras."

Mentioning the scheme was enough to send Hedison off on another of his tangents. "It's a trick I picked up reading about Mack Sennett, the silent-movie guy. He was always watching the papers for something he could build a film around, a ship launching or a car race or something. He'd sneak a camera in and get his footage. I do the same thing: take advantage of whatever comes along."

"Sounds like one of your kids has studied Sennett, too. What exactly do you want Hollywood Security to do, Mr. Hedison?"

"I want you to join the *Duo-Glide Rider* company as special security for the concert trip. Tag along to Avenal and make sure nobody sells any drugs from one of our trucks."

I would have been looking around for my hat if I still wore one. "Call the police. They'll help you free of charge."

"Hell, no. Police mean arrests and publicity. I can't afford any of that. People let their kids go to my movies because we don't have stuff in them like drugs or race riots or wars. No. This has got to be kept quiet."

The old refrain. If I had a dollar for every time I'd heard it, I could have retired Paddy and maybe myself.

I got up and took a step toward the door. "Sorry. We don't keep drug dealing quiet. We make it extra noisy, when we get the chance. Call it a prejudice."

"But I've already told the crew you'd be on the job tomorrow."

"Untell them."

"I'll make you a deal," Hedison countered. "Find out who's behind this, and I'll see they never get on another Mexico junket. But that's as far as I can go."

"It isn't far enough. We don't look the other way when drugs are involved. You'll have to find another firm."

"You've helped actors hush up their drug habits, I know that for a fact."

I was almost to the exit, or else I might have asked Hedison where he'd gotten his information. "We've helped users trying to get clear. Not pushers. My boss would never run interference for a drug dealer. He hasn't many principles, but that's one of them."

"It's not drugs, Elliott. It's pot. It's harmless. I have it on good authority that it's going to be legalized anytime now. By 1972 at the latest."

I delivered my last line from the doorway. "I'll remember you said it first."

EIGHT

The phones in the outer office of Zodiac Productions had cooled down considerably. I borrowed one of them and checked in with Gabby. She sounded tired and said the same thing about me. That mutual weariness was all we had to talk about. No calls had come in from Fort Ord or the Pentagon or anywhere else.

Next I dialed Hollywood Security's number and got one of Mary Jordan's professional phone minders. They all tried to sound like early Ava Gardner, and this one worked at it overtime. She took down my very terse assessment of the Hedison project—"no soap"—and promised she'd pass it on to Paddy right away.

I knew that wouldn't be until he got back from his meeting with the doctors. I also knew that I could have waited a while and called him at his home number. But he might have come up with yet another job he hadn't inquired into closely, maybe running interference for Ted LeRoy's new mob-backed rivals from the porno film industry.

I had another plan in mind for my day. I drove down to Venice Beach near Santa Monica. The area had always been popular with the local kids, and it had lately become a draw for their transient cousins. Whole blocks of shops near the strand had been given over to the kind of hippie merchandise I'd seen in the Infinite Pad, only these shops had customers. I hit every one and then worked the beach itself, giving Miranda's likeness the kind of exposure agents dream about. All I got in return was sand in my shoes.

Afterward I stopped at a bar in Santa Monica proper that had once been a great spot to get a Gibson, the longtime mixologist being a genius with a cocktail shaker. That genius was now a full-time fisherman, so the bar was a safe place for a temporary teetotaler like myself to rest his feet. I rested mine and ordered a ginger ale from the fisherman's replacement. While he thumbed his bartender's guide for the recipe, I called Jordan's Jingles, getting the same Ava Gardner admirer I'd talked to earlier. She told me that Paddy wanted me to call him right away, her tone adding that I should settle my affairs first.

Sure enough, my boss came on the line mad. "What do you mean throwing over that Zodiac job? Didn't I tell you it would be a big check for us? How are we supposed to come back from the dead with you turning away work?"

In the old days, there would have been ten minutes more of the same, complete with charts and graphs. And I would have sat for the whole routine. But not today.

"It's drugs, Paddy," I said, still making the mistake I'd made in Hedison's office, assuming Paddy didn't know the details. "He wants us to keep a drug dealer clear of the cops. I told him we don't do that kind of work."

"What I heard him say was he wanted us to keep some marijuana from reaching some kids. I'd do that for nothing, and here Mr. Hedison is offering to pay us for it. What the hell is wrong with that?"

"That's just his fallback position. He wants us to protect his in-house pusher so Zodiac's production schedule doesn't slip. I told him we draw the line at that. I've seen you figure the odds before you turned in a murderer, but never a drug dealer."

"Stop talking about drugs. This is a little Mary Jane. If you held this town upside down and shook it, you'd get more stems and seeds than pawn tickets. You'll be campaigning against beer next. Your nose has always been cocked too high, Scotty. It's one of the things that's held us back."

I'd been accused of corrupting Paddy with my morals before, but never by the victim himself. "If it's just the money, you know Ella and I will help you out."

It was the wrong thing to say and then some. "I still intend to earn my bread if I'm given half a chance to do it. You may be content to live off Ella, but I'm not."

I thought of Peggy curled up in her bed and swallowed hard. "I already told Hedison no."

"Lucky for you, he took that for a negotiating tactic. He's upped his offer, providing you're on site tomorrow morning. See that you are, or I'll get somebody else."

"Who?" I asked, but Paddy had hung up by then. The question was really for me anyway. I certainly knew the answer. I knew I should have quit years before, when the job had still been something I played at, as Ella had recently observed. In that same burst of candor, she'd pointed out that I was Paddy's last hard case. It was me or no one now.

As recently as two days ago, I'd still had Ella to talk things over with. I tried to do that as soon as I got home, but the cone of silence was still clamped down hard. All she wanted to do was sit and wait for word of our son. I waited with her for a time, with my arm around her, but she was somewhere else, maybe a whole ocean away.

That left one other sounding board, my poet daughter, but I already had her loaded dangerously. Instead of piling on more, I decided to give Gabby a break. I called the mother of one of her girlfriends and explained the situation. Shortly afterward, the mother showed up in a station wagon full of kids and dragged Gabby off to a double feature.

Ella and I spent the evening together, in a manner of speaking, me listening to records from my Duke Ellington collection—the oldest ones, for some reason, sacred seventy-eights—and Ella listening to the sound of our phone not ringing.

When it finally did ring around ten, she was in the bathroom. It was the first lucky break I'd gotten all day. If she'd answered it, she might have thrown it at me by way of passing it over.

The caller was Mary Jordan, forwarding a message herself because it gave her an excuse to ask about Peggy. The message was from someone who didn't want to leave their right name, in Mary's opinion. I thought her suspicions were understandable, since the name the caller had left was Petunia Seagull Sunrise.

Ella reappeared, and I told her I was going down to the corner for some tobacco. I was pretty sure I could have said Egypt and gotten the same disinterested response.

The evening was very still and almost cool. I decided to leave the Charger in its shed and walk down to the little neighborhood store that never seemed to close. There I bought some Captain Black for honesty's sake and retired with it and my pipe to a corner phone booth. Once I had the pipe drawing, I called the number Mary had given me.

Jill took up pretty much where we'd left off up in Topanga Canyon. "That you, flatfoot?"

"Arch supports and all." I opened the booth's door. Not in hopes of the night breeze, which still hadn't shown up, but to shoo out some of the pipe smoke.

"Have you found your runaway yet?"

"No," I said, warily, afraid I'd deserted my post at the house for a social call.

Jill wasted no timing putting my mind at rest. "I may have something for you. Some boppers came into the store this afternoon. I showed them the picture you left."

I was still scarcely listening, still mentally back up the hill with Ella. Then Jill yanked me to attention.

"You forgot to tell me the runaway's name. One of the kids said it was Miranda. Is that right?"

"Yes. What was this kid's name?"

"I didn't ask. But she told me something interesting. She said this Miranda is a big fan of a rock group called the Proposition."

I was so tired it took me a minute to remember where I'd recently heard the name. It'd been in Roland Hedison's shrine to USC. The Proposition was the band that had agreed to be filmed as part of *Duo-Glide Rider.*

"She's more than a fan," Jill was saying. "She's almost a groupie."

"A what?"

"A girl who's so gone about a group she follows it around. Like running off to join the circus, only you have sex with the clowns. The Proposition is touring the West Coast right now. I bet your little lamb is wagging her tail behind them."

"Could be." I couldn't see how following a rock group around would satisfy Miranda's apparent desire to publicly humiliate her father. Then again, as Combs feared, his daughter's new plan might simply be to hurt him by hurting herself.

I asked, "Have you heard about a concert coming up at a place called Avenal?"

"Everybody has, and everybody's planning to be there. You'll never find one groupie in that mob."

I might, if she'd attached herself to one specific group.

"Will you be going?" I asked for no particular reason.

"Why, flatfoot," Jill said. "Don't tell me you're interested. Or were you thinking of setting me up with your son?"

It was the obvious crack to make in that spot, but it hit me hard. "My grandson," I managed to say, but I couldn't put much into it.

"We even now?" Jill asked.

"Yes," I said. "And thanks."

NINE

I called Zodiac Productions the next morning from a familiar spot, Paddy's old office in the little building on Roe Street, once the home of Hollywood Security and now world headquarters of Jordan's Jingles, phone service to the stars.

When I pulled into my old space in front of the ersatz hacienda, I was only a short drive from Roland Hedison's office, so I might just as easily have shown up there. But after my exit of the day before, I didn't fancy standing at the producer's desk, hat in hand. Figuratively hat in hand, since Gabby and Ella had hidden all my hats except the one I wore to cut the grass. Thrown them away, probably.

Likewise, I didn't want to call Hedison from home, where someone I cared about might hear me bending my knee, or bowing my bared head, or whatever. Nor from some greasy spoon, either, where the breakfasters would be entertained by the meal I was making of crow. Not even from a drug store, my favorite place to make a call in the field. The local drug stores were all taking out their phone booths, as they'd earlier torn out their soda fountains, giving the floor space over to racks of important things, like comic books and panty hose. At Jordan's Jingles, I could phone and collect Hollywood Security's mail, what there was of it. And I owed Mary Jordan a visit. Her call the previous evening to pass on the message from Jill had been a subtle reminder of that overdue obligation.

When I'd first met Jordan a few years back, she'd dressed like a small-town librarian, a reaction, I'd decided, to living in a town whose average looks had been skewed toward gorgeous by a steady drip of aspiring Janet Leighs. Jordan, who'd been built by nature to withstand high winds, had refused to enter the beauty pageant, preferring comfortable shoes, spacious suits, and eyeglasses you could weld in. In the past year or so, perhaps in response to her business success, she'd loosened up a bit and now looked like a librarian on vacation.

For example, when I found her bustling about in Paddy's old redoubt, she was wearing a crisp white blouse and a khaki skirt that was short by her standards: It covered her knees but barely shaded her ankles. She still wore the safety glasses and her nose needed powder, as it always did, but her brown hair had escaped the bun of old and fell in almost natural curves toward her stout shoulders.

The private office had changed a lot since it had been Paddy's. For one thing, it was no longer private. Paddy had never shared the space with anyone on an ongoing basis, not even Peggy, but Jordan had squeezed in two additional desks, staffed by her two busy assistants. Peggy's old domain on the public side of the double doors, where I would have stuck the middle management, was now crowded with telephone operators.

Jordan gave me a big welcome, which for her meant a firm, dry handshake. She'd been a fan since Hollywood Security had handled a job for her in '66. The job hadn't ended well, but she'd come away from it impressed with me, Paddy having exaggerated my contribution, as he liked to do. When the handshake was over, she told her two assistants to catch a breeze, and they shut the door behind themselves.

I sat down in the chair where I'd spent many a meeting, comfortably and otherwise. It had been reupholstered recently and the drapes had been changed; Paddy's old horizontal stripes were now a wild plaid. And the carpet was new. The redecorating might have accounted for the room's single biggest difference: It no longer smelled like cigars.

Jordan noted my inspection. "Things change, Scotty. And sometimes, the change is overdue. Paddy held on too long. Peggy knew that, but she couldn't get him to let go. And he's still holding on. I've offered to buy this place from him outright. You know that. You know I'll give him a good price. When I bought back that little stake he and Peggy had in my company, I paid him twice what it was worth."

"I remember," I said.

"He's still dreaming of a comeback, but he's almost seventy. All his big scores are behind him. Talk him into selling, Scotty. Then he'll have that nest egg he thinks he'll find in some safe-deposit box."

"I'll talk to him," I said.

"Unless you think it would be better not to give him a lump sum. I've been thinking it over, and I'm not sure that would be wise. He might bet it all on one chance to get back on top. I was thinking it might be better if I told him I had to pay him over time. So much a month. Then he'd have a steady income for a few years."

I thought for a second I'd caught a whiff of cigar. The kindness Jordan was proposing was not dissimilar to the secret breaks Paddy had worked out for others in that same office. That he'd balanced those good deeds with an equal or greater number of not-so-nice ones didn't lessen the nostalgia for me.

"Ask Ella what she thinks would be best," Jordan said.

"Good idea," I said.

Someone knocked on the office door. It was nothing like Peggy's old crack of doom, which had sometimes caused even her husband to levitate. One of the assistants poked her head in and reminded Jordan of a ten-o'clock appointment across town.

Jordan pushed the manila envelope containing our mail my way and asked, "Is there anything else I can do for you?"

I mentioned the use of a phone.

"Use mine. I'll talk to you soon."

She gave my hand another workout and pointed to her chair, but I sat again in the one I'd been using and dragged the phone to me. I wasn't looking forward to fighting my way through the stampede of calls I'd witnessed from the sidelines the day before. Luckily, I didn't have to. The number Paddy had given me was the headman's direct line. Hedison didn't seem surprised by my change of heart, which was understandable. I was just another Hollywood hustler to him, trying to sweeten a deal. He told me I could meet the *Duo-Glide Rider* company that very morning. They were shooting at a mothballed airstrip that was south of the city but misleadingly named Whitman West.

Hedison sounded busy, which made me chatty. I put my feet up and asked him for something I hadn't bothered with the day before: a list of suspected pot smugglers.

"How many from this crew also worked on *Die, Zombie, Die?*"

"Not that many," Hedison said. "Let me see. There's Sol Riddle, the director; our star, Matthew McNeal, who's also one of the screenwriters; his writing partner, Jacqueline Jarret; and Robert Sears. Sears is a kind of a jack-of-all-trades. He handles the lifting and carrying. The other three are the creative talent."

"That's it?"

"I'm not sure offhand. There may be one or two others. Sol and Matthew take care of some of the hiring. I trust their judgment. You can ask around when you get there, see if there's anyone I forgot to mention."

His breezy impatience told me how serious he was about rooting out the drug smuggling as opposed to pulling a rug over it. It also made me less inclined to take my feet off the desk.

"Tell me a little about the big four," I said.

"I'm kind of busy doing my job, Elliott. If I find time to take yours on, I'll give you a call."

"Call me at home," I said. "I'll be watching *As the World Turns.*"

"Don't be that way. I only meant that they'll be more than happy to talk about themselves. Show me somebody around this town who isn't. They're all good kids, I can promise you that. Jackie and Matt are both film school graduates. UCLA, but I don't hold that against them. Sol's self-taught. He practically grew up in movie houses. No kidding, he can rattle off more facts about more old movies than any old-timer you'll meet. So can Matt. Jackie's more of a novelist gone bad. She did her undergraduate work somewhere back east, Penn maybe. I feel a little guilty about keeping her from writing the Great American Novel, but she's young. She'll write it someday. I expect to be a major character."

Between that and being mentioned in Oscar acceptance speeches, Hedison's future looked rosy. I said, "What about Robert Sears?"

"No college that I ever heard of. A school-of-hard-knocks guy. But the others would be lost without him to pack the trucks, throw together sets, or organize some stunt work."

"Sears packs the trucks?"

"Yes, but everybody pitches in. Don't read too much into that. I like Rob. He's blue collar from way back, like me. The other three had better starts. Matt teethed on the proverbial silver spoon, to hear him tell it. Maybe a golden one. He's kind of a golden boy in general. Sol grew up in the business, sort of. His mother was a story editor at Columbia. Jackie's dad is a dentist, I think. They all three dress like they shop at the Salvation Army, and they like to play the rebel. But a lot of well-heeled kids do. Don't let that turn you off."

"I'll try not to," I said.

"Now I really have to go, Elliott, no kidding. One of our other units ran into some trouble yesterday. Not your kind of trouble," he hastened to add. "They were using a tethered balloon as a UFO, and it got loose. Ended up in a swimming pool in Anaheim."

I expected him to say he was driving out to apologize, but that was underestimating him.

"I'm hoping to get some photographs before they haul it out, maybe get Zodiac's name in the papers. Our next release, *Queen of Blood*, is another space movie, coincidentally, so the tie-in is golden."

"Your lucky day," I said.

TEN

I didn't delay Hedison further by asking for directions to Whitman West. I knew the airstrip well, since the studios had been using it as an extension of their back lots for years. It was a World War II relic, one of the places where Lockheed and others had passed their planes over to the Army. Its big concrete runways were ideal for aviation pictures, of course, but almost as attractive were the paved roads the government had lavished on the property, including a mile-long straightaway as wide as a country highway. It had doubled for one in dozens of movies and television shows. You could film on it all day without worrying about blocking traffic or having a hitchhiker wander into your shot.

Just outside of Torrance, I came to the airfield's gate. Usually padlocked to keep drag racers out, it now stood open, its lock and chain hanging from a center post. Just beyond the gate, the fake country highway started, and at the midpoint of that, I found the *Duo-Glide Rider* encampment. It consisted of the two big panel trucks Hedison had mentioned, along with several cars and a van. Missing were the trailers every other movie crew dragged along to give the actors someplace to pout. In their stead were two big, olive drab tents, one with sides and the other without. I guessed that the complete one held the dressing rooms and makeup department. The marquee sheltered a couple of long tables, one of which, I noticed as I walked up, was covered with manuscript pages. The pages were protected

69

from the breeze by a variety of paperweights: soda-pop bottles, rocks, a pair of goggles, and a teddy bear.

The bear could have belonged to either of the two people working there, a man and a woman but both fairly new to those classifications. Either the kid was wearing a costume or he liked to overdress. Everyone I'd seen lounging around the caravan seemed to be in jeans, and he was no exception, but with his he wore a black cowboy vest and a long buckskin jacket. Like Hedison, he sported a scarf, this one red with white polka dots. I couldn't tell whether he was made-up. His heavy tan looked natural, as did his blond Fu Manchu mustache. His even blonder hair was parted a little off center, like Veronica Lake's, and was almost as long as the film noir vamp had once worn hers. His eyes, which might have settled the makeup question, were hidden behind dark aviator sunglasses.

Over her jeans, his companion wore a peasant blouse that could have been a souvenir of one of the Mexico trips. The shirt was the color and texture of burlap and long enough to double as a dress. A very straight dress, as the woman inside it was thinner than the poles holding the canvas over our heads. Or so she seemed at first glance, her straightedge lines accentuated by her afro, the biggest I'd ever seen. At the moment, it was somewhat asymmetrical, as she was tugging at the right side with a hand that wore a ring on every finger, all silver. Her glasses, which she had trained on me, were silver-framed and big and round. They had to be big for the eyes behind them, huge cat's eyes in that skin-and-bones face, eyes to make a man feel mouselike.

"What are you selling?" she asked me. "Insurance, I bet."

That stung. I'd worn an especially natty blazer that day, a gray one with buttoned-down flaps over the pockets. Gabby had insisted on picking it out for me when she'd heard I was working for the company that made her favorite beach pictures.

She'd tried to get me to skip the tie, too, but I liked to wear one when I was on a case. It gave studio heads and angry cops something to yank.

"I am in the insurance line," I said. "I'm from Hollywood Security."

"Oh, yeah," the kid in buckskin said. He stood and extended a hand. "Roland told us you might show up today. I'm Matthew McNeal."

He said it in the way a lot of the people in the movie business said their names, like he expected me to know it. I would have, even if Hedison hadn't prepped me. I'd seen it on a movie poster only the day before.

"The star of *Die, Zombie, Die?*"

"Right," McNeal said, as pleased as if the credit had been *Gone with the Wind.* "I was the screenwriter on that, too. One of them. Jackie here was the other. Jackie Jarret."

She nodded. "Welcome to Camp Zodiac, Mr. . . . ?"

"Elliott. Scott Elliott." So here were two of my suspects, front and center. They both seemed perfectly relaxed about it. Or they were until I asked a very innocent question. "Script trouble?"

At once, Jarret became as stiff as the stick figure she so resembled. "Just the normal rewrites," she said.

"Rewrites of the rewrites," McNeal added, a little too brightly. "It's tough working for a perfectionist."

"Hedison didn't strike me that way," I said. "And he told me your script was cute."

That brought Jarret back to life with a jerk. But McNeal answered me. "I wasn't talking about Roland. I meant Sol, our director. He's the perfectionist."

"What he is," Jarret countered, "is a guy who never wrote a thing in his life. He thinks rewriting a scene just naturally improves it, like practicing a lot improves your backhand. The truth is, a writer's first cut might be the best one. The freshest, the most inspired."

What she said hung together, but the way she said it—her too-rapid and too-flat delivery—made me think she was dancing around something else. The hunch got stronger when McNeal set out to change the subject.

"I thought Roland hired you for the Avenal trip. To keep an eye on the valuables in that mob scene."

"He did."

"We're not driving up there until Saturday."

It was currently Thursday, as McNeal seemed anxious to remind me.

"Just thought I'd memorize some faces," I said. "In case I have to find you later in a crowd. I'll stay out of the way."

"This weekend, too?" Jarret asked. She was busy gathering up loose pages.

"I'll do my best."

"Maybe we should write you into the movie," said McNeal, who was still as chipper as two Betty Huttons. "Can you act?"

I was saved from that bit of self-examination by the arrival of a messenger, a ten-year-old girl, barefoot and dressed like a Depression-era waif, in a dirty cotton frock. She told McNeal he was wanted.

"I'll introduce you to Sol," McNeal said as he guided me by the arm toward a stretch of road where a camera was set up and waiting. "Riddle's his last name. We all call him the Riddler, inevitably."

The nickname was inevitable, given the nation's recent obsession with the *Batman* television show. There were a number of ways to react to something like that happening to you. I would have considered moving to Uruguay. Sol Riddle had decided to embrace the situation, or so I concluded from his opening words to me.

"Riddle me this, shamus. What do my ex-girlfriends, bad luck, and you have in common?"

"I'll bite," I said.

"They're things I don't want hanging around."

The uncomfortable half minute that followed that exchange gave me time to develop a mental photograph of the director. Hedison had referred to the crew as kids, but Riddle looked a little older than the others, perhaps because his surprisingly short hair was thinning noticeably. What he had left lay flat on his large head in little swirls. Another suggestion of youth gone by was the pot belly pushing out the front of his T-shirt. The shirt bore the words "don't screw with me," and Riddle's expression underlined them. The look in his eyes did most of the work, his eyes being his dominant feature. They weren't extra large, like Jarret's, but they poked out of his head so dramatically they seemed to be dragging the rest of his face—the dark, almost continuous brow, the pug nose, the soft, lopsided mouth—along behind them.

"He's cool," McNeal assured him. "He won't get in the way."

"He's there already. I've been waiting for you for ten minutes. I say we blow off the whole day as a protest."

"We're wasting light, Solly. I'm here now. Let's get the shot." McNeal winked at me and pointed to the sidelines.

I stepped around the camera, getting a friendly nod from its operator, whose outfit consisted of pith helmet, cutoffs, and ancient Army boots. A row of motorcycles was parked nearby, and I headed that way. Three of the four were choppers, their fenders gone or severely cut back, their exhaust pipes like something from Lon Chaney's organ, their front forks jutting out like Sol Riddle's eyes, dangerously so in the case of a Harley-Davidson Duo-Glide, the bike from which the movie had taken the front half of its name. The Harley certainly looked like a title character, with its gleaming chrome and the fancy paint work on its khaki-colored gas tank. On each side of the tank was an Uncle Sam hat in a ring, the squadron insignia Eddie Rickenbacker had carried on his Spad. One of the other modified bikes was a Harley, too, an old Panhead painted in orange and yellow flames. Beside it was an even older Indian Chief. What paint it had left was black. The stock bike was a Triumph, a British make, and brand new. The model, Daytona, was one I hadn't come across before.

I was stooped over, looking at the Triumph's engine, when I heard a jingling noise behind me. Then someone said, "That's my bike."

I took my time straightening up. The speaker was a weight lifter, a little shorter than me and half again as broad through the chest. His head looked too small for him, as many weight lifters' heads did, but his jaw was plenty heavy. And, as Paddy had recently said of my nose, it was cocked a little high, as though inviting a punch. The jingling I'd heard was from a big ring of keys clipped to his belt.

"The wet head's dead, Pops," he said in place of good morning. "Or haven't you heard?"

I'd heard the hair-spray company's slogan often, along with the rest of America, but I hadn't taken it personally. "Nice bike," I said. "I had one once. Rebuilt it myself. A 1917 Indian Model O."

I was hoping to find some oil-soaked common ground, as I had with Glenn Starkey. The muscleman wasn't having any.

"I think I read about that, Pops. Your name is Tom Swift, right? Didn't you also have a flying machine and a giant searchlight?"

"No. My searchlight's pretty average. And my name's not Swift. It's Elliott. What's yours?"

"Sears."

Robert Sears, according to my telephone briefing. He had

ice-blue eyes that looked very out of place against his dark skin. His face was even more tanned than McNeal's, but the difference went beyond the shade of brown. McNeal had a poolside tan. Sears's reddish mahogany, cut by lighter streaks where his skin crinkled around those cold eyes, belonged to a working stiff.

"Hedison said you were a jack-of-all-trades," I told him. "What's that mean around here?"

"It means I'm too busy to fool with you. Go sniff around for your pot somewhere else."

So much for my powers of disguise. I waved my most recent Father's Day present at him, a pigskin tobacco pouch. "Mine's black cavendish."

"Don't put me on. Everybody knows why you're here. You were heard coming. A fucking elephant couldn't have made more noise. We get the word that nobody better be hauling grass around and then you show up. We're not stupid."

Stupid no, but definitely angry. I put away my tobacco and my smile. "So what do you know about it?"

"Nothing. I'll save you some time, Gramps. I haven't seen anything. Nobody's seen anything. Look around all you want, you won't see anything either. Not you or the next fucking elephant."

ELEVEN

Sears started the Harley with the hat-in-the-ring insignia and, without a backward glance at me, rode it over to where McNeal and Riddle waited. I walked to the nearest panel truck and looked inside. It held only two well-scarred packing cases, each reinforced at the edges and corners like a steamer trunk. Their stenciled labels stated that they contained lighting equipment, and they did. The other truck held metal scaffolding, some sheets of heavy plywood, big loops of cable, and some dust. There were none of the stems and seeds that Paddy thought so common and no hidden compartments, either, at least none I could detect with my Tom Swift penknife.

I'd given up being subtle because there seemed to be no point to the act after Sears's revelation. For that matter, there was no point to my hanging around, but I did anyway. And it wasn't because I had a feeling, as I'd had once or twice before, that something bad was going to happen. I was just being stubborn. The drug smuggler, with the able assistance of Roland Hedison and Patrick J. Maguire, had shot my day. I hoped to at least make his uncomfortable.

Or hers. Jackie Jarret joined me just before shooting got underway. I'd borrowed a camp chair that sat upwind from a barbecue grill whose load of briquettes was heating up for lunch. She took the chair next to mine, perhaps to keep an eye on me. I didn't mind. I liked the company.

I half expected Jarret to enter a guess in the when-pot-will-be-legalized sweepstakes. Instead, we had a literary discussion. It began with a series of unanswered questions.

"Did Roland really say that our script was cute?"

"Something wrong with cute?"

"Besides being condescending and dismissive?"

"He's filming it," I said. "How dismissive is that?"

"He can't help himself," Jarret said, breaking our string. "He's a prince."

Many Californians had brought their accents with them from somewhere else. Jarret's sounded a little like Peggy Maguire's, which I'd always taken for authentic Baltimore. Paddy's was more complicated, as he'd never completely shed the phony Irish brogue he'd used for years in vaudeville. In fact, it seemed to have increased in the years I'd known him.

"As long as we turn out the same kind of movie he's been making since 1958," Jarret said, "Roland treats us okay. He directed them all himself back then. Now he doesn't even bother looking at the dailies. He's seen it all too many times."

"At least you're working." That was an actor's standard consolation. I expected it to apply to writers, too, but it evidently didn't.

Jarret was twirling her silver glasses. Without them to act as a filter, her gaze was even sharper. "Tell me something, Mr. Elliott. At what age do you stop giving a damn? When does just having something to do become more important than doing something you care about?"

"I had my first bout early," I said. "Just after my discharge from the Army. I thought if I got the occasional Gibson and a warm place to sleep, the world could go hang itself."

The spinning glasses came to rest as though a bearing had seized. "Were you in a war? Which one? Korea? World War II?"

I jumped in before she had me back with Teddy Roosevelt and the Rough Riders. "World War II."

"What's combat like? Is it anything like the movies?"

"Exactly like them," I said.

"Really? I've always heard that war movies are pretty phony."

"Sorry. I didn't make myself clear. Combat isn't like war movies. It's like those musicals Busby Berkeley used to direct for Warner Bros. A lot of oddly dressed people doing crazy stuff, as crazy as dancing in the dark with neon violins or calling you-oo-oo-oo by a waterfall. And to see the pattern, you have to be way up high. At ground level, the choreography makes no sense at all."

Jarret actually smiled. It was amazing how it softened her bony face. "So if I want to write about war, I should study the work of Dick Powell and Ruby Keeler?"

"That's my advice."

"You had a good war at least. Not like Vietnam. A good cause. One worth dying for."

"They're all the same to the guys who die for them," I said.

It would have been tough to chat on after that. Fortunately, Riddle called for quiet on the set, with a very pointed glance at me. Sears had handed the chopper over to McNeal. The actor now drove it a hundred yards up the road and turned it around. The bike had a lousy turning radius, like all choppers, and Mc-Neal had to use the grass of both berms to get it done. When he was on the asphalt again and steady, he waved to Riddle and came on. The kid in the pith helmet followed him with the camera until McNeal braked to a stop next to the little girl in the cotton dress, the one who'd come to fetch him earlier. She was an actress now. As we looked on, she handed McNeal a flower, a big daisy. He removed his sunglasses, gave her the smile he'd used for his yearbook photo, and took off again. That was it, the whole scene.

It looked to me like they'd wrung it dry, but Riddle the perfectionist had them do the shot a couple more times.

Meanwhile, down the road a ways, Sears and two helpers were assembling the scaffolding and plywood sheets I'd seen in one of the trucks. The collection turned out to be a prefab ramp.

"What's that for?" I asked.

"Robby's going to jump a motorcycle over a car," Jarret told me.

"For the hell of it?"

"No. For the next scene we're shooting. It's just a gag."

"Does Sears know what he's doing?"

"Oh, yeah. I've seen him make that jump a dozen times. Roland likes the shot. He always uses it in the trailer."

The heat from the briquettes was now distorting the air above the grill. Jarret got up to start lunch.

"We all pull double duty on this crew," she explained.

As she said it, she dangled a long-handled spatula in front of me. I was hungry, so I lost my tie and jacket and pitched in. Almost immediately, memories of Billy sandbagged me again. I'd run many a backyard cookout for him and his buddies, kids almost old enough by now to be on the Zodiac payroll.

To distract myself, I watched Sears finish up his ramp and begin to test it, without a car in front. Using his shiny new Triumph—because, I guessed, the choppers' modified front forks wouldn't handle the impact of landing—he took the ramp at faster and faster speeds. McNeal and Riddle and the rest of the crew cheered every launch, which seemed to egg Sears on. After a jump that would have cleared a bus, he almost blew his touchdown. He got the bike in hand, but not before he was opposite my grill. As he wheeled around, our eyes met. He formed a gun with the fingers of his right hand and shot me through the head in dumb show. Before I could fire back, the smell of hot grease got Riddle's attention, and he called a break.

The cooking crew was served last. Jarret took her lunch and disappeared somewhere. I looked to the crowded tables under the tent. Duty was shoving me that way, but I didn't like the odds. I took my camp chair and set off for the shade of a nearby tree. Someone had sat under it earlier in the day, someone named Peter Reber. I deduced that from an object I found lying on the grass: a copy of the script of *Duo-Glide Rider* with Reber's name penciled on its cover.

The way Jarret and McNeal had reacted to my questions about script trouble made me anxious to read their work. I also wanted to see how the scene with the daisy fit into a pinchbeck beach-party movie. I wasn't sure my interest would be welcomed, given my treatment to date, so I took precautions. In addition to the script, Reber had left behind a copy of the *Hollywood Reporter.* I picked up the newspaper first, slipped the script inside it, and sat down to eat and read.

I hadn't read very far before I decided that my leg had been pulled. Whatever *Duo-Glide Rider* was, it wasn't an Annette Funicello comedy. It wasn't any kind of comedy. It was a road picture, as Hedison had said, but a serious one. The main characters were both male, two drifters on motorcycles. One, named Adam, rode a chopper called "Captain Eddie," which explained the First World War insignia on McNeal's bike. The other drifter, named Downer, was being played by the man whose script I held. Reber had carefully underscored all of Downer's lines.

In the early part of the story, Adam and Downer encountered a variety of people in one kind of minor trouble or another. They were careful not to get involved, despite a certain hothead quality in Downer. Their goal was always to make it to "the big concert" at a location that wasn't specified.

Though it was hazy on the concert's whereabouts, the script made clear how important it was, especially to Adam. In a long speech to a girl he'd slept with and was about to desert, Adam equated the concert to "a higher level of consciousness" and a "love-in" where people could find "purity and peace."

I fell into a reverie then on the subject of Miranda Combs. Maybe we had it all wrong, her father and I. Maybe she wasn't running away from something or bent on hurting herself or someone else. Maybe she was after her own slice of purity and peace. A guy who'd studied keyholes as long as I had could empathize with a dream like that.

Just as I got back to my reading, a shadow fell across me, literally and figuratively. The shadow wasn't entirely unwelcome, the shade from my tree being fickle, but I could see at a glance that the man casting it hadn't intended to do me a favor. It was Robert Sears, and he was mad.

I could have said still mad, since Sears had never warmed to me, except that this new mood made his earlier bad temper seem like mild irritation. The fists he was making had his biceps twitching. And his glacial eyes were giving off a scary inner light.

"Did I forget to toast your bun?" I asked.

"Get up," Sears said.

"Why?"

"So I can knock you down again. I hear you think combat's a joke, that it's like some Fred Astaire movie. I just spent a year in combat. I sent my best friend home in a body bag. I'm sick of people ranking on the war. Saying it isn't even a war. Spitting on soldiers."

Sears's head might have been too small for his chest, but his booming voice was a perfect match. His first words had turned heads, and his list of complaints was drawing a crowd. I looked for Jarret, who must have misquoted me and might now set things straight, and Riddle, who was supposed to be in charge, but both were absent.

"Is that you, Gramps?" Sears was asking me. "You one of those people who spit on soldiers? Try it on me."

I thought of mentioning Billy as a way of avoiding a fight. The idea made my skin burn. I stood up.

The nature lover in the pith helmet stepped between us. "We're all three veterans, Rob," he said. "We should stick together."

Sears shoved him aside. "Shut up, Maitlan. You did your time on a cruise ship. Don't tell me you know combat. And Sergeant York here thinks we don't count. Our war doesn't rate with him."

I set my feet, wishing I'd kicked the folding chair out of my line of retreat. Sears wasn't going to be a pushover, like the flyweight bandits at the Infinite Pad. He had me in every category except reach and guile.

I fell back on guile, winging my newspaper and script combo at his head while he was still staring down Maitlan. When he raised his arms to block it, I hit him in the stomach with everything I had.

He must have been neglecting his abs, because my right doubled him over. Before he could straighten up, Maitlan grabbed his left arm. McNeal, charging through the crowd, took hold of his right.

McNeal spoke with a quiet authority that surprised me. "Cool it, Rob. We've wasted half a day if we don't use this setup. You can't do the jump with two black eyes."

"His eyes'll be black," Sears gasped. His sunburned face had gotten even redder, mostly from embarrassment.

Riddle edged in, addressing the crowd in general. "Let's go. We're not paying you guys to watch a cockfight." To me, he added, "Roland won't be able to fire you fast enough."

That made me a leper. The little crowd melted away. All except the beanpole in the Clyde Beatty hat. The chest he displayed so proudly was almost concave, with a tiny patch of hair at its lowest point. His head was shaped like an inverted eggplant, but his expression was friendlier than most eggplants I'd met.

"Thanks for your help," I said. "How did you know I was a veteran?"

"I was listening when Jackie told Rob what you said about being in the war. I understood what you meant, but Rob's not into understanding these days. I don't know whether he was born with a chip on his shoulder or 'Nam made him that way, but bad is definitely his current bag. I hear your name's Elliott, by the way. Mine's Maitlan, Ben Maitlan."

"I owe you one, Ben."

"I'll say we're even if you can finish the following sentence. He's got more lists than . . ." He pointed to me like it was the spot in our routine where I did my buck-and-wing.

"Huh?" I said. It seemed like the only thing to say.

"Fill in the blank. He's got more lists than blank. Over lunch we've been doing detective talk in your honor. Crazy metaphors, you know, like this burger's hotter than Satan's insoles. Or this soda's flatter than George Gobel's crewcut. Like detectives talk."

I'd once believed detectives talked that way. Like my new friend, I'd gotten the idea from the movies, where I'd picked up more than one bad tip. Even after I'd learned that real detectives were more likely to grunt, I'd hung on to the habit of metaphor. It was a link to that naive guy who'd only wanted the odd Gibson and a warm place to sleep.

"Where do lists come in?" I asked.

"While we were eating, the Riddler came by with a bunch of them. Lists. Every morning and every afternoon, he's got lists made up for everybody. To-do lists. Or lists of things you screwed up yesterday. He's famous for them. So we tried to find a metaphor for that. The best we could come up with was 'Sol's got more lists than a supermarket full of housewives.' But it lacks snap. You're a real detective. You can do better."

Beyond Maitlan, things were coming back to life. Someone was positioning a car in front of the ramp, under Sears's very careful supervision. It was a generic patrol car.

The cameraman followed my gaze. "Almost time for the trick shot."

"Trick shot?"

"The jump. It's a big fake. The way we've got the camera set up, you won't see the ramp. It'll look like the bike just took off on its own. Speaking of which, I'd better go check my angles."

"Wait a minute," I said. "Sol's got more lists than an orphanage at Christmas."

Maitlan beamed at me and touched a finger to the brim of his comical hat. "I knew you were a real detective," he said.

I then proceeded to prove him wrong. While they finished the final preparations for the jump, I wasted time looking around for the script I'd tossed at Sears. Someone else had picked it up in the confusion, maybe its rightful owner.

Or maybe Riddle. He was standing near the camera now, but he seemed to be deferring to Sears and Maitlan. Jarret and Mc-Neal were in the vacated dining room, rewriting their rewrites again. I headed their way, intending to thank Jarret for putting me in right with the stuntman. I was halfway there when Sears, now dressed in a black leather jacket and a white helmet, revved his engine and started his run.

The ramp was as hidden from me as it was from the camera, so I didn't actually see it collapse. I heard something like a sharp slap and then the sound of an express train hitting a roundhouse. The patrol car was shoved sideways across the asphalt. Glass shattered, most of the glass in the world. The taillight of the bike traced a high parabola across the flawless sky. All around the camera, people fell as though blown down. And somewhere in the middle of the mess, Robert Sears died.

TWELVE

I sent Ben Maitlan after the police. He wasn't hurt; none of the tenpins around the camera had been. They'd all hit the ground from reflex. Maitlan, the Navy vet, seemed to collect his wits faster than the others. And he knew of a working phone at the mothballed airstrip's mothballed office.

Before sending him off, I verified that Robert Sears was beyond hope. I checked though I'd known what the verdict would be the instant the bike hit the car. He was as dead as my hairstyle, as the jack-of-all-trades might have put it himself.

After that, I went back to the survivors. If Sol Riddle's shirt had had a collar instead of a warning label, I would have loosened it. As it was, I considered slapping him to bring him around. His bug eyes were glassy, and the drool coming out of the low side of his mouth had a foamy quality. I passed him to Jarret and McNeal, who were only a little better off. Luckily, the little girl in the shabby dress had been sent home before lunch. But no one in the crew seemed much older just then.

None of them had gotten closer to the dead man than the spot where the camera sat. Not until I went back to give Sears a second look. On that visit, the two wranglers who had helped him assemble the ramp tagged along.

It was very quiet by then, the stillness broken only by some muted sobbing from the makeup girl and the last of the patrol car's glass tinkling down onto the asphalt like musical snow. Sears had knocked a lot of that glass out himself. He'd gone through the rear side window and ended up in the backseat. His autopsy might not reveal a whole bone, but he wasn't the mess I thought he'd be when I'd first run up. His neck had obviously been snapped, and, in one of those sleight-of-hands that wind or water or violence can work, his right foot was bare—boot and sock both gone. But he wasn't badly cut up, despite his bed of glass. His leather jacket and gloves and his now-shattered helmet had done him that much good. The Triumph hadn't fared so well. It was so accordioned it looked too small for Sears ever to have ridden.

The two assistants I'd inherited, who answered to Mike and Jake, asked where I wanted the body. Their spokesman, Mike, sounded relieved when I told him not to touch it. And at the same time, a little offended. Leaving the dead alone went against some strong genetic impulse to treat them like stubborn sleepers. To fold their hands for them and cover them with blankets they didn't need. I felt the impulse myself, but I resisted it.

To distract my volunteer morticians, I asked them to tell me how the ramp went together. It now looked much like it had in the back of the panel truck, like big sections of scaffolding with plywood sheets lying a little askew on top. The metalwork consisted of three pieces. Two of them were rectangles roughly ten feet by six. One had a raised lip to hold the plywood sheathing and the other didn't. The naked frame, Mike explained to me, was intended to rest on the ground. The frame that held the plywood sat on top of it, pinned to the lower frame on one end and raised up on the other by the third element of the structure, a long truss of welded pipe. This support now lay flat on its side directly in front of the lower section of the ramp. It was covered by the upper section, which had moved forward when the structure collapsed.

"I told him we needed to fasten that thing together better," Mike said, Jake nodding vigorously behind him. They both pointed to what had been the thin edge of the wedge when the ramp had been intact.

"Robby designed and built the thing himself. He wanted it light, so we could take it down and put it up fast. The thing was never rigid enough. It was vital the upper section didn't move forward at all when the bike hit it. Vital, man. If it did, the front support would just collapse forward, too, which is what happened. For the thing to work, the leading edge had to stay together. But, look, it didn't."

From a distance, the sound of a siren came to us like the first tentative notes of a teakettle.

"How was the thin end fastened?"

"The top section was just a little bit wider than the bottom. See? The outside supports of the top came down on either side of the bottom frame. There's a hole drilled through both sides for a cotter pin."

"That's it? What about this steel plate?" A six-foot-by-six-inch length of sheet steel lay nearby.

Jake spoke up. "That was just to get the bike up from the road to the ramp. Kind of a ramp for the ramp. The pins carried the whole load. Look at them. They snapped clean off."

I examined the four pieces of what had been two pins and wondered at Sears trusting his life to them. Neither was as thick as the average pencil. As Jake had observed, the break in both was clean. But not perfectly clean. Both pins were slightly bent at the point where they'd snapped.

During the latter part of our chat, the siren we'd been hearing was joined by another, even shriller one. The first belonged to a highway patrol car, the second to an ambulance. Maitlan evidently didn't trust my ability to take a pulse. That was okay. We'd eventually need someone to cart the body off. Another, less helpful example of the cameraman's initiative arrived an hour later: a very unhappy Roland Hedison.

I spent that intervening hour questioning everyone on the set. The two patrolmen who were actually in charge didn't seem to mind. They were busy taking statements of their own. Their questions concerned the accident itself, which I knew because I was the first one they quizzed. I had a choice to make then. I could tell them I didn't like the looks of things, but that would have meant telling them why I'd been hired, which would have been it for my employment with Zodiac Productions and maybe with Hollywood Security, not to mention my entrée to Avenal and my chance to find Miranda Combs there. So I settled for looking unhappy and asking them to give the cotter pins a close examination.

Since the cops had the accident covered, I pumped the crew about the hour before it happened. The lazy lunch hour, when the ramp that had performed so well in testing had been left unguarded. The hour the actual guard—me—had spent looking for clues in the pages of a script.

No one could remember anybody going near the ramp but Sears himself. Not for the record. I was reminded of what Hedison had said about the code of the school yard. "No tattling to the teacher." I was the stand-in authority figure, and no one was "peaching" to me, to use the slang of my own school days. The recovered Riddler was more up-to-date: "Why was the big pig so lonely? Because nobody would squeal to him."

My time wasn't completely wasted. I also asked everyone I talked to about *Die, Zombie, Die*. Everyone except the three I knew had worked on the film: Riddle, Jarret, and McNeal. Hedison had hinted that there might be other *Zombie* veterans on the *Duo-Glide Rider* roster, but no one claimed the honor. Not even my pal Ben Maitlan. He'd acquired a shirt sometime after the accident, though true to his principles, he hadn't buttoned it up. He told me he'd been working on another Zodiac project when that first invasion of Mexico had taken place. A space picture. He looked like he wanted to discuss something more important, but he never got around to it.

Hedison, on the other hand, had plenty to tell me. He started off badly shaken, going from one knot of crew members to another to console and be consoled, an unlikely father figure in matching leather jacket and pants that made him look like an extremely large hair dresser. When he got to me, he shifted to plain angry, though whether it was for letting Sears get killed right under my nose or for informing the cops of same, I couldn't say.

Whoever had sold Hedison on hiring Hollywood Security seemed to have convinced him that we were miracle workers. I gathered from his rant that he expected me to have swept Sears's broken body under the nearest concrete runway. Instead, I'd called in the very police he'd been trying to avoid.

Those same cops kept me from being placekicked by Hedison into the unemployment line. He was working himself up to do it when I cut him off, tactfully.

"Shut up a minute," I said. I'd been given ear calluses by some of the biggest front-office names in Hollywood history. Harry Cohn, Louis B. Mayer, and Darryl Zanuck, to name just three. The idea that I had to take the same treatment from Roland Hedison, king of the zombies, made me sore in spirit. "Nobody's firing anybody yet."

"Think not?" Hedison gave the seams in the shoulders of his jacket some serious stress testing. "What are you going to do to stop me? I hear you sucker punched Robby right before he died. You going to try that on me?"

"No, I'm going to threaten you. Shut up, or I'll go over to that guy in the uniform and whisper 'drug smuggling' in his ear. After that, whatever fines you're looking at for letting Sears play stuntman are going to seem like parking tickets. I haven't done it yet, for which you can send me flowers later. For now, stop riding me."

The big man dropped a shirt size. "You don't think this accident is connected with the marijuana, do you?"

"We'll talk about that later."

Hedison was getting a little taste of what it meant to bare your soul to Hollywood Security. If I knew Paddy, the producer would soon be eating a five-course meal at the same hash house.

"In the meantime," I said, "here comes someone you'll want me to handle. A cop who hates the movies."

A pale-blue Ford had snuck up behind Hedison's Avanti. The sedan had "government issue" written all over it. So did the man who climbed out, a thin, dark guy in a wash-and-wear suit that had seen too much of the latter and too little of the former. His wavy hair made mine look fashionable, and the skin of his habitually sour face was badly pitted. So were his insides, I had reason to believe.

He was an LA captain of detectives named Grove. I'd known him since the forties, when he'd worked for Hollywood Security, in a manner of speaking. Paddy had slipped him something to be our eyes and ears inside the police department. Grove had found out, as Hedison was learning now, that doing business with us could be complicated. Paddy had kept Grove in his reed section for a couple of years, using the threat of advertising those early bribes as his baton. Then the detective had wiggled free. I had more than once asked Paddy how, but he'd never told me.

Since his escape, Grove had risen steadily through the department, all the while maintaining a lively interest in Hollywood Security. It seemed to be the goal of his life to put the cuffs on Paddy someday. Or to pull a sheet over him.

All of which meant that by offering to handle Grove for Hedison I was putting a good face on a bad situation. There wasn't much chance Grove would give the producer any trouble. Or even the time of day. He was there to see me, period. How he'd discovered my connection to Sears's death, I couldn't guess.

For form's sake, I said to Hedison, "Go hold somebody's hand. I'll do my best to keep you out of this."

As I expected, Grove hardly gave Hedison a glance as they passed one another. He was too busy running over his first line in the scene: "Here we are again."

As Grove's greetings went, it wasn't much. Lately he'd been working in my right to an attorney.

"A little off your beat, aren't you, Captain?"

"Hollywood Security's my beat. You know that, Elliott. How'd you screw up this time? I know a scared kid called in an accident report and babbled your name in passing. Start from there and work back."

So Grove's visit was something else I could thank Maitlan for. It occurred to me that I actually should be thankful, that I might have more to gain from the captain's arrival than the points I'd scored with Hedison. So far, the police hadn't paid much attention to the failed pins that had caused the accident. I wanted to know more about them, but even in its fat days, Hollywood Security hadn't had a metallurgist on retainer. We certainly couldn't afford one now. But the LAPD could. So I made those pins the point of my story.

Which turned out to be exactly the wrong way to play it. I should have used Grove's natural suspicion against him. Refused to talk about the ramp. Claimed not to know what a cotter pin was. Trying to lead Grove to them only made him sarcastic.

"We'll ship that hardware off to Washington right away. The FBI's been bugging us for work. When they hear some kid killed himself on a homemade motorcycle ramp held together by knitting needles and spit, they'll want in. They may want to know how you happened to be here, Elliott, a top investigative brain like you. So tell me, just in case."

Grove had a gaze that had often left lumps on the inside of my skull, but today he was reluctant to make eye contact. He seemed fascinated instead by the lines of a pretty nondescript hill in the distance.

I trotted out the story of the concert in Avenal and how I'd been hired to protect Zodiac's hubcaps. Grove on the scent would have tossed that thin tale back at me. This Grove said, "What, all the crossing guard jobs taken?"

I was ready by then to say uncle. I'd expected him to dig for some way to blame me and Paddy for Sears's death, some angle that would paste Hollywood Security in the scrapbook once and for all. There wasn't much material to work with at Whitman West, but that had never stopped Grove before. And it wouldn't take much to topple us these days. Not the way we were tottering.

Instead of digging, Grove lit a cigarette, after absentmindedly offering his pack of Larks to me. Then he said, "I heard about your son. That he's missing in action. That so?"

"How did you hear?"

The detective shrugged. "From the friend of a friend of a friend."

Grove didn't have a friend to get that chain started, but I didn't call him on it. He was trying to work himself up to say something else, and I let him.

"I'm sorry, Elliott."

I believed him. He'd actually met Billy once, way back when my son was sporting diapers. I thought how ironic it would be if Grove turned out to be the person I'd been looking for. The one I could talk things over with. It was so ironic, I didn't try.

He devoted himself to his Lark for a time. When he had it smoked down to its charcoal filter, he said, "Must be killing Maguire."

He didn't smack his lips as he said it. Still, I hated to hand him the very harpoon he needed to bag his great white whale.

In the end, I gambled. "Paddy doesn't know."

Grove finally turned to face me. He had his trademark, dead-eyed look firmly in place. "He won't hear it from me. But if I picked it up, the old mick will."

He dropped his cigarette on the hardpan and ground it underfoot. "Tell your wife I . . ."

"I will," I said.

THIRTEEN

I didn't keep my promise to Grove to pass on his elliptical condolences to Ella. Not right away. As soon as the detective drove off, I collared Hedison and talked him out of Sears's home address. Then I stopped the ambulance men in the act of zipping Sears into one of the body bags he'd spoken of so passionately moments before his death.

"We need his keys," I told them. "We can't move the trucks without them."

The keys were still clipped to the dead man's belt. After a uniformed cop okayed the move with a nod, I unhooked the ring. The keys were surprisingly heavy, but that might just have been my guilty conscience at work. One of them actually did belong to the panel truck that had held the ramp. I left it in the ignition, to whom it may concern, and pocketed the rest.

The address Hedison had given me took me to South LA, to a stretch of old pavement that claimed to be a street but was more of an alley. That fit, since the place Hedison had described as Sears's house was really a garage, one of a row of garages and little machine shops, some of which customized cars. Or so their signage claimed. They might actually have cut up stolen cars or they might have cut up or customized as the mood struck them. It looked like a street that would do what it had to, to make ends meet.

Sears's garage was two bays of concrete block and heavily

94

padlocked, which fit with the late stuntman's sunny personality. I expected a big dog to be chained up somewhere, too, but when I rattled the door, nobody barked.

I did get someone's attention, though. A little guy in dirty gray overalls that were stripped like a railroad engineer's hat stepped out of the shop across the alley. He wasn't over thirty, but he could have taught a college-level course on male pattern baldness. The exposed top of his head was as waxy as a fruit-basket apple.

I waved at him. "I'm going in there," I said, jingling my borrowed keys. "If you want to watch to see that I don't take anything, that's fine with me."

The winesap sauntered over. "Robby won't like that."

The name sewn in fancy script on his overalls was Birdie. I had no idea what impulse caused mechanics and repairmen to wear their names on their chests, but I admired it. The world would be a nicer place, I thought, if everyone wore embroidered ID.

"Robby's joined the silent majority," I said.

"Huh?" Birdie said.

"He died this afternoon." I described the accident in twenty-five words or less.

Birdie then echoed Mike the wrangler. "I told him that ramp was underbuilt. He wanted it to be collapsible. You pulled the pins out and the thing would just fold up. You could carry it away as a unit. Only as a unit it was too heavy to carry. You needed ten guys to lift it. So he was stuck taking it apart every time. That's amateur engineering for you. Overbuilt in some ways and underbuilt in others. Why do you want into Robby's garage?"

I showed him my card. "I'm looking into the accident for the production company he was working for."

"For insurance?"

"For whatever." I started to try keys in the padlock.

"Maybe I should call the fuzz," Birdie said as though asking for advice.

"Call them from in here. You can keep an eye on me at the same time."

The third key fit the lock. It opened like it had been oiled that morning. The garage door went up the same way. The inside was neat but well stocked with odds and ends. It was a single open space except for a cubbyhole bathroom in one corner. Next to that was a camp stove and an Army-surplus iron bed, so tightly made up I was tempted to bounce a quarter off it for old times' sake. That bay also held a long workbench. Near it stood an acetylene torch, its gas bottles neatly strapped to a handcart. A black wall phone hung above the other end of the bench. Birdie made no move to use it.

The second bay held the makings of two or three more choppers. There was also a stack of the steel L-beams and pipes the ramp had been built of. What there wasn't was any sign of marijuana. Not the bulk shipments I'd been looking for. Not a private stash. I couldn't even find an ashtray.

"Robby wasn't a smoker," I observed.

"Not his thing," Birdie said. "Didn't smoke cigarettes or anything else. He was in Vietnam. You know that if you met Robby. He couldn't go ten minutes without telling you. Different ways that'll take you, Vietnam. It took Robby the Puritan way. His body was a temple. He wouldn't even put white bread into it."

"How did he feel about other people using pot?"

"You getting personal?" Birdie asked, shuffling his booted feet.

"*Other* other people."

"Rob was no evangelist. He thought most people had their heads up their asses. As long as they didn't cross him up, he didn't care."

I walked to the workbench and looked around for the things that had crossed Sears up, the cotter pins he'd bet his neck on. I found a cardboard box that still held a number. I tried bending one in my bare hands and couldn't.

Birdie was at my elbow. "Good luck with that," he said.

"How would you snap one of these if you wanted to?"

"You mean besides sticking it in some cockamamy ramp and running a hog over it?"

"That's what I mean."

He thought about it, his focus on the wall behind me. "Metal fatigue isn't that hard to come by. The real trick is avoiding it. You could bend that thing a bunch of times, like a piece of wire you were trying to break. It'd snap by and by."

"Only this doesn't bend," I reminded him.

"Not in your hands. You'd have to put it in a vise." He pointed to a nice example on one end of the workbench. "And maybe heat it."

We both looked to the cart that held the torch. Beyond it was some carefully stacked scrap lumber. Carrying my souvenir pin with me, I went to examine the pile. Toward the bottom, I found two pieces of two-by-four about a foot in length. On one end, each piece held the clear impression of a pin. I placed my pin in the grove of one board and then pressed the second board on top, like I was assembling a mold. The end of the pin that held the eyelet stuck out about three inches. Where it emerged, the wood was charred.

"Well, I'll be Governor Reagan," Birdie said. "Look, you can still see the marks the vise made on the wood."

I handed him the assembly to examine at his leisure and returned to the workbench. The cardboard box of pins had a label on one end. It told me that the box had originally held twelve examples. It now held six. The one I'd left with Birdie made seven, an odd number. That bothered me so much I instituted a search. I didn't find the missing pin on the bench or in any of its drawers. But I did find a flashlight. I got down on my hands and knees and pointed it under the bench. The beam glinted on something round and silver against the back wall.

"Well, I'll be Senator Murphy," said Birdie, who was now kneeling beside me.

"There's a yardstick up top, Senator."

He retrieved it. The ruler just reached the shining object. Birdie knocked the thing toward the nearest open ground and then scrambled to collect it. He returned with eyes as round as the eyelet end of the fragment he carried. It was snapped off exactly like the pins I'd seen at Whitman West.

"Don't tell me," I said. "You'll be President Nixon."

"How did you know it would be there?"

"I'm a top investigative brain." I pocketed the broken pin. "Excuse me a minute."

I crossed to the wall phone and dialed the number for Paddy's bungalow. It was his normal time to be visiting St. Anne's Home, but I was hoping he'd given himself a night off for once. He didn't answer. I called the Hollywood Security number next and left a message for him.

Stuck behind one corner of the phone was a color photograph. It showed a small ranch house in a yard of dirt. A worn, brown mountain appeared in the background. In the foreground was a motorcycle, Sears's shiny new Triumph Daytona, now deceased. I carried the photo to Birdie.

"Robby's place," he said. "His mom's old place. He inherited it when she passed. It's out near Lancaster. I'm not sure where exactly."

"Thanks for your help," I said. "I'm locking up."

"Wait a minute. You haven't said why Robby would fool with those pins. Why would he do that?"

I handed him the business card I'd flashed him earlier. "If you figure that one out, send us your résumé."

FOURTEEN

I drove home with the feeling that the rest of my day couldn't go wrong. The idea was born less of optimism than very low expectations. If Ella had come around, all well and good. If she hadn't, I'd take to my quiet sofa in the den without complaint. There was a third possibility lurking in the background, of course. News of Billy might have come in at last. There'd be no quiet place where I could hide from that.

When I sighted our house—an eccentric nineteen-twenties villa worth less than its hilltop lot—that third possibility lunged at me from the shadows. There was a sedan I didn't recognize parked in our driveway. Like Captain Grove's Ford, this brown AMC Matador had a lowest-bidder look about it. I thought it might have brought some Army representative, a chaplain maybe, and the worst possible news.

I parked in the street, ran up the front steps, and found Forrest Combs installed in my living room. He was sitting on the sofa with Gabby, pretending to admire her collection of doll heads, which she'd been rescuing from secondhand shops and dustbins for as long as she could walk. If Gabby had been showing him shrunken heads, Combs couldn't have been less comfortable.

"Scotty," he said, holding a baseball-size example sans eyes as close to arm's length as he could get away with. "There you are at last. Any news?"

"No news," I said.

I asked the same question of Gabby with a glance. She shook her head. "No news, Father."

She'd pulled her dark hair back with a plastic hair band and draped a thin cardigan across her bony shoulders. It was a costume she'd improvised especially for Combs, I decided.

"I'm afraid I've been straining your daughter's powers as a hostess," Combs said as he carefully placed the eyeless baseball in a row of heads on the coffee table.

"Not at all," Gabby said. She sounded nearly as English as Combs, and I wondered who had been entertaining whom. Gabby knew exactly how Charles Addams her collection was, and she loved to shock people with it. As happy as I was to see the laughter back in her eyes, I decided her current mark had suffered sufficiently.

"Where's your mom?" I asked.

"Upstairs, I think," Gabby said, dropping the Greer Garson.

"How about telling her I'm home?"

"Will do, Chief."

I offered Combs a scotch, and he accepted it gratefully. I poured a fistful of Dewars for him and a glass of club soda for myself. Making him drink in the middle of a doll mortuary seemed ungracious, so I took him out back, to the cracked stone verandah I'd never gotten around to replacing.

"No pool?" Combs asked. "I thought I remembered seeing one here once."

As far as I could remember, Combs had never been to our place before. I had no idea whose house he was remembering and no interest in finding out. He busied himself by lighting a cigarette, which reminded me that I'd left my jacket—and pipe and tobacco—in the Dodge. I didn't trot down to get them. My day hadn't consisted of much more than reading and flipping hamburgers, but I was worn out.

"I enjoyed spending time with Gabrielle, Scotty." He pulled

at the crease on one leg of his dark trousers. With them, he was wearing another short-sleeved shirt, one with a seersucker stripe. The combination wasn't as casual as it had been when the outfit was new, around 1963. The fashion world had moved on too far.

I wondered if Roland Hedison didn't have the right idea. Maybe it was better to dress like the kids and risk looking silly in some future family album.

"You're lucky she didn't read you her poetry," I said.

"We started with the poetry, actually. Some of it was quite good, I thought. You have a very talented daughter."

The last word was a death knell for his happy mood. He sucked down most of his free scotch and then hung his head.

"I'm sorry, Forrest," I said. "I don't have much to report."

I told him what I'd been up to so far, starting at the beginning, as Paddy had trained me to do. Paddy had also taught me to omit embarrassing details when addressing clients. In this case, I edited out Roland Hedison and *Duo-Glide Rider*. If Combs thought I was two-timing him, he'd be twice as hard to get rid of. When I got to the hot tip about the Proposition, the actor started off doubtful and worked his way up.

"I'm afraid I pay more attention to the volume of Miranda's music than the musicians. Music was one area where we had to agree to disagree. I began listening to classical music years ago when I was teaching myself to be a proper gentleman. Then I found I actually liked it. I could never convert Betty Ann—she liked Dick Haymes—and I never had any luck with her daughter. The Proposition? The name does seem familiar. The Proposition. Yes, I'm sure I've heard Miranda mention them. She took some of her record albums away with her. Theirs, probably. Will you go to Avenal, Scotty? I'd go there myself, but I'd be lost. It's terrible of me to ask you, given what's happened. Ella told me about your son. Why didn't you tell me, old man?"

In the yard next door, my neighbor was having a pre-dinner catch with his kid. I couldn't see them for the overgrown landscaping, but I could hear the sound of the ball hitting their gloves: a smacking sound when the father threw it and a soft "pock" when the kid tossed it back.

"Would it have gotten me off the hook?"

"Probably not," Combs admitted.

His golden hair looked phony in the early-evening light. Especially sprouting from his china-white skull. It looked like the hair on one of Gabby's severed heads.

"But it would have explained Ella's strangeness on the phone. Poor woman. And your reluctance to pitch in."

"How did Ella seem tonight?"

If Combs thought it odd that I was asking for an update on my own wife, he didn't show it. "She's quite used up, Scotty. I'm worried about her. Seeing her this evening made me think of that film she wrote years ago, the one about the woman whose wartime lover comes back to haunt her."

"Private Hopes," I said.

"That's the one. When I saw that picture for the first time, I thought, 'That laughing, golden wife of Elliott's wrote this? She has depths I never guessed at.' This evening I thought I could see straight down into those depths. It frightened me. It's all been stripped away, all the layers of persona, the loving wife, the Hollywood success. It's like seeing a person laid open by a terrible physical wound. Forgive me for being blunt and stupid about it, Scotty. I'm not saying exactly what I mean. But *you* know. You've seen the same thing yourself. You understand it better than I do."

I let that true-confessions opportunity pass. Combs was still on the trail of his point, holding his cigarette out before him like an ineffectual candle.

"You'll think it flippant of me, but the other thing I remembered while speaking with Ella was my early, terrifying brush with television. Live television, I mean, which was frightening enough all by itself. The strangeness of it, the pressure, the awful cables running everywhere underfoot. But what made it even more sweat-inducing for me was working with young actors from New York. Real actors, not movie stars. Method actors. Until I met them, I thought of acting as a process of putting things on. Costumes, of course, and makeup, but characterizations also. Acting meant burying oneself under layers of something else, and the best actors were the ones who hid themselves so completely they were unrecognizable.

"Those young firebrands from the east saw things differently. Acting for them was stripping everything away, all disguise and pretense. Laying everything bare. It frightened me, I remember that clearly. It went against so much, not just the way I did my work but the way I lived my life."

He toppled a towering ash from the tip of his Parliament. "It's a hell of a thing to get to our age and find everything you believed was true is not. Do you suppose the young people are right, Scotty? Are we so inauthentic?"

Combs's language certainly was. It was the language of a self-made gentleman. A figment of his own imagination. But in our zip code, who wasn't a figment of somebody's imagination?

"I'll ask Gabby," I said. "She might have a poem on the subject."

"Or a replacement head for me," Combs said, rousing himself. "I should let you have some time with her. And with Ella."

We followed a flagstone path that led around the house. At the head of the drive, Combs suddenly remembered why he'd come.

104

"It wasn't just for a progress report. I've heard of a group that helps runaway teenagers here in Los Angeles. Some well-to-do people who open their homes to them. A friend of mine saw an article about them in the *Times*. He suggested I contact them. They call themselves the LA Lodgers. Is that a play on the LA Dodgers, do you suppose?"

"I suppose," I said.

"I wondered if it might be worthwhile checking with them. One of their members might have taken Miranda in. Though the thought of her staying with strangers, however well intentioned . . ."

My thought was that a well-intentioned stranger would beat the hell out of the common variety. But I was tired of holding Combs's hand, so I was careful not to stir him up again. "I'll check it out," I said.

"But the concert—"

"Isn't till Saturday."

"Good. You'll let me know what you learn."

"I will," I said.

FIFTEEN

I went inside. Gabby was downstairs, alone and dressed to go out, not as an English hostess now but as herself, in bell-bottom jeans and a striped sailor's blouse.

"The Murrays asked me over to dinner," she said. "I'm suddenly very popular. It's all your fault, Dad. We're on the jungle telegraph now."

Meaning that the woman I'd called to get Gabby a night at the movies had spread the word of the limbo in which we were living. I wondered if that was how Grove had heard the news. Or how Paddy eventually would.

"What did your mother say?"

" 'Be back by eight.' I'll be back a lot sooner than that. She's better, I think, Dad. She's taking a shower."

Now that she'd mentioned it, I could hear the water running through our old pipes. A car horn called up to us from the street below, and Gabby headed for the door, giving me a peck on the cheek as she passed.

"I almost forgot," she said at the door. "Paddy called again. He wants you to call him right back."

"He always does," I said.

I followed her as far as the front steps, so I could see her safely into the convertible waiting below and wave my thanks to the woman at the wheel. They'd be bringing over covered dishes next. That would be something else Ella could kick me for.

Back inside, the water heater was still taking a beating. I

decided I had time to call my boss.

"You've never been the easiest man to get hold of, Scotty," Paddy said for openers.

He might have led off with a conciliatory word, our last conversation having ended abruptly. But that wasn't Paddy's way. I settled deeper into the chair I'd selected, a worn leather club chair that had survived all the redecorating to date, thinking I should extend my own olive branch. I never even considered pointing out that I'd left the first message in the current exchange. Paddy might have lost his office, but he'd retained all his prerogatives.

"What did the doctors tell you yesterday?" I asked.

"Doctors," Paddy said derisively. "I haven't run into so many experts who don't know what they're talking about since Dewey beat Truman. They don't think Peg's getting any better. They don't think she ever will. I don't give *that* for the lot of them."

I heard the sound of his fingers snapping. It was loud enough to summon a dead maître d'.

"Every day she seems better to me," Paddy said. "Just tonight, when I told her how close you were to a fatal motorcycle accident, it was all she could do to keep from railing at me for putting you in harm's way for the hundredth time."

"How did you hear about that?"

"On the radio, the way I usually get my reports. Me and Dick Tracy. Only I have to wait for the evening news."

"They didn't mention my name, I hope."

"No, but they did squeeze in Roland Hedison's. So I knew you were nearby. He's pleased with our work so far, I expect."

"Thrilled to death," I said. I gave Paddy the full story then. Around the point where I punched Sears in the stomach, I heard Paddy lighting a cigar. But he didn't speak again until I described what I'd found in Sears's workshop.

"Here's one for the funny papers," he then said. "Did Sears

seem like the kind who'd take his own life?"

"Only if he could take everyone else's first. But stranger things have happened, I guess."

"We could fill a book with them. How does the pot smuggling fit in?"

"I'm not sure," I said.

"Not sure or haven't idea one?"

"Take your pick."

I realized then that the water had stopped running sometime during my recitation.

"Hedison's going to try to slip the hook," I added quickly. "He didn't want the police called in on the smuggling. He's never going to pay to have this accident turned into something else."

Paddy replied as I'd hoped he would. "We'll see about that. It sounds like I should give Roland a call. To explain his civic responsibilities to him. I'll let you know how he's bearing up."

I climbed hand over hand out of my chair and then went up the stairs slowly, not because I was expecting an ambush but because my feet felt like lead. But there was an ambush waiting, of a sort.

Ella was seated at her dressing table, brushing her hair. There was nothing odd in that, except she usually had something domestic on, a robe or pajamas or one of my undershirts. This evening she wore a nightgown, an old favorite of mine. It was a flashback to wartime pinups, but that wasn't the reason I looked forward to its every appearance. Ella called it her dancing attire, "dancing" being our code word for "sex." The lace and silk signaled that she was in the mood and usually got me there a heartbeat behind her.

This evening, though, I was so sure we had our signals

crossed I said, "Sorry," from the doorway and started to back out.

"Scotty, don't go," she said. "I want to talk with you."

Gabby had been right; Ella did sound more like herself, though it was a hesitant, distracted version. I crossed to the bed and sat down. From there, my view was of the deep, straight line of her spine disappearing in a swirl of silk. It was a view that never failed to get to me. It got to me now, despite the gravitational pull of the pillows behind me.

"I talked with Forrest Combs this evening," she said. "He told me about Miranda running away." She was still speaking haltingly, like someone who hadn't used her voice in years. It scared me to think how long it had been since we'd really talked. How close we might have come to never talking again.

"I'm sorry I didn't give you a chance to tell me what you were doing, Scotty. If you could have told me."

"Forrest didn't swear me to secrecy."

"I meant, if you understood what you were doing."

"There's generally room for doubt," I conceded.

She put down her brush and swiveled on her stool. She ended up sitting with her knees together but off center, her hands gripping the stool's sides. She was leaning forward slightly, as the late Betty Ann Combs did in her memorial oil painting. Ella could have held her own in that competition if she'd been wearing a sweat suit. In her dancing attire, she won by a mile. Then she smiled, and I actually forgot the possibility of sex.

"What I'm trying to say is, you might not understand why you're doing it."

"It's not a favor for an old friend?"

"No, not just that. It's not an excuse to run away, either, Scotty. I'm sorry that I thought it might be."

So was I. "What is it?"

"A transference," Ella said. "A substitute. You can't help

Billy, so you're trying to help Miranda. You're trying to make the universe owe you one, to buy Billy a break by proxy. I'm sorry I didn't see it earlier."

I couldn't feel smug about that, since I still didn't see it. In fact, I thought that Ella was plain wrong, that she'd fallen into the classic storyteller's trap. It was the belief that you only had to knit together the story behind a certain event or condition to understand the outcome. And control it. That is, if you could make a story of the chain of events leading to X, you'd have X where you wanted it. In this case, the chain was a short one: Detective hears of son being lost in a faraway land, detective hears of girl being lost close to home, detective compulsively searches for girl.

As a sometimes solver of mysteries, I was a regular victim of the storyteller's trap. I'd often followed a story back to its once-upon-a-time, trying to understand a smashup by tracing the skid marks. But that wasn't why I knew about the pitfall. I knew because Ella, a professional storyteller, had lectured me on it. She considered it one of the banes of modern life, born of too many Hollywood happy endings and a growing but misplaced faith in psychoanalysis. In the power of storytelling, in other words, to give us that happy ending. A surprising number of our friends and acquaintances served time on doctors' couches, looking for the missing pages of their personal stories and never finding them.

The real problem, according to Ella, wasn't that it was impossible to hammer the million fragments of your life into a coherent narrative. That only took patience. The problem was that faith in the healing power of storytelling was misplaced. It assumed the thing at the end of the story—depression or heartache or the desire to take a life—would go away if the distant first cause were known.

But it didn't work that way. Figuring out a story didn't

explode a problem any more than figuring out what had caused Peggy's stroke would make her rise out of her bed. Or poking around in a garage would bring Robert Sears back to life. The most storytelling could do was set your foot on the long road to forgiving yourself or keep you from falling into the same hole twice. So said Ella.

But now my cynical wife was herself playing Freud, and I was stretched out on the couch, figuratively. I thought I might be there in reality very shortly. Ella was looking at me like she wanted to consummate her forgiveness. When she joined me on the bed, she didn't sit in my lap, but she came awfully close.

I wanted her as much as she appeared to want me, but not at the cost of leading her on. If she thought her revelation about my motive for finding Miranda Combs was going to make me give up the quest, we were in for another blowup. A record one, once she knew that I was off to Avenal with the rest of the Mod Squad.

"Forrest wants me to check into a group called the LA Lodgers," I said, starting us off in low. "Have you ever heard of them?"

"Of course," Ella whispered in my ear. "Winnie Mannero is involved in that."

"I should talk to her."

"But not tonight," she said.

"No," I said. "Not tonight."

Honesty had been served, I decided. Ella knew I wasn't giving up, and she wasn't kicking. Mentioning the concert and the job I'd taken on for Paddy could wait. Everything could wait but one thing. For a moment, we could step outside the story we found ourselves in, the long lead-in to this moment and whatever lay ahead.

"Tonight I need you to do something for me," Ella breathed.

"Name it," I said.

"Hold me, Scotty."

Sixteen

Around eight, we heard Gabby come in. The sound woke Ella, who'd been dozing with her head on my arm. She sent me down to check on things, saying she might follow later. She was asleep again before I'd left the room.

Gabby already had the television on. She was lying on her stomach, her head propped on hands and elbows. She answered, "Okay," to my question about dinner without turning her head from the tube. I pulled a footstool over and sat beside her.

"Something wrong?" I asked.

"Something else, you mean."

"So?"

"They all act like Billy is dead, Dad."

On the small screen, Elizabeth Montgomery, daughter of the man whose movie we'd watched earlier that week, was trying to undo a magic spell cast by Agnes Moorehead.

"It's how we act that counts," I said.

Gabby chewed on that for a while. Then she held one hand out to me behind her back and we shook on it.

"The Charger's still in the street, Dad."

It would have stayed there, too, if I hadn't remembered for the second time that evening that I'd left my pipe and tobacco on the front seat. I went down to collect them and the jacket that held them and moved the Dodge into the driveway while I was at it. That was a waste of effort, as it turned out.

When I got inside and unzipped the tobacco pouch, I found

a premium the tobacco company hadn't put there. It was a folded square of notepaper. Unfolded, it turned out to be a typed set of directions I badly wanted but hadn't asked for: "Sears Ranch, Highway 138, three miles west of Lancaster."

I called Paddy, using the extension farthest from Gabby's television.

"Feel like a drive?" I asked.

"Always," Paddy said. "As long as I'm not doing the driving. What particular drive do your have in mind?"

"To Lancaster."

"The actor or the town?"

"The town."

"That's not a drive, it's a sleeper hop."

I told him about the color shot of the ranch house I'd found in Sears's garage and the note that had turned up in my black cavendish.

"Put there by whom?" Paddy asked.

"Anybody," I said. "My jacket was on the back of a lawn chair most of the afternoon."

"It wasn't a request for a meeting, since it didn't specify a time. So it's what, do you suppose?"

"An anonymous tip," I said. "Like the ones Hedison got."

"Pointing you toward the pot? Or just trying to get you off someplace lonely?"

"One way to find out."

"Right. I'll be ready when you get here."

I broke the bad news to Gabby, who took it stoically. Especially when I added that her mother was probably down for the count. I based that hopeful prediction on how tired I felt myself.

Before I left, I unlocked the cabinet where I kept my automatic. Gabby got less pleased with me, but didn't say anything. At one time, I would have made a joke about mountain lions, but she was too old for that now. So was I, for the moment at least.

"Just being careful," I said.

"Be real careful, Dad," Gabby replied.

As Paddy had said on the phone, he'd always loved being driven around, and I was his favorite chauffeur. He climbed into the Charger wearing the slacks from that day's suit, a windbreaker, and the gray straw fedora he sported when he vacationed out of state. The hat implied, as its wearer had joked earlier, that Lancaster was halfway to Reno. Actually, it was on the other side of the San Gabriel Mountains, just past Palmdale.

We climbed the Santa Monicas first and crossed Forrest Combs's valley very near where the actor sat drinking the night away. Then we picked up Highway 14 and took it through a high pass in the San Gabriels called Antelope Valley.

Paddy had started the drive with his window rolled down and a cigar going, his favorite way to travel. But as we climbed and the night air thinned and cooled, he tossed the last of his corona away and rolled up the glass. With the wind noise gone, he was free to tell me how he'd handled Roland Hedison, and he made it his usual dramatic reading.

I sipped coffee from a paper cup and listened with one ear. With the other, I imagined I heard Ella's regular breathing as she slept. I caught myself holding my own breathing shallow, as though her head still rested on my arm and any movement might wake her.

Paddy was saying, "So the problem isn't Mr. Hedison. It's his crew of junior geniuses. They don't want you along on this Avenal trip. They've threatened to throw the whole thing over if you insist on going. Our twisting Hedison's arm does no good if he isn't able to twist theirs. From what he tells me, he isn't. This gang doesn't need him that much anymore. They've all of them got the credits they need to go it alone. And they'll go anytime, Hedison thinks. If this little mutiny comes to a head, they'll go all the faster."

"And do what for backing?" I asked.

"They've no respect for money, these young people," Paddy said with a sigh.

"When hasn't that been true?"

"Never, I guess. If twenty-year-olds had any sense, Peg and I would still be in Baltimore. And you'd be in Indiana, practicing law. But the kids today are crazier than we ever were. I may have thumbed my nose at Rockefeller, if I'd run across him in, say, 1919, but it wasn't because I thought money was the bunk. I was cocky enough to think I'd do at least as well as old J.D. had. These kids don't seem to give a damn about that."

"Hedison's kids care about doing good work," I said. "They're artists, maybe."

"Where's Hollywood going to be if those types take over?" Paddy demanded. "Having one Irving Thalberg around is okay, especially if he's got a Louie Mayer watching the books for him. Everyone treats him like a pet. When he dies young, the studios all shut down for the day and everybody has a good cry. But a whole town of Thalbergs? I shudder to think of it."

He shuddered in silence for a long stretch of road. In Palmdale, we picked up Highway 138. Between Palmdale and Lancaster, the highway ran due north. At Lancaster, it turned west. I checked the odometer. Paddy unzipped his jacket and produced a snub-nosed thirty-eight. For years, he'd carried a forty-five that was the twin of mine, but recently he'd switched to the revolver, at the recommendation of Jack Webb, or so he always claimed. He broke open the cylinder and snapped it shut again with a flip of his wrist. Three miles later, we came to a turnoff marked by a rural mailbox on an extra tall post.

"Must deliver on horseback out here," my passenger said.

The box was rusted generally but was a little less so where the shadow of old paint spelled out the name Sears. I turned into the lane, the Dodge nearly bottoming out in a gully that might have doubled as a drainage ditch. A series of washouts kept our speed down to a crawl. Finally, the headlights illuminated a barn and the house from the photograph. I switched off the lights and the engine, and we sat listening to the V-8 tick and the more distant sound of a coyote looking for a date.

"Your lead, I think," Paddy said.

I opened my door and climbed out, without the benefit of the car's dome light, which I'd disabled the day I'd driven it off the lot. I carried a flashlight, but I didn't need it yet. The moon was up, and this far from the city, the sky was incredibly clear.

The little frame house had a porch roof that ran across its entire front but no porch to go with it. The overhang's supporting posts, which looked like the trunks of old saplings worked over with an ax, were set directly into the packed earth. An old rain barrel flanked the leftmost support, and an even older wagon wheel leaned against the weathered siding next to it. In the moonlight, everything seemed a bluish gray, a light gray in the open and a battleship gray in the shadows.

I guessed the wagon wheel to be a decoration, the West Lancaster equivalent of a lawn jockey or a reflecting ball. If so, it was the only frill the old place had. The two front windows carried all their glass but no shades or curtains that I could see. The effect made me feel exposed, both to the blank, black stare of the house and to anyone hiding within. Between the windows was a modest door. If it had ever been painted, the wind coming down off the mountains had long since scoured it clean.

I knocked on that door and then tried the knob. The door was locked, twice. Luckily, I still had Sears's key ring. Paddy stepped up behind me as I was turning the dead bolt. He moved very quietly for a big man. He spoke even more so.

117

"Any thoughts of a booby trap? Would you put that past Mr. Sears?"

"I wouldn't put a minefield past him," I said.

I pushed on the door and got well to one side before it opened. No bouncing grenades disturbed the peace of the night.

"I'll stargaze for a bit, I think," Paddy said, by which he meant he'd watch my back.

I went inside, preceded by my flashlight beam. The furniture and decorations were early John Ford, but there were enough feminine touches to convince me that the place was more a reflection of the dead mother than her dead son. If so, the neatness I'd observed in the South LA garage was a family trait. The family was also represented in photographs: an old one of a raw-boned man and a smiling girl, a newer one of the girl as a wrinkled woman with hooded eyes, and a faded color print of Sears as a boy, astride a bicycle with no fenders and what looked like a length of straight pipe for handlebars. He'd been a customizer even then.

I found no drugs or drug money or anything else worth pausing over, with one exception. There was a box of shotgun shells, twelve gauge, in the drawer of the little writing desk where Mrs. Sears might have done her bills. There was nothing odd in that. If I'd lived in that lonely spot, I'd have had a tommy gun in the umbrella stand. Only there was no twelve gauge to go with the shells, not hanging on the wall, not propped by the door, not under the bed.

Outside, Paddy actually appeared to be gazing at the stars. There was such a splash of them, I was tempted to join in. I headed for the barn instead, which was small and even grayer than the house. Its double doors were secured by a heavy hasp with a stick though the staple. That stick was another off note. For one thing, it seemed insufficiently neat for the very neat Sears family. And it was way too trusting for one of the Searses, the one I'd met. I thought of the boat-anchor padlock on the LA garage. If the stuntman hadn't used a lock on this door, maybe he'd used something else. I remembered Paddy's booby trap comment and then the promise I'd made to Gabby.

I handed my backup the flashlight and removed my belt. I carefully slipped the stick from the staple, holding the door in place with my foot. I pulled back the hasp's hinged strap and threaded my belt through its slot. The buckle, pivoted, made the connection secure. I was about to give it a real test when Paddy tapped on my shoulder.

"A little insurance," he said and handed me his belt.

I knew there was no danger of his pants falling down, in spite of the weight he'd lost, because he also wore suspenders. I fastened his belt to the end of mine and motioned him to get clear.

The door didn't swing open on its own as I stepped away, but the slightest pull started it going. When it was open about a foot, it stopped. I gave it a tug. An instant later, a blast of light and sound tore the night apart.

SEVENTEEN

I ended up flat on my back. So did Paddy, I saw when a little of my night vision came back. By the time I scrambled over to him, he was sitting up and laughing. It'd been a while since I'd heard that full-bodied, up-from-the-diaphragm boom. I joined in, and between us, we scared off whatever wildlife the shotgun blast hadn't scattered.

"Imagine us almost falling for that one," Paddy said. "With all the experience we have under our belts."

"We're not wearing our belts," I reminded him. I'd never wear mine again. The blast that had made splinters of a chunk of the door had shortened the strap to its prewar length.

Paddy said, "You'd think two guys with our know-how would walk around the blooming barn and look for a window. But God knows what Sears would have wired to that. One of your old howitzers, maybe. Where's my hat?"

As I helped him to his feet, he added, "I hope when you hit that guy he knew it. His little greeting card will bring the police if there're any to bring. Let's have a quick look at what he was trying to protect."

We first examined the booby trap. Sears had made a thorough job of it. The shotgun I hadn't been able to find in the house was wired to a heavy sawhorse that was itself staked to the barn's dirt floor. The gun's double barrels had been sawed off dangerously short. And recently, I thought. The cut was rough to the touch, and the bare metal hadn't started to corrode.

The barn was set up as a stable, with four stalls, none of which contained a horse. They weren't entirely empty, though. In one of them we found the marijuana, covered with old feed sacks. The pot was in two rough bales, bound in burlap.

Paddy whistled. "I've seen this stuff in bales before, on that freighter where old Morrie Bender ended his days. I didn't think two-bit operators like Sears were bringing it in like this. God help us."

It was a spot to remind him of his recent dismissal of "Mary Jane" as no big deal. But neither of us would have enjoyed that comeuppance. And I understood Paddy's change of heart. It was hard to shrug off the threat when you were faced with that much of the stuff. I couldn't help thinking of Gabby and the carload of friends who had taken her to the movies. How many bags would those bales produce, I wondered, to be bought by how many kids? "What's the street value, do you suppose?" was how Paddy phrased the calculation.

"Don't worry," he added in response to a sharp look from me. "We're not going into that business. I was just trying to figure what Sears stood to make from this. It might tell us what dream he was trying to finance."

"The money was the dream," I said.

"Maybe. But it's been my experience that money's only dream fertilizer, at least in our little corner of the world. That's why we see so much of it plowed into the ground."

I didn't want him getting autobiographical just then, so I asked, "What are we going to do with this stuff? We don't have much time to decide."

Paddy was a man St. Peter couldn't rush. He rocked on his heels and said, "We've been hired to keep this quiet, which will be hard to do once the police get here."

"Damn near impossible," I said. I'd been straining to hear an approaching siren. If the cops were coming, they were sneaking up on us.

"I think a little bonfire is called for. We'll be destroying evidence, but Sears has passed beyond the reach of the law, so where's the harm? We can keep Hedison's skirts clean and stop this stuff from poisoning anyone, all for the price of a match."

With a wave of an apparently empty hand, he produced one of the kitchen matches he favored.

"These bales won't burn very well without help," I said.

"How will the barn do for kindling? Look around for what the arson boys call an accelerant."

I found the can of kerosene that fed the lamps in the house. After checking for headlights on the washed-out drive and seeing none, I doused the bales.

Paddy struck his match and said, "Out of here now. If Ella smells this on your clothes, she'll take away your pipe. You'll be down to dipping snuff."

I went as far as the door. Paddy joined me there, after pausing to give the shotgun a last look while the flames flared up behind him.

"I suppose we should have dismantled that contraption," he said. "Oh, well. It'll give the police something to teethe on. If they ever get here."

I was anxious to be gone before they arrived. It didn't seem possible that we could make it back to the highway before somebody showed up, but we did. We took the first turnoff we came to, a southbound road of well-packed dirt with a sign for a place called Quartz Hill. Then we stopped on a little promontory to smoke and admire our handiwork.

The pyre was just hitting its stride. The flames were sending a nice tower of sparks into the starry sky, hot red points of light that died before the cold blue ones high above could even notice them. It was a sight to make a man philosophical, but it didn't take Paddy that way.

"Where are the damn cops? If I ever decide on a life of crime, this is where I'm setting up shop. Ah, at last."

Headlights were speeding along the road from Lancaster. Above them, a red beacon rotated lazily.

"The question now," Paddy said, "is what to tell Roland Hedison. We could pretend we didn't find the stuff and string him along for another paycheck or two."

"The cops will connect the barn and Sears's death," I said. "They'll probably talk to Hedison."

"That doesn't mean he'll hear about any pot. Sherlock Holmes himself couldn't sift those ashes from the pile that barn will leave. Still, Hedison may put two and two together. I guess it's best we take credit for this and hope for a bonus and a nice letter of recommendation down the road. It's a pity we can't cash in on that concert. But our leverage with Hedison is useless if he doesn't have any with his troops."

"I might have some," I said. "Leverage with his troops, I mean. When you talk to Hedison in the morning, tell him I want to meet with his front line. Their names are Jarret, McNeal, and Riddle. Don't take no for an answer."

"That'll be the day," Paddy said.

It was well into the next morning when I parked the Dodge in my driveway again. Gabby was asleep in front of the television. The station she'd been watching had gone off the air, leaving only a glimmering screen and a comforting hiss, like a surf retreating from a pebbled beach. The house sounded way too quiet when I shut it off.

I thought of trying to carry Gabby up to bed, but I didn't need another reason to feel old and tired. I woke her just enough to get her on her feet and then led her upstairs by the hand.

Ella was still asleep. It seemed to me she hadn't even rolled over since I'd last seen her. I wanted very badly to crawl into bed beside her, but I thought it would be better if I first showered away the three or four kinds of smoke I'd been exposed to.

I made it as quick and quiet a shower as I could, but when I came out, our bed was empty. I searched the house for Ella and found her on Billy's twin, curled into a tight ball.

EIGHTEEN

Winnie Mannero was a Beverly Hills hostess, the widow of a silent movie star named Carlos Mannero. He had been one of a score or so of Valentino imitators, one of the better ones, I always thought. His career had been slowed by rumors of homosexuality, which his long marriage to Winnie had never quite silenced, and stopped in its tracks by the coming of sound. After that watershed, his Spanish accent had demoted him to playing heavies and guys who lost the girl to fast-talking Americans, and Carlos had gotten his fill of both roles in a hurry. So he and Winnie had settled down to being givers of dinner parties, a respectable second career in Beverly Hills.

Ella had known the Manneros longer than she'd known me. She'd introduced me to them and later volunteered me to be one of Carlos's pallbearers, a tough assignment, given that three of the others had been old silent names and not much help. Buster Keaton, I was pretty sure, had been lifting in pantomime. Being a family friend, I didn't call ahead for an appointment. I just made the familiar drive to the big, pink stucco house with the wrought-iron balconies on its upper windows and the regulation two palm trees out front.

Down the street, a tour bus was making a slow pass in front of Jack Benny's place. I waited in Winnie's drive, not wanting to make her open her front door while the bus was there. That gave the tour guide the chance to point me out to her charges, maybe as "a former Paramount hopeful who couldn't find his way out of town." She didn't bother.

Winnie's smile of greeting more than made up for the slight.

"Scotty! So good to see you! I was just thinking of giving Ella a call. It's been forever since we were together."

It'd actually been about two months, but that felt like forever to me just then.

"You look tired, Scotty. Have you been keeping late hours?"

"They've been keeping me, I think."

Winnie was a short, plump woman with hair as high and stiff as any first lady's. Her face was dominated by black-framed eyeglasses too big and too young for her face. The skin of that face was sun damaged—wrinkled and spotted both—but she seemed okay with it. She'd never had a face-lift that I'd been able to detect. Nor had Ella, and she could spot a tuck job a mile away. Winnie's outfit today was a jacket and skirt of matching brocaded blue. She looked like she was dressed to go out, but she never mentioned it or acted rushed.

She sat me down on a living-room sofa so tightly stuffed I barely made a dent, offered me a number of beverage choices, and then perched on the cushion beside mine. When I told her I was looking for a lost young woman and asked her about the LA Lodgers, her ravaged skin reddened.

"Scotty, I'm not doing that anymore. It got to be too much for me. I think that it's a worthwhile idea . . . that it started as a worthwhile idea: people opening their homes to runaway children, giving them a safe place to be. There's so much danger out there for children, so many people trying to take advantage of them. People who want to sell them drugs or prostitute them or photograph them doing horrible things."

"You're talking about pornographic films?" I was surprised that Winnie even knew about them. She seemed so like Central Casting's idea of a grande dame.

"Oh, yes. Just the other day Helen Silverman—she's the driving force behind the LA Lodgers—called to tell me about a new danger. Girls are being recruited right off the street for these underground films. Kidnapped almost, to hear Helen tell it. They're given drugs to control them and to get them to . . . perform, I suppose you'd say. Certainly it isn't acting. Not in that kind of film.

"Helen called to get me to reconsider, to get me to take in more teens. It made me weep to turn her down, Scotty, but I had to. I'm too old for it. The first two young ladies Helen— she's the one who pairs the children and sponsors—sent to me were so sweet. It broke my heart to think of them out in the world on their own. But the last one! Scotty, she was loud and dirty and crude. She left cigarette burns in everything. She brought a man into her room, a man she hardly knew. And she stole from me. Some earrings and a pair of silver candlesticks and a cup Carlos won at the polo club. His team beat Spencer Tracy's that year, and you wouldn't believe how proud Carlos was. The police recovered the jewelry and the silver, but not the cup. I tear up every time I think of it.

"That was it for me and the LA Lodgers. It's a serious problem, I know, but it's too big for me. It's too big for the entire city. Why should we be responsible for the lost children of the whole country?"

Because greater Hollywood had done so much to make those children the restless souls they were today, a sociologist might have answered. I said, "It was very nice of you to get involved at all."

Winnie's small hands fluttered in her lap. "I did it because I'm lonely, Scotty. People envy one a long marriage, and they should. It's an achievement, especially in this day and age. But it leaves you so empty when it ends. It's like all the loneliness you didn't experience—all the loneliness the people who have no one feel every day—has been saved up for you and delivered to your door all at once. Enough of that," she said, making fists of those fluttering hands. "How are Ella and Gabrielle? How is that soldier of yours?"

"Not good," I said.

I hadn't gone to Winnie's intending to spill my guts to her. But I did. I told her about Billy being missing and how hard it had been on Ella. I didn't tell her because she'd admitted to being lonely and telling her created the illusion that she was family or because she reminded me of a favorite grandmother who'd always been a confidante. Not even because she was an old friend and entitled to know. I told her because I was more worried about Ella now than I'd been before last evening's reconciliation. I'd thought the talk we'd had and the desperate clinging afterward were steps back to our normal sense of being one, but they hadn't been. If anything, Ella was more withdrawn than ever. I was secretly fearful that last night's interlude had been her way of saying good-bye to me before she set out on some journey alone.

Winnie listened to it all calmly. Very calmly for a woman who cried at the thought of a stolen polo trophy. Then she said something that caught me off guard.

"You think Billy's dead, don't you, Scotty. You know in your heart he's dead. Is it a father's instinct or is it because you've been to war yourself? 'Missing in action' doesn't mean the same thing to you as it does to a civilian. It isn't a reason to hope for you. It's just a way of putting off the truth."

Her insight made me feel much the way I had when Robert Sears had accused me of spitting on soldiers. Only hours earlier, I'd told Gabby that it didn't matter what anyone else thought, so long as we believed that Billy would come back. It shamed me to remember now that I hadn't told Gabby I believed her brother was alive. I'd said we had to act as though we believed it. We had to play a part.

Feeling threatened, I stuck to what I thought was the point. "I'm worried about Ella."

Winnie paused for a few ticks of the mantel clock before replying. "Of course you are. But I think you're doing the right thing by giving her the time she needs to work through this. She's a little lost now and wrestling with problems no one can solve for her. She's like the runaway children we've been discussing. Most of them find their way back to their families."

"But not all of them," I said.

"No," Winnie said. "Not all of them."

We listened to the clock count off another century's minute. Then Winnie said, "I'll call on Ella. But I'll wait a day or two."

"That might be best," I said.

She walked me to the door. On the way, at my request, she stopped at a rococo secretary and jotted down Helen Silverman's address. At the front door, Winnie had a last-minute thought of her own, one that frightened her so much she never finished it.

"There was Ella's brother. Another Bill . . ."

"Thanks for listening," I said.

I followed up that unannounced visit with another, this one to the Los Angeles home of Helen Silverman, the woman who distributed runaways to the idle rich. She was tall and fortyish with the brittle look of someone who had married movie money and then found her time hard to pass. She wasn't interested in passing any of it with me, however, especially after I told her why I'd dropped by. She tried to send me packing and then reluctantly agreed to look at Miranda Combs's photo. As a reward, she got to tell me she'd been right from the start.

"It's as I said, Mr. Elliott. Our runaways are from other parts of the country, not other parts of the county. Children don't run away to get a few miles from home."

Edna May Oliver couldn't have sniffed her way through the line any better. Her frostiness kept me from asking a follow-up question about the porno-film menace she'd spooked Winnie with. I had another, better source in mind in any case.

That source was a cop named Ed Sharpe. I found him in his cubbyhole office in downtown Los Angeles, with his sleeves rolled up and the knot of his tie yanked down toward his waist. Sharpe was a safe cop to approach. Unlike Captain Grove, he bore no grudges against Hollywood Security or me or anyone else, as far as I knew. Not even against humanity in general, which was rare in a man who'd dealt with so much humanity for so long.

Sharpe was grayer than I was, and he clung to a dated, clipped mustache that gave him the look of a faded lounge lizard, a look that probably served him well in his current assignment, vice. Though he looked older than I did, we were of an age. I knew Sharpe had served in Burma under "Vinegar Joe" Stilwell. That experience might have been what helped him keep things in perspective. Or maybe it was the space program. Pinned to the corkboard on the wall behind his head was a photo cut from the *Times*. It had been taken from an Apollo spacecraft in orbit around the moon and showed the earth as a not particularly big ball against a whole lot of black.

I was hoping Sharpe would dismiss the idea of porno films made with or without the consent of underage draftees, that it would turn out to be something Helen Silverman had cooked up to keep her volunteers motivated. But the policeman not only confirmed it, he tied it to something Ted LeRoy had told me in the opening moments of the case.

"It's mob money, Elliott. That's what we're hearing. It's found its way into the blue-movie business, and it's changing it like you wouldn't believe. Think Las Vegas in the forties."

"Gambling's legal in Nevada," I said, "which makes it a good place for the mob to invest their money. Where's it legal to kidnap kids and film them having sex?"

"I dunno, but it's happening somewhere not very far from that chair you're slouching in, if the rumors are true. Though kidnapping is probably too strong a word. These scumbags wave a little money or a little pot in front of some cute kids and lead them back home. Then maybe the kids don't have such an easy time getting away. That's the word on the street, as they say on television. Unfortunately, actual witnesses are hard to come by. The kids that come through it are too scared or embarrassed or plain strung out to step forward."

"But where can your scumbags hope to show movies like that? It'd have to be strictly underground, like the old stag films."

"Not necessarily. It's a big world out there. The mob's gotten used to thinking internationally. The drug business has done that for them. They're financing films you can just get away with showing in the bigger American cities, films made with consenting adults, and, if these rumors are right, they've got a hand in other films, ones you can only show overseas. So far, anyway."

As usual, Sharpe didn't seem too put out about any of it. It made me wonder how tough Stilwell had been. The policeman did a little chair-slouching of his own, loosened his tie even more, and asked, "What's your interest, Elliott? Or is that confidential?"

I only had a couple of photos of Miranda left, but I thought it was worthwhile spending one on Sharpe. "Missing kid," I said as I dealt it onto his desk.

He didn't reach for it right away. "A kid you know?"

"A little. Why do you ask?"

"You don't look so good. You look like Sonny Liston looked after Cassius Clay got through with him."

"Muhammad Ali," I said.

"Right. You look wrung out, which isn't like you. I've always admired your positive attitude, given the business you're in. Nothing seems to get you down."

"There's a coincidence."

He picked up the photo and said, "All-American blonde," with a connoisseur's appreciation. "Yeah, she'd be the kind they'd want for some romp they intended to show in Hong Kong or down Argentine way. Assuming 'they' really exist. Of course, she's the type most shady guys want for most shady things. I'll keep an eye peeled for her."

NINETEEN

I drove home to Doyle Heights and found Ella on the phone. She was sitting on the living-room sofa looking very small, holding the handset to her ear like it was a gun she'd put to her temple but couldn't decide to use.

The call's come in at last, I thought, and started into the room to join her. She waved me away without breaking her eye contact with the far, bare wall. Gabby, who'd made her usual noiseless approach behind me, hustled me into the hallway.

"Who called?" I asked.

"No one. Mom called them. She's mad today, Dad. You can't hang around. She's getting madder, too. They keep putting her on hold, transferring her, and putting her on hold again. But she won't give up."

I liked the sound of that. If Ella was fighting back, she couldn't be on her way to someplace beyond my reach.

"Maybe I'd better hang around," I said. "I don't want her throwing things at you. You can't catch."

"But I move fast," Gabby said, which may have been a criticism of me. Certainly at that moment I wasn't moving at all, though she was pulling me hard by the arm.

"There's another thing, Dad. There are ladies coming over to see her. Brenda's mom and Nancy's mom. I heard about it last night at dinner. You don't want to be here when that happens. Mom's going to blame you."

"Why?"

"Because it's your fault."

That wasn't unreasonable, but I was. "Why didn't you tell me last night?"

"I thought it might be a good idea if someone did come. So Mom could let off steam."

My first reaction was to call the women and warn them, but Gabby had a point. Maybe giving Ella some other living people to react to wasn't a bad move. I was still trying to decide, when Gabby stopped pulling.

"I almost forgot. Somebody did call. Paddy. He wants you to call him right back."

Which I'd have to go somewhere else to do. The force of that argument was so strong that Gabby didn't resume her yanking.

"Don't forget to duck," I said and kissed her good-bye.

I drove down to the corner store where I'd bought several thousand quarts of milk and borrowed the outside phone booth from which I'd earlier called Jill the groupie expert. Paddy had had his way with Hedison, and he gave me a blow-by-blow account of the fight. I was afraid my change would be gone before he got to the knockout. Two nickels shy of the crisis, he told me I had a one-o'clock appointment with Jarret, Riddle, and Mc-Neal. Then he read off directions that covered half of the envelope I happened to have in my pocket.

I knew before I'd finished scribbling that I'd have to leave right then if I was going to make it, which meant leaving Ella and Gabby to face the women's auxiliary alone. It was yet another opportunity to throw the whole thing over, to tell Paddy my gambit wouldn't work after all, that we'd have to settle for Hedison's current tally. But then I'd also be giving up on the concert and the chance to search there for Miranda Combs. Since talking with Ed Sharpe, I'd been clinging to the hope that Miranda was following the Proposition. Even if she was playing house with one of them, it was far and away the lesser of two evils.

I signed off with Paddy, picked up Route 10, and took it west to the Pacific Coast Highway. Then I followed that road around the long curve of Santa Monica Bay, the traffic thinning as I drove. The land and sea breezes must have been jostling each other just then. I alternately smelled the sea and the pines of the passing hills.

At Malibu, I started watching my odometer, as I had heading out of Lancaster the night before, though that drive seemed like an hour before or maybe a month. Six miles later, when I was almost to Point Dume, I turned off the highway, taking a road next to a sign for a bird sanctuary. The road wound between hills that had once been sand dunes themselves. They were now miles from the surf and covered in the tall grass and stunted trees that liked the sand. After two more changes of road, I spotted the drive I'd been told to look for. It squeezed between hillocks and ended in a sandy parking area. I'd seen the cars parked there at Whitman West: an old Willys station wagon with wooden sides and a somewhat-less-old Plymouth Valiant. The teddy bear who'd been part of the rewrite team the day before was propped in the Valiant's rear window, looking sad. A pal of Robert Sears, I thought as I parked behind the sedan.

The dead stuntman might have visited this remote spot once himself. Between the parked cars were motorcycle tire tracks that didn't look particularly fresh. They ended at a footpath that circled one of the smaller former dunes. It led me to an almost flat, treeless area the size of a couple of tennis courts. In a far corner was a house trailer on pilings of concrete block.

Earlier, I'd wondered how old railroad cars had found their way into Topanga Canyon. Getting a trailer into this hollow had been another engineering challenge. But just then I was thinking more about loneliness than logistics. I felt a little like I had back at the Sears ranch, only without Paddy and his trusty thirty-eight to back me up. It didn't make any sense to feel that way—Sears was dead and he couldn't have booby-trapped all of Southern California—but there it was.

I was as stealthy as Gabby crossing the baby dunes of that lot, but somehow I attracted Jackie Jarret's attention. She opened the trailer's door before I got close enough to knock.

"You made a long drive for nothing, Mr. Elliott," she said.

"If I don't get anything else done, at least I can thank you for setting Sears on me yesterday."

Jarret wouldn't be distracted. "You're not going to Avenal. We told Roland that's a no-no. If you go, we don't."

Which would have had me wondering why they'd agreed to meet me if I hadn't been a little distracted myself just then. Jarret was wearing a dress of broad horizontal stripes of white and green, a dress so simple and straight and short it might have been an untucked shirt. The legs it exposed had been wasted in yesterday's jeans. She had her silver glasses pushed up into her hair, the better to glare at me. I gave her a chance to get tired of that and then closed the range. She stepped out of the trailer's doorway to let me enter. I caught a whiff of her perfume as I did, and it reminded me of the orange groves that had surrounded Los Angeles when I'd arrived in the thirties.

Then the perfume gave way to smoke—all from cigarettes, my trained nose told me. The small space was hazy with it. Riddle and McNeal were wedged behind the trailer's little dining table, poring over loose script pages. McNeal climbed out to shake my hand. He'd lost his Wild West jacket and vest of the day before, but not his jeans. With them, he wore a pink, buttoned-down, oxford shirt that went not at all with his George Armstrong Custer locks.

"Welcome to my beach house," he said. "The best place in the world to get writing done. No neighbors, no phones, no distractions."

"And no beach," I tagged on impolitely. "You could write a whole book on your walk down to the water."

"True. It's not exactly ocean view, but it's cheap. Someday, when we hit the big time, I'll move the trailer to Malibu. If the property owners association doesn't object."

"We're a pretty broadminded bunch."

McNeal raised his golden eyebrows. "You live in Malibu?"

"Only on the weekends."

"There must be money in the shakedown business."

"Funny you should mention shakedowns," I said, leaving it at that for the moment.

I expected Riddle to be the least friendly of all—he was still wearing his don't-screw-with-me shirt from the day before—but his opening remark was almost cordial.

"I thought I recognized your name yesterday. It took me all night to remember an article I'd read in *Film Scene*. You were with Carson Drury in 1955 when he went back east to try to restore the ending of *Imperial Albertsons.*"

"That's me," I said.

Drury was Hollywood's favorite failure, a onetime boy genius who'd gone from world-beater to has-been in two pictures flat. He'd always maintained that his big flop, *Albertsons*, had been sabotaged by his studio. In '55, he'd put the last of his money where his mouth was and gone to Indiana to try to restore the film's original ending. I'd been a member of that doomed expedition, one of the lucky survivors. Ten years later, *Film Scene* had asked me for an interview for an anniversary article, and I'd consented, in part because it seemed to be the punch line to a very old joke. Drury had told me that my brief association with him would be a claim to fame one day.

It figured that Riddle would see Carson Drury as an iconoclastic forefather. A lot of the self-proclaimed rebels of

Hollywood did. I was tempted, as I'd been with the gushing reporter from *Film Scene*, to tell the Riddler about Drury's taste for Cuban cigars and handmade shoes and of his inability to tell the truth for two sentences running. But I didn't. Never throw away a bargaining chip, as Paddy always said.

"It would have saved him, man," the pop-eyed director was saying, his enthusiasm almost reverence. "If he'd been able to salvage that film, it would have been a win for the little guy against the system. That's why the studios got together to stop him. That's what happened, wasn't it? It was a conspiracy of the big studios, right?"

"We'll talk about it in Avenal. Over a campfire, maybe."

"No maybes about that," McNeal chimed in. "You're not coming along. There's no reason for you to, now."

"Meaning what exactly?" I asked.

Jarret was backed against a mini refrigerator, her arms folded across her spare chest. "Let's just say it. If we'd dropped the bullshit yesterday, Robby might still be alive. You were called in because Roland got an anonymous tip about pot smuggling. That's all over now. The smuggler's dead. No pot's going to Avenal courtesy of Zodiac Productions. And no you, either."

"So you all knew what Sears was up to?" No one answered me. "Which one of you sent the note to Hedison?"

"It doesn't matter now," Riddle said. "It's over, like Jackie told you. What Sears did was his own business, until it threatened the picture."

"Then it became your business." No one replied to that, either, but no one looked away guiltily. "I got my own anonymous note yesterday. Whoever slipped it to me might be interested to know that it paid off. A lot of coyotes got a free high last night."

That wasn't news to them, of course. Paddy had bragged of it to Hedison, and the producer had surely passed it on. I didn't add anything about me almost getting my head blown off, the atmosphere already being strained. I asked instead, "Why was Sears smuggling drugs?"

"You understand that we'd be speculating," McNeal said. "You do what you do for the love of it or you do it for money."

Or beach houses in Malibu, I thought but didn't say. I had decades of experience treading carefully around artistic pretensions.

"Rob did things for the money," Jarret added. "Zodiac didn't pay him enough to keep him happy."

"Why did you say he might be alive today if we'd had this chat yesterday?"

She shrugged, sticking a bony shoulder through the oversize neck hole of her dress. "I don't think what happened to him was an accident. I think he knew things were closing in on him."

"So he killed himself?"

McNeal answered that one. "He's been acting like he wanted to, as long as we've known him. Probably since he came back from 'Nam. His way was to pick a fight with the world, like he did with you yesterday, and do wild things and run with wild people, like the creeps he smuggled drugs for. The way he died, that's the death he's been flirting with for months. If I was writing it in a script, that's the suicide method I would have picked for him."

"You'd never get away with putting that in a script," Riddle said. "Suicides do simple things, not Rube Goldberg things. For my money that was a timely accident."

Jarret didn't like the "timely" crack. "If someone had called the police at the start, Rob would have ended up in jail, but he'd be alive. He could have gotten help."

She hadn't exactly delivered that recrimination to Riddle, but he reacted as though she had. "What's done is done, Jackie.

Sears did his own thing and paid the price. None of us is going to get a better deal than that. Which brings us back to your services no longer being needed, Elliott. Drive carefully on your way home."

"You may not need me," I said, "but I need you. I'm trying to locate a runaway girl who's a big fan of that band you're going to Avenal to film. She may show up at the concert. Or somebody in the band may know what happened to her. I could drive up there myself and maybe connect with the Proposition. Or maybe not. If I ride along with you, it's a sure thing."

"And Papa Hedison pays for you to find someone else's kid," Riddle sneered.

"He can afford it."

"We can't, Elliott," McNeal said. "We're going to have exactly one chance to get the footage we need. No retakes. We can't afford to have any distractions. If you want me to ask the band about this girl, I'll be happy to."

I was sorely tempted to take him up on that. But then he added, "Besides, it won't be safe for you up there."

"Why not?"

"Rob was going to sell that pot to someone at the concert who planned to resell it at a considerable markup. The way he told it, the buyer he had lined up is a real hard-ass. He was one of the dangerous people Rob liked to hang with, like I was telling you. If he finds out you're the one who kept that pot from arriving, it could get ugly."

"It could get ugly for anyone connected with Sears and Zodiac," I said. "Any one of you."

"We can take care of ourselves," McNeal said.

It was a young person's standard boast, almost the motto of the current generation. In fact, it had been one of the last things my son had said to me before he'd shipped out.

"If I'm there to play lightning rod," I said, "you won't have to take care of yourselves. You can work without looking over your shoulder."

"Thanks but no thanks," McNeal said, his arms folded now, like Jarret's.

Riddle, slouched behind the table, couldn't be bothered. "There's no way you can talk us into taking you."

I had one more bit of talk to try, one of the shakedowns McNeal had jokingly referred to as the source of my beach house. I pointed to the script pages Riddle had carefully collected and placed beneath his ashtray. "Has Hedison seen those?"

"He approved the script for *Duo-Glide Rider,*" Riddle said. "He approves every picture before shooting starts."

"Then he gives you the longest leash in the business. That's what he told me. What you told me yesterday backs that up," I said to Jarret. "You said he doesn't even look at the dailies anymore, not the ones shot by an experienced crew like you three. It'd be possible to get him to approve one script, a teenage comedy with motorcycles, say, and then film something entirely different, something like the story I started reading yesterday after lunch. It was an artsy thing about a big love-in, with no comedy whatsoever, also featuring motorcycles.

"I'm guessing you plan to present Hedison with a fait accompli, a finished picture that isn't what he'd ordered but that he can't afford to shelve. Only without that concert footage, *Duo-Glide Rider* is a fait half accompli. Hedison can still pull the plug on you if he finds out what's going on."

They didn't try to deny the basic charge. There was no point in that, not when, at my prompting, Hedison could demand to see the footage they'd shot so far. So they tried a different bluff, Riddle leading off.

"Roland will go along with anything we say. If the movie's evolved as we shot it, he'll dig it."

"And he doesn't want to piss us off," McNeal tossed in. "He

knows we'll walk if we get mad, and we're the best he has."

"He's expecting to lose you soon whatever happens," I told them. "When he finds out what you're up to, he'll figure you're working out your own severance package. How's he going to like being played for a sap? He has a little temper, from what I've seen."

Jarret, who'd left the dodging to the others, finally spoke up, but only just above a whisper. "He may like what we've done."

"Maybe. Or maybe he'll think you're trashing Zodiac's reputation on your way out. Will the folks in Kansas trust their kids to him when you three get through?"

Riddle muttered, "If they let their kids see *Die, Zombie, Die,* they're trusting him way too much already."

McNeal took a step my way. "We can't go on making that kind of crap, Elliott. It was fun at first, and it was a way to learn our craft, but now it's killing our souls. We deserve a chance to make our own films."

There were any number of good answers to that. They could try to sell their project to Hedison honestly. They could quit Zodiac and try to sell the idea to someone else. They could lay bricks or mow lawns or do whatever it took to become their own backers.

But I wasn't in Point Dume to lecture anybody. I was thumbing a ride, the hard way.

"You don't have to go back to making crap," I said. "You just have to put up with me for a day or two. Talk it over. I'll expect a call by quitting time."

TWENTY

I caught a break that evening. Ella joined me of her own free will on the front steps of our house, where I often sat to smoke my last pipe of the day.

That was after I'd spent some time on the telephone. My first call was to our answering service to get my messages. Hedison's wonder trio had made up their collective mind. I was to report bright and early the next morning for the ride up to Avenal. My second call was to Paddy to ask after Peggy—he'd seen the usual hopeful signs—and to report my success. The last call was to Forrest Combs. I told him I'd struck out with the LA Lodgers, but that, with any luck, I'd be interviewing the Proposition the next day. Combs was sure I'd come back with the answer, if not the girl herself. His optimism had the same forced note as Paddy's, with an added flavoring of alcohol.

I hadn't gotten a report from Gabby when I'd returned from Point Dume. I'd found her asleep in the den when I'd gotten in and I'd left her at it. I'd figured that as a family we were at least thirty hours in the hole as far as sleep was concerned. And Gabby was the one I would have picked to catch us up.

Ella had been in our bedroom with the door closed. Hoping she was also finding some rest, I'd gone downstairs without looking in and made my calls. I'd eaten a sandwich standing at the kitchen sink and then retreated with my pipe to the front porch.

I'd no sooner sat down there than I'd been waylaid by a

memory of Billy and that same porch, which he'd used as his office when he'd set himself up as a private detective around age seven. By age eight, he'd decided he'd rather be a soldier than a private eye. He'd yet to outgrow that career choice.

Ella showed up before I dug myself in any deeper. She sat down beside me, but well to the other side of the step, as though she was expecting us to be joined by someone. Her hair looked fully blonde, a trick of the twilight's I'd often enjoyed. She wore an old tan dress shirt of mine, worn through at the elbows, white pedal pushers, and penny loafers. That everyday outfit cheered me almost as much as last night's lacy nightgown had. But her opening speech made me hold my breath.

"I'm going down to the beach house tomorrow, Scotty. I want to be alone. It's too hard on you and Gabby to have me here. You should have heard me this afternoon when a couple of the PTA mothers showed up to hold my hand."

"They still speaking to us?" I asked, tapping out my pipe with elaborate nonchalance.

"God knows. I'm surprised you're still speaking to me, after the awful things I said to you."

"We made our apologies last night."

"Last night," she repeated wistfully, as though I'd mentioned Paris in the fifties. "I just don't want to spoil things again. That's why I think I should go off by myself."

I was sure she shouldn't, sure it would be the first leg of a trip she'd never finish. I asked, "What did you find out on the phone today?"

"Nothing. I don't think we'll ever hear anything from those people. Billy will just show up someday and tell us it was all a mistake."

Her voice almost broke on that line. I put my hand down on the cool concrete between us, and she placed hers over it. We sat like that for a while. I was breathing shallowly, as I had on the drive to Lancaster when I'd imagined her sleeping beside me and hadn't wanted to wake her. Tonight I didn't want to frighten her away. So I stayed very still, until she drew her hand back and squared her feet to stand.

At the last possible second, I said, "Would you mind holding off a day or two?"

"Why?"

"I've gotten involved in something for Paddy. I have to go up to Avenal tomorrow, maybe stay overnight. Somebody should be here with Gabby. I can take over when I get back."

She didn't say anything, and I plunged on. "We're working for Roland Hedison of Zodiac Productions. Somebody on his payroll, a stuntman named Sears, was smuggling pot up from Mexico in Zodiac's own trucks. Hedison thought the latest shipment was heading for Avenal."

It felt perfectly natural to be talking a case over with her. I'd been doing that since before we were man and wife. It felt even better than natural when I saw that she was actually listening to me.

"To Avenal?" she asked. "To the Roads of Destiny concert?"

Even at half speed, she was more aware of the world outside of Hollywood than I usually was. "Right. Sears got killed yesterday trying to jump a motorcycle over a car. I was standing twenty yards away and never saw it coming. The ramp he was using for the jump collapsed; the pins that held it together failed. I went to Sears's workshop yesterday and found a pin that had been made to fail. Then Paddy and I drove out to a ranch Sears owned. We found the marijuana, a lot of it."

"And immediately didn't call the police."

"No," I admitted. "But we saved them a match."

"So case closed," Ella said. "Smuggling stopped, smuggler dead, probably by his own hand. But you're still going to Avenal."

That was my cue to drag Miranda Combs in. Then Ella could have taken up last night's refrain—Miranda was a substitute for Billy—and we would have been done. But as often happened when I recounted a case for Ella, I was seeing the pieces in a different arrangement.

"Something else is going on," I said. "The creative team making this movie, *Duo-Glide Rider,* are three bright kids named Jarret, McNeal, and Riddle. They're pulling a fast one on Hedison. He thinks they're making a drive-in-grade comedy. Actually, *Duo-Glide Rider* is an art-house film, maybe with antiwar themes."

"Good for it."

"They see it as their chance to break free from Zodiac and do some important work. Sears's little sideline threatened that. Hedison was tipped to the drug smuggling by anonymous notes, which is also how we found the pot last night."

"You think one of the three is the anonymous source?"

"All of them, probably. They seem to be joined at the hip. It would have hurt them all professionally if Sears had been caught by the cops and the business got into the papers. And there was an even worse possibility, from their point of view," I continued, figuring it as I went. "A scandal like that would have killed their baby, this film they're making behind Hedison's back. Not by letting Hedison know what they were up to, though that could easily have happened. The bigger threat was that *Duo-Glide Rider* would get tied to a drug scandal. That would have tainted it in a lot of people's minds, tainted its message. Even if these kids had been able to finish it and persuade Hedison to release it, no mainstream reviewers or audiences would have given it a chance."

Ella's role in these sessions, besides logic teacher, was devil's advocate. She slipped into it easily now, perhaps finding as much relief in the old routine as I was. "Tipping Hedison off, anonymously or not, threatened their movie, Scotty. Anything that drew attention to that crew did. Why would they run that risk? And how did they know Hedison wouldn't call in the police himself?"

"They know him pretty well, or think they do. And the first time they tipped him, they were working on a picture they didn't care about, a zombie movie. Hedison didn't bring the cops in then, so it was pretty safe to assume he wouldn't this time. It's harder to figure why they didn't name Sears in their notes. Hedison could have fired him and that would have been that. And once they knew what Sears was up to, why did they agree to work with him again?"

"He might have had something on them," Ella said. "Maybe he knew that they were planning to switch scripts on Hedison. They would have had to keep him around then, to keep him quiet. They would have had to do anything he told them to do."

"That could be why—" I cut myself off in mid thought, not wanting Ella to follow me there. As usual, though, she was a thought ahead of me.

"You're afraid these kids killed Sears, aren't you, Scotty? When Hedison brought you in, they saw the notes had been a mistake. They killed Sears, picking a way that could pass for an accident if nobody looked too close or suicide if they did. You're afraid of that, aren't you?"

"Yes," I said. "They pushed the suicide angle pretty hard today. Too hard. But if it was murder, it can't have been something they improvised because I happened to show up. They had to have planned it." I finished the thought I'd cut short, the thought Ella's speculation had inspired. "Sears must have been using his leverage to control the film, maybe to change it in ways they didn't like."

"It was premeditated because they had to tamper with the pins, I assume. What about that, Scotty? What about the broken pin you found in Sears's own workshop?"

"If it was murder, I was meant to find it and the other things that suggested the pins had been doctored there. Using Sears's own equipment to do the sabotage was a master stroke. It would have meant getting his keys away from him somehow, but that would have been a minor challenge for these three."

"Slow down a little. Wouldn't killing Sears jeopardize their movie? There isn't much that stays hidden in a murder investigation."

"What investigation? You're right, though. They would have been running a big risk. That's a vote for its not being murder. I hope it's not."

Two of the neighborhood children zoomed past on the street below, one on a bicycle pulling the other one on a skateboard with the aid of a third party's clothesline. The skateboard rider waved to us as they passed. I thought the sight might derail Ella, but after a moment she spoke again.

"You like these whiz kids, don't you?"

"I like one of them. I admire all three."

"Because they're betting everything on a movie," Ella said. "You've always been a sucker for people who do that. If the movie in question is doomed from the start, you fall even harder."

"This one's not doomed yet."

"Are you going to Avenal to save it or because you need to know what really happened to Sears?"

"Yes. Plus some other reasons." For example, now I was going to keep Ella from running off. But I stuck with reasons that were safer to discuss. "The crew might be in danger up there. The guy Sears was selling drugs to might come looking for them."

It was another chance to mention Miranda and the Proposition. I would have, if Ella had still needed selling. But I could see that she didn't.

"As long as you know why you're doing what you're doing, Scotty," she said, giving me as good an opening as I was going to get for a question I really didn't want to ask. "It's when you don't know that I worry about you. You lead with your right then."

"With my chin."

That almost got a smile. I hated to kill the mood, but I knew I had to. "Speaking of motives," I said, "are you sure you know why you want to go away?"

"Speaking of leading with your chin," Ella said in warning.

"I went to see Winnie Mannero today. About the LA Lodgers."

"I remember."

"We talked about Billy. Winnie remembered something that scared her. About what happened in 1944 when you heard your brother Bill had been killed."

"Before your time, Scotty," Ella said, meaning: "None of your damn business."

"Winnie scared me with it," I said. "I'm still scared."

"Scared of what? That I'll party too much and sleep around?"

That was how that death in '44 had taken her. At least, those had been the outward signs of the wound.

I said, "While I'm gone, think about why you want to be alone. We can talk again when I get back."

TWENTY-ONE

Our rendezvous was Oxnard, north of Los Angeles on the 101. I got there earlier than the sun, expecting to find something like the flea-circus caravan I'd seen at Whitman West. But when I located the gas station named in the phone message, its lot contained only two idling vehicles: one of Zodiac's panel trucks and an old, short-bed school bus.

McNeal explained the situation to me, after describing himself as our wagon master. He was dressed for the part, as he was again wearing his buckskin jacket and black vest.

"We're traveling light, Elliott. Only three actors, me, Pete Reber, and Polly Hayden."

He introduced me to them, though I'd already met Reber, whose script I'd briefly kidnapped. I'd questioned him in the aftermath of Sears's accident, along with the other cast and crew. Reber was a big bear of a kid, the resemblance heightened by hair as long as McNeal's but much less manageable and by a full beard. Polly Hayden hadn't been at the airport location, so we were meeting for the first time. She was maybe twenty-one and "thrilled to make my acquaintance," which told me, along with her big dewy eyes and perpetual grin, that this was probably her first picture.

McNeal was grinning himself, so hard the corners of his Fu Manchu were hiked up almost to his cheekbones. "We have to take the motorcycles and a camera and the portable sound equipment, of course, but that's pretty much it. No lights, no food, no tents. Our goal is to get in, get the shots, and get out. We'll redub some dialogue later, probably, and shoot some close-ups, maybe. Today we're going for the cast-of-thousands stuff. Take good notes, Elliott. *Film Scene* will be calling you someday for another interview. Maybe on the tenth anniversary of this very day!"

I asked myself what McNeal was high on and decided it was nervous energy. We'd come to the make-or-break point of their make-or-break movie. Even the hard-to-flap Ben Maitlan, gypsy cameraman, was a little overbright for the early hour. He'd traded his pith helmet for an Australian bush hat, the brim tacked up on one side in the regulation manner. As a concession to the predawn chill, he wore a windbreaker that showed a lot of wrist and waist. He pumped my hand longer than was necessary and invited me to ride with him in the truck.

No glance had passed between Maitlan and McNeal—or between the cameraman and either the sleepy Riddle or the pacing Jarret—but I thought the plan was probably the big three's idea, their way of isolating me for the three-hour drive.

I agreed on one condition. "I'd like a copy of the script."

I addressed our wagon master, but the suddenly-wide-awake Riddle answered me. "We're the ones setting the rules, shamus. Here's one for you. No shootin' irons."

I was wearing a windbreaker over a golf shirt, chinos, and desert boots, the better to pass for the world's oldest Pat Boone impersonator. I thought the loose jacket hid my holster and gun, but evidently I was wrong.

"Sorry, Elliott," McNeal said. "But that's final. This concert is about peace and love, not guns."

He was standing shoulder to shoulder with his director. Jarret, dressed in a long quilted coat that looked like a sleeping bag with sleeves, stepped up to form a united front. Maitlan

151

wandered off to join Reber and Hayden and the rest of the crew.

I said, "You told me yesterday we might meet up with a disappointed drug dealer."

"We also told you we could handle that," Jarret said. "Besides, you won't get in with a gun. The security people will kick you out."

"And us with you," Riddle said.

Hiding a gun in a truck that had previously gotten a couple of bales of marijuana through customs didn't seem like that big a challenge, but I didn't quibble. I didn't want to give them an excuse to turn me away, now that it was too late to threaten them with Hedison. Before I could even get the producer out of bed, they'd be safely on their way to the concert. They'd come back with all the footage they needed to finish the picture, with or without Hedison's permission.

I removed my jacket and the holstered automatic, which I locked in the trunk of the Dodge. Then I asked McNeal again for a copy of the script, interrupting him in the process of checking his watch for the tenth time.

"Why do you want it?" he asked back.

"Your story caught my interest the other day."

That was true, but it was also a lure designed to snag a writer's heart. It worked, too.

"You're already in the know, so I guess it's okay. Have we got an extra copy, Jackie?"

"He can have mine," Jarret said, passing over a dog-eared example.

She was part of the package, as it turned out. As we were loading up, she stepped between me and the truck's passenger door.

"Can't ride with Sol," she said. "He'll give me a list of scenes he wants rewritten before we get there."

152

That was easy to believe, given what I'd heard of Riddle. But as I mounted the truck's step, I remembered a feeling I'd had about Maitlan just after Sears's accident, which was that the cameraman had wanted to tell me something. That was a lot less likely to happen with Jarret along.

Not that her presence kept Maitlan from talking. We'd no sooner pulled out behind the bus than he was telling me all about growing up in Garden Grove, outside Los Angeles, where his widowed mother still lived. From there we moved to the Navy and his service in Vietnam, a place he'd mostly seen on shore leave. He paused only for widely spaced breaths and to say "excuse me" to Jarret every time he had to shift gears. She might have passed the apology along, since she was pressing her knees against mine on every shift. Then again, she might have been counting on the intervening layers of her insulated coat to make the contact impersonal, which they did.

After a short run on the 101, we picked up 399 and headed north. I should say the sum total of our progress was north. The road wound as it climbed into the mountains, never holding the same heading for more than a mile.

"Why aren't we going up Ninety-nine?" I asked our driver as he slowed for yet another curve.

"Matt thought we'd miss some traffic going this way. There were reports of backups going into the concert site last night, and the show isn't even starting till today."

"How did this Roads of Destiny group pick Avenal? I live a lot closer to it than they do, and this'll be my first visit."

Maitlan laughed. "It kind of picked them. The Roads wanted to hold the concert at Golden Gate Park in San Francisco, but they couldn't get the permits. I guess Woodstock is too recent a memory for the local taxpayers. They tried a couple of other places in the Bay Area and were turned down, too. Then somebody got the idea of holding it between Frisco and Los

Angeles and drawing from both places."

"That's a long way to draw," I said. I could imagine Duke El-lington getting the job done, but not some skinny English kids.

"The Roads are that big," Maitlan assured me. "At least, the citizens of Avenal think they are. The city council or whatever offered a site outside of town for the concert."

They'd be petitioning for a state prison next. Our road was going through a high pass, twice as high as the Topanga Canyon cut where I'd met Jill the hippie shopkeeper. Jarret's sleeping-bag coat made good sense by then, since the truck's heater was working no harder than a union rep. She was bundled up to the eyebrows and napping, apparently. I decided I might never get a more private moment with Maitlan.

"Anything on your mind, Ben?" I asked. "I had the feeling the other day you wanted to unload something."

Maitlan didn't jump on that chance to do that unloading. And then suddenly it was gone. Jarret poked her nose out of the covers and said, "Any chance I can get some sleep? If I'd known you two were going to yap the whole way up, I'd have ridden in back with the bikes."

"Sure, Jackie," Maitlan said, not sounding half as disap-pointed as I was.

I opened the script to *Duo-Glide Rider*. A mountain to our right, maybe the Pine Summit I'd seen signs for, was trying to hold back the dawn, but enough was getting past to read by. Nor was I hampered by the film's still being in typescript. I'd had a lifetime of experience visualizing movie scripts, starting back when I was a young hopeful like Polly Hayden and continuing up to my present sideline: proofreading the works of my talented wife.

When I'd left the movie's Mutt-and-Jeff team, Adam and Downer, they'd been on their way to the big concert after pages and pages of just talking about it. According to the last line of dialogue I could remember reading, they'd been in search of "purity and peace." I'd been interrupted at that point by Sears, in search of a piece of my hide. I was almost derailed again by memories of that confrontation and the violent death that had followed on its heels, but I dodged them, hiding, as I so often had before, in a movie.

I skipped a page or so of directions for Adam and Downer's ride to the concert, much of it describing the music to be played under the shots. The script was less specific on the concert site, which was understandable. In the world of Zodiac Productions, you took your scenery as you found it. I got the impression, though, that the movie concert was taking place in some kind of park, perhaps the San Francisco one the Roads of Destiny had originally tried to use.

Once there, Downer set out to get stoned and Adam met a girl named Eva, presumably the part to be played by the dewy Polly Hayden. If so, she was good casting. The Eva of the script had the same youthful glow Hayden had used to light up sleeping Oxnard.

She was also something of an evangelist. She hadn't known Adam for a full typed page before she was trying to convince him that there was more to life than cruising and concerts. America was "on its knees," in her opinion, and it was up to young people like Adam to save it.

So far there hadn't been much for the parents of Roland Hedison's regular customers to object to, except maybe the absence of sight gags, but following one of the musical numbers to be supplied by Miranda Combs's favorite group, the Proposition, Eva produced some mysterious pills and offered them to Adam. His subsequent trip took the form of a montage, first of concert clips and then of scenes from earlier in the film, including a shot of a mission church Adam and Downer had visited in reel one. Only now it had a naked Eva dancing on the front steps.

That was sure to catch Hedison's eye at the premiere.

Following the montage, Adam and Eva settled in for an idyllic night under the stars, another sequence that might not play in Iowa City. Adam awoke the next morning to find Downer poking him in the shoulder and Eva gone. In fact, the script implied that the entire concert had somehow packed up and moved on during the night like a one-elephant circus.

On their own way home, Adam and Downer came across an antiwar rally about to turn ugly. Adam, taking Eva's message of involvement to heart, decided to wade in. So did Downer, without the benefit of a lecture. He waded in so deep that he ended up shot to death by a rookie cop.

The last scene in the script was the one they'd filmed at Whitman West while the grill had heated for lunch, the one in which Adam accepted a flower from the child by the roadside. According to the script, he was setting out on a trip across America, though whether he was going to search for Eva or to spread her gospel or both wasn't clear.

The sun was fully up when I finished reading. Up and heating the truck cab nicely. It helped that we were descending into a little valley, the school bus ahead of us hitting eighty on the downgrade and Maitlan swearing softly under his breath.

When we were safely on the valley floor—endless rows of apple trees passing on either side—Jarret struggled out of her cocoon. I handed over her brainchild.

"Well?" she asked. And then, before I could mince my first word, "The drug stuff turned you off, didn't it? I knew it would. I knew you wouldn't see the symbolism."

Maybe I'd seen too much unsymbolic pill popping in my time. I had a flashback of my own then, to a starlet in a black evening dress with a belly full of pills and skin like sweating marble. Had her last moments been a collage of bright images

with an up-tempo musical accompaniment? I doubted it somehow.

"I liked it overall," I said. "I think Hedison will, too. I think
you could be honest with him."

"Roland Hedison can go screw himself," Jarret said, catching
me by surprise. "We're not bowing and scraping to him."

Before I could ask what Hedison had done to her, Maitlan
chipped in. "I don't know. I think the antiwar part is going to
be hard to sell to Roland. He's not as hip as his wardrobe."

"Is that it?" Jarret asked, still looking for a reason for the bad
review I hadn't given her script. "All that stuff you said about
war and Busby Berkeley was a put-on, wasn't it? You're behind
Vietnam like all the other guys too old to get drafted."

"My son wasn't too old to get drafted," I said. "He's over in
Vietnam right now." Somewhere in Vietnam. "If I thought your
movie would shorten the war by a day, I'd sell tickets."

"Sorry, Elliott," Jarret said. "I didn't know."

"I'm sorry, too," Maitlan said. "I—Oops. Looks like we're
pulling over."

Twenty-Two

McNeal wasn't stopping to let us stretch our legs. The sun was high enough and we were close enough to Avenal for the workday to begin. We'd reached a beauty spot called Blackwells Corners, which was a good thirty miles south of the concert site on State Highway 33. Already, there were signs of the Roads of Destiny's appeal. Along the shoulder were parked cars and pickup trucks containing sleeping music lovers who had gotten this far before deciding to turn in. Some were stirring, and these watched us unload the motorcycles and set up Maitlan's camera in the back of the truck.

"Don't worry," Maitlan told me when I gave the fish-eye to the ropes holding the camera in place. "We do this all the time."

"That's what they said about Sears jumping cars."

McNeal, his eyes hidden again by his dark aviator sunglasses, interrupted my safety inspection with a question. "How'd you like to make yourself useful, Elliott? We're short a driver this morning. Jake didn't show. We could use someone to drive the truck while Ben's in the back filming. Sol's lying down in the bus. He gets carsick. And Jackie can't drive a stick."

I said I'd do it, and McNeal handed Jarret a walkie-talkie. "I'll give Ben directions with hand signals. He'll radio them to you in the cab."

"Then you tap them out to me on the dashboard in Morse code," I side-mouthed to her. It failed to get a smile.

Mike, the wrangler who had shown up, was driving the school

bus. He told me he'd stay well ahead of us. He was as good as his word, too. By the time we got Reber's chopper to start, the bus was a speck on the northern horizon.

I thought Jarret might be a more relaxed passenger on this leg, now that she was no longer standing guard between Maitlan and me. Instead, she seemed to grow more tense with every mile we drove. When her walkie-talkie crackled to life as we were crossing the intersection of 33 and Highway 41, she actually jumped in her seat.

I could just hear the message that Jarret then relayed. "They want you to speed up. Try about seventy."

At sixty, the truck's front end had a shimmy that would have made Clara Bow jealous, but I gave it the gas. The steering wheel settled a little in my hands as we approached the target speed. In the big side mirror, I could see the two motorcycles weaving back and forth, Reber and McNeal waving to each other and laughing like kids playing hooky.

"We're creating art," I informed Jarret.

She grunted in reply, which I considered an opening. I said, "How'd you meet up with McNeal and Riddle? Did Hedison bring you three together?"

"Not Matt and me. We met in film school. Lived together for a while." She glanced left to see if I'd dropped my false teeth over that. I hadn't, so she didn't follow it up. "We met the Riddler when we signed with Roland. Matt took to him right away."

"But not you?"

"I know what I like. I know what's good and what's junk. I don't need a second opinion."

"McNeal does?"

She didn't answer, leaving me free to speculate aloud. "You were his second opinion once. Now he lets you and Riddle fight over the job. It keeps him center stage, but that's probably just a coincidence."

"If you're trying to drive wedges, Mr. Elliott, you'll need a bigger hammer than that."

"Just a student of human dynamics." I added, "And truck driver," as the radio crackled again.

"Slow down up here where these people are walking." Then, to prove she was still joined with McNeal on some astral level, Jarret read his mind. "He wants to play to an audience."

As though on cue, McNeal began waving to the hikers, who smiled and waved back. There were more cars parked by the northbound side of the road, many more than there'd been back at Blackwells Corners.

"They can't be walking into the concert," I said. "We're still five miles out."

I said it even though I could see the traffic backing up ahead of us. When Maitlan passed along McNeal's instruction to speed up again, it was already too late. We slowed to twenty for a mile or two and then dropped to a crawl.

Avenal was in sight by then, what there was of it. I could see our line of traffic going into the little knot of one- and two-story buildings and another line exiting to the east, heading toward a line of low hills. The land running up to those hills was one big parking lot, the dust from it rising up to filter the sun.

So much for our plan to zip in and zip out. I bought hot dogs from a roadside vendor for Jarret and me. It was too early for lunch, too early for some peoples' breakfasts, but something told me it might be our last chance to eat.

We could see our school bus, twenty or so cars ahead of us. After we'd crawled so close to Avenal that I could read the sign on their Rexall drugstore, a pale Riddle came back to us on foot. Jarret was out of the truck by then and wiggling out of her sleeping-bag coat, revealing the regulation jeans and a serape top so loosely woven it looked macraméd. She headed off for a conference I wasn't invited to attend. I watched it in the side

mirror instead. Jarret's comments on her relationship with Mc-
Neal and Riddle had suggested a tug-of-war with McNeal playing rope. I watched that acted out, Jarret and the director standing on opposite sides of McNeal's chopper and arguing what
appeared to be opposing points of view. It didn't seem like Mc-
Neal was listening to either one of them, but when he rode past
me, heading into town along the berm of the road, I could see
that Riddle had won. His color was back and he was scratching
his belly contentedly. Jarret was looking after the departing Mc-
Neal like she didn't expect to see him again.

If so, she was wrong. McNeal came back, and not alone. His
gaudy bike was followed by a second chopper, ridden by a guy
way too wide for it. The newcomer was bearded, like Reber, but
his head was shaved, the better to show off the scars that made
a patchwork quilt of his scalp. I saw them as he cruised slowly
past my open window. I tried to catch the name painted on the
back of his black leather jacket and finally did, reading it
backwards in my mirror: the Ninth Circle.

I knew the gang by reputation. They were hell-raisers, less
well-known than the Hell's Angels and even less personable.
Though traffic was still inching forward, I decided to find out
what was going on. I got as far as opening the truck's door.
Then Jarret, running forward, waved me back inside.

"Stay put!" she called as she ran. As she climbed up beside
me, she explained. "We're going to get an escort."

"From an outlaw motorcycle gang?"

"From the concert's security company, which happens to be
a motorcycle gang. The Roads hired them to watch their equipment."

"Who's watching them?"

Jarret was shaking her head too hard to hear the question.
"Matt thinks he can bluff his way in. He told this guy we have
permission to film."

161

"Don't we?"

"We have a verbal agreement with the Proposition, but they're just one of the warm-up acts. We don't have any kind of agreement with the Roads. The guy on the bike, Hector, made it sound like there's a film crew up there already. One the Roads brought in. If we should run into them . . ."

"They'll ask us to leave," I said, trying to make it sound like no big deal. It wouldn't be, either, if I found Miranda Combs first.

I didn't convince Jarret. Her grim expression made a death's head of her thin face and confirmed my hunch that she and her partners had way too much invested in *Duo-Glide Rider*. The idea of the trio informing on Sears and then killing him to protect their project suddenly seemed less farfetched.

Hector rumbled past and disappeared into the town, leaving me to wonder what even a motorcycle gang could do to move us through that mob scene. That was exactly what the population of Avenal looked like to me. Not like a mob, which is ugly and active, but like a mob scene, a scene from a movie being filmed with a lot of patient, cooperative extras. The streets were almost gridlocked, the sidewalks jammed, the few stores overflowing with customers. But there was no yelling, no pushing or shoving. Not even any horns sounding. On any Los Angeles road that backed up, the brass section would have splintered safety glass. The purity and peace Jarret and McNeal had written about—naively, I'd thought—really seemed to be in evidence, as far as these pilgrims were concerned.

An hour after Hector left us, after we'd made a right in downtown Avenal and started on the outbound leg, we watched our bus pull off into a side street. The turning was guarded by several bikers, I saw when we crept up to it sometime later. The guards waved us in to where the bus and Hector were waiting. Impatiently. As soon as we started to turn, they took off, leading us through more back streets than I would have guessed Avenal had.

We left town on a dirt track that passed almost immediately through a gate in a wire fence. Passed onto private property, I guessed. A man in a cowboy hat, who might have been the property's owner, sat on the hood of a parked pickup. He didn't challenge us as we passed, but he didn't wave howdy, either. His look, resentful but resigned, reminded me of the ones I'd seen on German burghers as my artillery unit rolled past them in 1945. The next meeting of the Avenal city council promised to be a lively one.

I still had that lonely pickup in sight when heavy bass notes boomed in the distance. Then another sound came to us over the nearest hill. A welling cheer.

"The concert's already started," Jarret said. "God help us."

Twenty-Three

I almost seconded Jarret's prayer when we topped a rise and I got my first real sight of the Avenal concert grounds. There were probably thousands of natural amphitheaters tucked among Southern California's barren hills, but there can't have been many better matched to the Roads of Destiny's drawing power than this little valley east of Avenal. Our dirt-track service road was bringing us in behind the stage, three levels of scaffolding and sound equipment that was dwarfed by the humanity on the rolling valley floor. And that ground-floor contingent was no more than two-thirds of the total crowd. The rest were spread out on the hills to the right and left of the stage. I could even make out movement on the high ground that boxed the far end of the valley. To those people, the stage must have been no more than a rumor.

On a much nearer hill, the one we were circling to reach the backstage parking area, I could see individual heads, if not individuals. They were packed in too tightly for that, as tight as the seals on the rocks of Monterey Bay, a surging earth-toned mass still wearing the blankets and ponchos they'd slept in last night.

Whenever I'd thought ahead to the concert, I'd imagined the jazz festivals I'd been to, usually the famous one at Newport, where Ella and I had seen Duke Ellington make his comeback in 1956. I'd been told that I'd never find one girl at a concert the size of Avenal, but I'd considered it no worse than a long shot. Now I saw how right the doubters had been. Unless Miranda had actually joined the Proposition, maybe as second tambourine, I didn't have a chance.

I wasn't the only one taken by surprise. Maitlan's voice, coming through the walkie-talkie's tin-can speaker, sounded like a man reporting a fire. The dead-calm Jarret translated.

"Ben says to drop back. We're getting too much dust from the bus." She tacked on a joke of mine, her lifeless voice cutting it off at the knees: "We're making art again."

But only for a moment. The bus was already inside the parking area, which was defined by tractor trailer rigs arranged like a wagon train expecting an Indian attack. We rolled into this compound, joining a couple of big house trailers and a lot of smaller vehicles. A little way beyond the protective ring was an impressive stand of motorcycles, probably the mounts of our guardians.

The group onstage—not the Proposition, according to Jarret—was doing its best to fill the surrounding hills with noise, but the speakers hadn't been made that could get that job done. The amplifiers on hand were all pointed away from us, so, even with the echo effect, it was possible to converse normally on our side of the stage. Jarret barely had to raise her voice to address me as I slipped us into a space beside the bus.

"Listen, Elliott. You're a truck driver today, okay? That's all. Not a security guy. These Ninth Circle creeps won't notice another truck driver."

"Are they the ones Sears was meeting?"

"I don't know. I only know they're bad news. They won't put up with any kind of heat, private or otherwise."

Her thinking sounded solid to me. Unfortunately, Jarret didn't get a chance to brief the other members of the triumvirate. McNeal had already dismounted and joined Riddle in front of the bus. They were speaking to Hector and to a second

165

biker. Hector stood a respectful half step behind him, though the newcomer wasn't nearly as large as our late escort or as battle scarred. He wore the Ninth Circle's regulation black: jacket, jeans, and boots. And a look of genuine menace, a look Hollywood tough guys, on screen and off, aspired to but seldom pulled off. Richard Widmark had, early in his career, when he'd played ticking bombs in zoot suits. The bomb listening to Riddle jabber about the drive reminded me of early Widmark. He was thin and hollow-cheeked, with a hank of dirty blond hair that fell across his forehead the way Hitler's had when he'd gotten himself worked up.

I was hanging back by the truck, playing its protective driver while trying to stay close enough to listen in. But McNeal, turning as Jarret walked up, spotted me. He ignored his writing partner and waved me over.

"This is the security guy I was telling you about," he said to Widmark, Jr. "Our boss insisted we bring him along. So we don't need anyone to look after our stuff. We've got him to do it. It wasn't our idea, but we're stuck with it. His name is Elliott. Elliott, this is Russo, one of the concert's security team."

There went another perfectly good disguise. I expected McNeal to add something like "Oh, by the way. Your buddy Sears is dead." He didn't add it, and Russo didn't ask for the stuntman, probably because I was there. He certainly wasn't happy about that. He was looking at me the way my cop friend Grove often did, like he was measuring me for pine.

Russo hadn't extended his hand when we were introduced, so I kept mine in my jacket pockets. Tensed into fists, as it happened. Back at McNeal's trailer, I'd offered to play lightening rod for the crew, but now that I could feel the crackle of an approaching storm, I was regretting the impulse. I didn't relax until the biker turned and stalked off, forcing Hector the giant to dance out of his way. As Russo showed his profile, I saw that

I'd been wrong about him lacking battle scars. A livid one started on his left cheekbone and ran straight into a ravaged ear.

The two weren't out of sight before Jarret opened up. "Matt, I thought we agreed—"

"Don't freak out on us, Jackie," Riddle told her, holding a flat hand up almost to her mouth. "We're improvising today. No script and no goddamn idea how anything's going to turn out. Ben, you ready?"

Maitlan had his camera on a shoulder mount that looked about as sturdy as his earlier rig in the back of the truck. "Ready when you are, C.B."

"Polly, you set? Peter? Okay, let's see if we can get around to the front of the stage."

McNeal said, "Somebody ought to touch base with the Proposition, Sol. Let them know we're here."

"Fine," Riddle said. "Jackie can do it."

I volunteered to go with her, and the director turned on me, eyes bulging dangerously. "You'll stay by the truck. Period."

McNeal's voice was as silky as his golden hair. "He wants to ask about that girl, Solly. That won't take him five minutes. Nobody will be nosing around here before then. Mike can watch the truck till he gets back."

"Five minutes," Riddle snapped at me. "Now everybody come on. We may not have much longer ourselves."

They trooped off, Maitlan giving me a cheerful salute as he passed. Then he called to his companions, "Remember where we parked, kiddies."

Jarret stood watching them go, until I thought I'd have to poke her arm to wake her up. The band on stage did the job for me by finishing a number. The sudden silence was filled by a roar that rose up from the crowd, coming to us in surging waves as the more distant hillsides joined in. Someone on the stage started to thank the audience for "being so groovy."

Jarret said, "We've got to move. If that's the end of a set, we may be too late already."

We settled Mike on the front bumper of the truck, where he immediately began rolling a reefer. Then we headed for the big house trailers, which had to be the concert's dressing rooms. That was confirmed by the first guy we bumped into, a harried young man with a clipboard and an English accent crisper than Forrest Combs's.

"The Proposition? Trailer on your left. They're on in five, tell them. As soon as we get some equipment changed out. Ask them if they want an escort to the stage." He ran a nervous hand up a broad expanse of forehead. "My recommendation would be they do without."

It was an opening for a question that had been giving me the bends. "Who had the idea of hiring an outlaw motorcycle gang for security?"

I'd managed not to use the words "who in God's name" or "stupid idea," but the man with the clipboard still looked hurt.

"We were advised that it's always done," he said. "They're not security, really. We were told that the concert organizers give them a keg or two in exchange for watching equipment. It's a form of tribute, really. We pay it, and they stay off by themselves and don't bother anybody. That's what we were told. This lot is taking a more active role." He'd whispered most of that. In a louder voice, he said, "But they're good chaps, really."

Jarret had marched off early in the exchange. I caught up with her as she knocked on the trailer's door.

"No goddamn greasers!" someone inside yelled in reply.

"He can't mean you," I said and opened the door.

The trailer was much newer than the one on McNeal's Point Dume lot and twice as big, but there were similarities. Like the fog bank of smoke we stepped into. McNeal's had been plain, old-fashioned cigarette. This was acrid and unabashed marijuana. I'd let Jarret precede me, gentleman that I was, and that was a mistake. The members of the Proposition lived up to the band's name, firing off three or four explicit invitations to her before she'd topped the last step.

"Warm it, Momma. Right here," a particularly shaggy one was saying when I spoiled the fun by stepping up behind her.

The shaggy one's name was Hound. I learned that when Jarret introduced herself as a representative of Zodiac Productions. There were three other band members present, all as stoned as Hound. All four were wearing crushed velvet jackets and frilly shirts, which must have been the uniform of the day. For company, they had three young women, two very young, but none of them Miranda Combs.

"Why'd you bring your grandpa?" Hound asked in reference to me. Jarret introduced me, using my first and last names.

"Beam me up, Scotty," Hound said, laughing as only the truly wasted can. I'd been hearing that one a lot lately. The other band members picked up the chorus, and the trailer started rocking. When Hound caught his breath again, he added, "I thought we said no greasers."

Jarret ignored that lapse in manners and rushed through her speech. "I just wanted to tell you we'd be out front filming. In case you saw us during your set."

"Yeah, about that," Hound said. "The Roads are making their own film of the concert. We didn't know anything about that when we talked with you guys, but, you know, five minutes in their movie is worth more to us than an hour in yours. You know what I'm saying? We can't let you screw that up for us."

"We won't," Jarret assured him. She followed up with some of her speed talking. "We'll clear everything with the Roads. We won't use any footage they want to use."

Hound was either too stoned to know what that promise was worth or to care. "I'm just saying, you know. It's not like it's even up to us. That fucking goon squad they hired is calling all the shots. If they see you trying to slip something over, there'll be trouble."

"We'll stay clear of them," Jarret promised. Then she stepped toward the door, running into a stationary object. Me.

I said, "I'm trying to find a girl who may be following your band."

"Beam me up, Scotty," someone in the back called out.

I handed Miranda's picture to Hound. "She's a big fan of yours. Also underage. Her father wants her home, no questions asked."

The musician studied the picture, passed it around, and, when it came back to him, studied it all over again.

"Never seen her," he finally said. "Tell you what, though, Pops. If you find her, bring her to me. You can have seconds, no questions asked."

It was my turn to bump into Jarret. I'd taken a step forward to get the picture back and maybe shake Hound by his frilly shirt. Jarret let me snatch the photo and then started pushing.

"You're on in five," she told the band. "Do great out there."

TWENTY-FOUR

Mike, the crew member we'd left to watch the truck, was nowhere in sight when we got back. The truck itself was still locked up tight.

"What next?" Jarret asked, burying the silver rings on one of her long hands deep into her afro, exactly as she'd been doing when I first saw her. "We'll never get everybody rounded up when the time comes to get out of here."

"When will that be?" I asked the question above the sound of rhythmic chanting from the audience. Its patience with equipment changes was running low.

"We should split *now*," Jarret said. "Drive and just keep driving. Drive right into the ocean and say to hell with the whole thing."

I wondered if we'd stayed inside the marijuana den too long. The whites of her big eyes were clear, but a lot of that white was showing. And when her fingers weren't pulling at her hair, they were fluttering around like Winnie Mannero's.

"To hell with *Duo-Glide Rider*?"

"Yes. It's screwed and we're screwed. It's not worth it."

"Not worth what?" I could see by her reaction to that—a general seizing of the tiller—that she wasn't about to blurt out any confessions. I followed it up anyway. "Not worth today or not worth what led up to today?"

"You should head on out of here, Elliott. While you can. You can walk to Avenal. We could pick you up there on our way

171

out." She added, "If we get out," not in words but in a furtive glance toward the used-motorcycle lot. The choppers reminded her of another possibility. "Or you could take one of our bikes. No one could catch you then."

"I'm not leaving you to deal with Sears's buddies. Besides, I have to guard the truck."

"You can't stay with the truck," Jarret said.

"Because that Russo character will be back looking for what Sears was going to bring him?"

"Matt thinks having you here will scare them off. I know that's why he told them who you are."

She raced through the second line, and I remembered that her words always hit ninety when she was selling something. Whether she was pitching to me now or to herself, I couldn't say.

"Maybe he's right. Maybe that'll work."

"Not here," Jarret said. "Not today. If you won't head for Avenal, you should move around. Look for that lost girl of yours. Get into the crowd and stay there until the Proposition finishes. Then get back here quick. I'm going to find the guys. Remember: be back here five minutes after the Proposition wraps up."

"Speak of the devils," I said.

The band members were passing behind Jarret on their way to the stage, their prom-night attire looking even more ridiculous in the light of day. That light seemed to be bothering them quite a bit, though they all wore sunglasses, tiny, inadequate ones framed like Ben Franklin's spectacles. Hound was especially troubled, shading his eyes with one hand and looking around like he'd gotten off at the wrong stop. I knew the feeling.

Jarret took off after them. I wanted to see her safely to wherever McNeal and the others were filming, but my promise to Forrest Combs was tugging me the other way, toward the trailer lately occupied by the Proposition. I got there just as the English kid with the domed forehead emerged, shooing the Proposition's groupies before him. In daylight, they were older than I'd guessed. Quite old suddenly.

"You'll miss the concert," the man with the clipboard told them. "Hurry."

None of the women looked capable of hurrying or interested in anything but a rest cure, but they wobbled off on their platform shoes, trailing articles of clothing behind them. Sending them half-dressed and stoned into that crowd wasn't the sporting thing to do, and the stage manager knew it, refusing to meet my eye as he mumbled his excuse.

"We need this trailer for the Roads. They'll be arriving anytime now. By helicopter," he tossed in when I failed to ooh and ah.

"Are you in touch with them?"

"No. We don't have a radio. We don't have anything. There was supposed to be a telephone line, but they didn't get it strung. We're quite cut off here." His stiff upper lip was wilting, but he wouldn't admit it. "Why do you ask?"

"You know why. Your so-called security squad. The more free beer they drink, the worse this is going to get. Right now it's balanced on the sharp end of a knife. You need help. Have someone drive into town and call the highway patrol."

There was a fair amount of self-interest in that suggestion, but it was still good advice. And like most good advice, it got the bum's rush.

"Everything will be fine. Once the Roads get here, everything will be fine."

Meaning it would all be someone else's problem. I gave it up and reached for the trailer's door.

The kid hopped to one side but asked a question for form's sake. "What do you want in there?"

"I think I left my autograph book."

My pal the stage manager had opened all the windows, and that had improved the trailer's ambiance in a big way. I tossed the place, wishing I'd brought rubber gloves. I found a lot of evidence that Western Civilization was crumbling but none that Miranda Combs had ever been there, no pocketbook or purse or love notes, no locks of blonde hair tied in ribbon or scented handkerchiefs with the initials MC woven into them.

I was satisfied by then that I'd done my best for the Family Combs. There was only one forlorn hope left to try. The Proposition had begun playing—the latter part of my search through their leavings in the trailer had been accompanied by an impressive guitar solo. I could scan the crowd for Combs's daughter, on the off chance she'd worked her way stage-side. I could do that and look for the Zodiac crew at the same time.

I headed toward the wall of scaffolding, past a humming generator truck and through a sea of crushed bear cans. All around me were people for whom the music was of secondary interest at most. One of these was dancing nude, a woman of perhaps two hundred pounds. She was being filmed by a two-man crew. The Roads of Destiny's filmmakers, maybe, or *National Geographic*'s. I didn't stop to ask.

I expected the area right in front of the stage to be packed, for the weight of that giant crowd to be pressing against the platform like Lake Meade pressed Hoover Dam. Instead, the crowd didn't really get going for a good fifty yards. I ran through a couple of explanations for that—the band playing was only a warm-up, the speakers I'd undervalued backstage were deafening out front—before hitting on the right one. Members of the Ninth Circle were everywhere around the stage and even on it. The ones patrolling out front with their backs to the music carried interesting staffs of office: pool cues. The long sticks should have looked comically out of place but somehow didn't.

The gang's numbers scratched my first plan, which had been to get onto the stage itself and scan the crowd from the safe side of a woofer. My second plan was to slip into the crowd itself, where I blended in not at all. Thanks to the threatening bikers, the first dozen feet or so of that mob was spread out enough for me to move about easily. The downside was that twelve feet was also about as far as I could see in any direction before the overlap of bodies choked off the view.

The band's current number seemed to be all refrain, the tag line of which was "don't beaumont that joint." I knew that the last name of my dead actor friend Tory Beaumont had made its way into the vernacular as a synonym for grabbing more than your share, and I never heard it without wondering what he'd make of the additional pinch of immortality. I pictured him grinning sardonically now, but that might have been his reaction to my presence in that swaying throng.

I didn't spot Miranda, not that I'd really expected to. She was starting to take on a mythical quality, like the basilisk or peace in our time. But I did expect to spot the *Duo-Glide Rider* crew. A group that big should have been sending out ripples through the fringe area I was walking, clearing a work space for itself and otherwise attracting attention. It should have been, but wasn't.

I was attracting attention all by myself. It was obvious to the soberer members of the crowd what I was up to. A kid in a leather cowboy hat with an eagle feather in its band started following me around, calling, "Where are you, Sissy? Please come home. All is forgiven. Mommy's waiting in the Studebaker!"

I turned to thank him for his help, and he immediately directed his attention to the stage. I glanced that way myself, in time to see Hound launch into another guitar riff. While he played, he skipped down to the end of the stage where three members of the Ninth Circle had made themselves comfortable. At first, they were all smiling, the bikers treating the gesture like a command performance. Then Hound started thrusting his pelvis at the biggest of the three, each thrust accompanied by a wail of the guitar.

Beside me, the citizen in the leather hat said, "Oh, shit."

Hound turned his back on his target, but kept up the gyrations, looking over his shoulder occasionally to see how his act was going over. It wasn't, not from what I could see. The Ninth Circle patrol in front of the stage was closing in, and Hound's principal victim, who was bearded like an Amish farmer, was looking about the way Queen Elizabeth would have looked if Sidney James had mooned the royal box.

"Oh, shit," my friend with the feather said again.

He and I were the only two on the paying side of the footlights who seemed concerned. Everyone else was cheering Hound on. That they didn't have his best interests at heart was clear a moment later, when the bearded biker got to his feet and bore down on the guitarist. The kid beside me waved to him—one warning hand in a crowd of thousands—but Hound's first real alert was a fist on the collar of his velvet jacket. The biker spun him around, the Fender producing a long "zip" that was the perfect sound effect. Then Hound was flat on his back.

I took an instinctive step forward. Before I could have my own second thoughts, someone had them for me and grabbed my arm. It was Jarret. If the screenwriter had been frightened before, she was terrified now. She tugged me deeper into the crowd, only stopping when a solid wall of teenagers blocked our path.

"Run, Elliott! You've got to get away!"

She had to shout a line that should have been whispered because the surviving members of the Proposition had had the good sense to keep playing. By then Hound himself was joining in, having somehow made it back to the safety of center stage. I thought I could make out a trickle of blood from one corner of his mouth.

I cupped my hands close to Jarret's ear. "What's happened?"

"Russo got into the truck. He knows the pot isn't here. He's after you. Matt told him . . . Hell, just *go*, okay?"

"Where's the crew?"

"Scattered. Russo won't let us finish. He took the camera."

All around us, people were suddenly pointing toward the stage. Hound was at it again, I thought, incorrectly. The new attraction was a column of black smoke rising above the scaffolding.

"They're burning our truck," Jarret sobbed.

I knew she was right, but I still headed that way to make sure. Jarret didn't follow me, which I understood. I was the last person in greater Avenal she wanted to be seen with. That was fine by me. I preferred her safely hidden in the crowd.

I couldn't stay hidden myself, not and make any time. I worked my way forward again, almost to the buffer zone controlled by Russo's brothers-in-arms. I still had the foremost fringe of the crowd as cover, but it wasn't enough. Before I'd reached the end of the stage and a clear view of the fire, I saw movement in the bodies to my right, heads and flailing arms jerking this way and that. Then the spectators nearest me were shoved aside, and Russo stepped into the gap, followed by Hector and one of the stage sentries, his pool cue at quarter arms.

"There's the bastard man," Russo said. It was the first time I'd heard his voice, and it made me think again of early Widmark, being high-pitched and singsongy, with psychotic giggles thrown in where none belonged. He hadn't had to shout as Jarret had. The band had finished a number and was still huddling for the next.

"You owe me some grass, bastard man. Or some money. What's it going to be, grass or cash or your wrinkled hide?"

"Take a check?" I asked. I'd always had a talent for the soothing word.

There was no reason for Russo to goad me—no jury was going to rule my beating death justifiable homicide, not even if I got in the first punch—but he goaded away, just for the pleasure it was giving the grinning Hector, maybe. He even picked the very spot where his late partner Sears had stuck the needle.

"You're a soldier man, I hear. A big hero soldier man. You're not looking so brave now, soldier man. I bet the only things you ever killed were little babies. You're a baby killer, I bet, like those fucking baby killers in 'Nam. The father of a fucking baby killer, I hear."

The left I led with would probably have knocked Russo down all by itself, but I got in a right before his knees completely buckled. In the movies, killing the Indian chief took the fight out of the tribe, but I couldn't take a chance on that. Even if I'd been in the mood to. My second punch had sent Russo into the man with the cue. That settled the question of who to tackle next, if my desire to wipe the grin off Hector's fat face already hadn't. I jerked the elbow of my extended right arm into the biker's nose and tried to follow that up with a jab to his windpipe. Before I could land the blow, the cue came down on the back of my head. I staggered around to block the next swing and instead caught it square on the skull.

For an instant, I was back on the hillside outside Lancaster, watching doomed sparks throw themselves at indifferent stars. Then even the stars blinked out.

TWENTY-FIVE

My last memory had been a glimpse of Lancaster, California, from two days before. I woke up much further back in time, circa 1944, somewhere in France. Or almost woke up. Someone was laying down a barrage, but whether it was my unit or one nearby I couldn't tell. I tried to sit up, didn't get very far, and decided the battle could get on without me.

Maybe the whole war could. I was wounded, I was sure of that. Every time the artillery fire made the ground beneath me throb, the pain curled my toes. I was convinced, in a confused, half-conscious way, that mine was a million-dollar wound, one that would send me back to Hollywood with a medal on my chest and a discharge in my pocket. I actually saw Ann Sheridan waiting on the Union Station platform for my train. Then the picture did a slow fade.

Sometime later—hours, maybe—I decided that what I'd been hearing wasn't artillery. It was music, elemental and pounding. I found the substitution disturbing and struggled against it, but again the tar pit I was swimming in won the fight. That was okay. I knew it was because someone a long way off kept telling me so, cooing the words as though to a baby.

The next thing I heard was rain pattering against cloth. It was the least threatening sound so far, but it was the one that finally got my eyes open. I was lying in the dark on what felt like bare earth beneath a scrap of leaky tent. Then my eyes adjusted themselves to the very feeble light. I saw that the fabric overhead wasn't olive-drab canvas. It was checkered like a farmhouse tablecloth. That didn't shake my belief that it was 1944. We'd often commandeered our shelter, my buddy Merritt Jackson and I, and usually from a farmhouse. Sure enough, there was someone lying beside me. I looked over, expecting to see Jackson, a man who had crowded me in many a foxhole. Instead a saw a woman, a young one, her shoulders moving to silent sobs.

I couldn't quite make out her face in what I now decided was predawn light, but it seemed to me I knew her. Then she spoke to me—not in French—yanking me forward to 1969 with such force I had to squeeze my eyes shut to keep from fainting away.

"Thank God, flatfoot. I thought you'd never wake up."

The woman with the trembling voice was Jill, the shopkeeper I'd rescued in Topanga Canyon, the tipster who'd landed me flat on my back in Avenal, if that was where I'd come to rest. I could see now that our tablecloth tent was a lean-to, held up on one side by stacked milk-bottle crates and pegged to the ground on the other. Beyond the tent's open end, I could see only rain.

"Where are we?"

"At the concert, what's left of it. You okay?"

The pain was making my head feel like a walnut shell between a bricklayer's palms. There was blood in my hair, some of it almost dried, some ominously sticky. My ribs were so sore I couldn't believe I'd stayed down for the count with only a thin blanket between me and the hardpan. But the barely suppressed panic in Jill's question told me to keep the medical report brief.

"I'll be fine. What happened? How did you find me?"

"I saw you fighting with them. One against three. I couldn't believe it."

"Did they get tired of kicking me or did they leave me for dead?"

"Once you were down, the two on their feet tried to help the one you'd knocked out. They couldn't wake him up. They carried him to the front of the crowd to get him some air. That's when I got you away."

"Alone?"

The picture of her lugging my dead weight solo should have been an excuse for her to smile. Instead, she drew as far away as our lean-to allowed. She was wearing the peasant blouse and jeans that had been her work clothes, but they were muddy now, as were her very pale face and strawberry hair. Her blue granny glasses were missing, which was a shame. I could have borrowed them to protect my splitting head from the strengthening light.

"I had help," she said. "Everybody wanted to help. Even the ones who were too afraid to try wouldn't tell where we'd taken you."

"Tell who?"

"The biker you knocked down. He came back looking for you with twice as many guys. That's what I heard."

"What else did you hear?" I was after an explanation for the tearing-paper quality in her voice. She was a world removed from the unflappable clerk I'd met at the Infinite Pad.

"I heard they killed somebody last night. While the Roads were playing. I'm not sure why."

"For the hell of it, maybe. You stayed with me, knowing it was that dangerous?"

"It probably didn't even happen. Probably it's just a rumor. Kids saw you attacked and started the story going around and pretty soon they were saying you'd been killed."

"I would have been, if you hadn't stepped up."

The idea that my life had depended on the million-to-one chance of the only person at the concert who had a reason to help me being on hand when I needed her made my bloodied head swim.

"You saved me from bad guys," Jill said. "So we're even."

"We already were, remember? You told me about Miranda and the Proposition. So now I owe you."

"Good. I may need you someday."

That exchange reminded me of people who needed me now, the skeleton crew of *Duo-Glide Rider.* Had they managed to get away or were they holed up somewhere like me? I'd never find out on my back. I tried to sit up and saw fireworks again.

Jill got an arm under me before I hit the ground. She kept it there after the spasm of pain had dropped back to the earlier steady crackle. My windbreaker had been serving as my blanket. She drew it over both of us, squeezing against me to make the arrangement work.

"You're freezing," she said.

That was true, though she was the one who was trembling. It wasn't hard to understand why. She'd just passed a long, hard night. Alone, for all the company I'd been. That ugly night was now an ugly morning, though the rain did seem to be letting up.

I moved my head too fast and let out a groan. Jill said, "Bad?"

"Nothing an amputation won't cure."

"Wait a minute." I heard our windbreaker blanket rustling and then a match being struck. A second later I smelled the kind of smoke the Sears's barn had exhaled with its dying breaths.

"Try this," Jill said, her voice a raspy giveaway.

"No thanks."

"It'll help with the pain. It's all I've got."

I accepted the joint to please her, which didn't work out for me.

"Don't puff on it. Take a hit and hold it in."

"Sorry."

We passed it back and forth like old friends. My head did

start to feel a little better. And I got chatty.

"Who's minding your store?"

"You met her. Myrna."

"The giant brunette? She your assistant?"

"I'm hers. Assistant for life, that's me."

"You and me both. Tell me about home."

"Home? I sleep over the store."

"I meant your hometown in Minnesota. Little Canada, wasn't it?"

"That pool cue didn't hurt your memory," Jill observed, sounding like she wished it had. When she handed me the shrinking joint again, she'd attached something to it. An electrician's alligator clip to act as a handle.

"There's not much to tell about Little Canada," she said. "It's north of St. Paul, which is no place to be north of. More lakes than people. More mosquitoes than lakes. A lot more."

"We had a few of those in Indiana. Mosquitoes."

"That's where you're from?"

"Born and raised," I admitted.

"I would have guessed you were a California native."

"You don't meet many of those."

"No," Jill said. "You don't." Then, for no particular reason, she started sobbing again, burying her face in my shoulder.

Mentioning her hometown had been a mistake, I thought. But, then, any small talk would have been, given the tension of the moment.

I broke an uneasy truce with my sore ribs by reaching over to pat her hair. "Don't worry," I said. "We're going to get out of here. I've got promises to keep."

Twenty-Six

After an hour or so, I tried getting up again. With Jill's help, I managed to prop myself up on my elbows, which brought my skull into contact with the sopping fabric of the makeshift tent. The resulting cold shower cleared my head more than somewhat. I rolled onto hands and knees and started to crawl.

The view that greeted me outside made me think of war again, but not of my relatively modern one. The scene was more like something Matthew Brady might have photographed, maybe in the aftermath of Gettysburg. The colors were damped down nearly to Brady's monochrome by the gray light, the overcast sky, and the mud. There were bodies everywhere, lying singly and in pairs or sitting up in a kind of sodden shock. Here and there, a figure picked its way along like a scavenger working the battlefield. Everywhere underfoot were the casings of spent shells, by which I mean beer cans. I decided there hadn't been an unexpended round. To complete the battlefield effect, there was a stench in the air of smoldering garbage. I could see one or two of the fires, lit for warmth, I guessed, and somehow kept going in spite of the rain. From the thickness of the haze hanging over the little valley, there must have been dozens of them.

Jill and her helpers had smuggled me well away from the scene of my last stand, almost to where the backstop hill began. It was no wonder Russo hadn't found us. In the middle distance, the stage looked like what it had been for Jarret and her friends: the set of a movie, now abandoned.

On the hills around me, there was more and more movement as the gray day and the rain raised more and more of the dead. Here and there where the hills met the sky, little figures appeared and then disappeared, showing that the exodus was well underway.

My eye was drawn to an exception to the outbound trend. It was off to my left, the direction of Avenal, an old Cadillac ambulance making its way slowly down a dirt track that was doubling as a streambed.

I tried to bend down to address Jill and ended up kneeling in the mud. "I'll be right back," I said when my head cleared again.

"What about the bikers?"

"They're halfway to Canada by now."

"Here, then," she said and passed me out my jacket.

It was ungallant to take it, but I was already shivering. I struggled into it, pulled one knee out of the ooze at a time, and staggered off.

There followed a long nightmare during which I was sure the ambulance would waddle away before I could reach it. I couldn't walk a straight line for all the late risers and the casual water, and the best pace I could manage was a teetering shuffle, but the ambulance was still there when I arrived—sweating—at the start of the rising ground. Two men in muddy white were strapping a young woman to a stretcher. A short, fat man in a plaid hunting jacket and a red cap that looked like Robin Hood's without the feather was looking on.

He turned and saw me and blinked. "What the hell?" he said.

"I came to hear Harry James," I said. "Turned out he wasn't on the bill."

The gnome had zeroed in on my scalp. "So you asked for your money back or what? Art, take a look at this."

One of the kids in white came over. He gave my head a quick look and then stared into each of my eyes in turn.

"You need a hospital, bud," he said. "We're kind of full, but we can try to squeeze you in up front."

"He can have my seat," Friar Tuck said.

The attendant had a hand on my arm, which I now removed. "I'll take the next run. I have to find some people first. I heard someone died last night."

"We know of five dead so far," the little man said.

"It'll be six if we don't get her out of here," Art told him. To me, he added, "Drug overdose." Then he went back to his job.

"How did they die?" I asked the game warden.

"Two were run over by a pickup while they were asleep in their sleeping bags. Two overdosed, like that little girlie there."

"And the fifth one?"

"Beaten up," he said, looking at my head again. "That's what the highway patrol boys told us. You sure we can't do anything for you?"

"I'll take some water, if you have any."

"Ours is long gone. Seems it was the last thing anybody thought to pack. But, here, I've been saving this."

He dug under the front seat of the ambulance and produced a bottle of Coke. I'd left my church key in my church suit, but my new best friend looked like the kind of guy who'd have an opener, and he did, one dangling from a ring chained to his belt, à la Robert Sears. The warm cola burned more than usual going down. Still, it was all I could do to keep from draining the little bottle. I offered the rest to its rightful owner. He waved it off.

"What the hell happened here last night?" he asked.

"Purity and peace," I said. A little more of that and he would have been dragging me into the ambulance like it or not. Luckily, Art reeled him in instead.

I started back, the open bottle safe in my jacket pocket. I almost didn't find the tent; there were so many nearly identical

186

shelters and I'd forgotten to drop bread crumbs. Finally, though, I recognized the farmhouse print.

I tapped on one of the milk-crate tent posts and said, "I found breakfast."

No one answered me or ever would. Jill was gone, lock, stock, and roach clip. I waited around for a time, though I knew she wouldn't be back. Then I finished the Coke and started down the valley toward the stage.

It was a trek that took me hours or what seemed like hours, not because of the distance involved but because I wandered around like my bruised mind. I found I was looking every kid I passed in the face, like an eyewitness trying to pick someone out of the world's longest lineup. That wasn't odd in itself. I'd come to Avenal in the first place to find someone. And I'd just passed up my chance to get away so I could locate some rebel filmmakers. I may even have started out looking for Miranda Combs or Jarret and McNeal. But before I'd gone very far, I switched over to looking for Billy. Even when I realized what I was doing, I didn't try to stop. I needed that hopeless search to keep myself moving.

By the time I finally reached the stage, the area around it wasn't the ghost town it had seemed from a distance. A small crew was already dismantling the electrical feeds, watched by a long row of gulls on the bare top bar of the scaffolding. Many more of the birds were picking through the garbage strewn everywhere about. They reminded me of Petunia Seagull Sunrise, my joke name for Jill, and worrying about her helped to bring me back from my search for Billy to the here and now.

I didn't waste what was left of my Coke buzz working out why Jill had wandered off. As Jarret had demonstrated the previous day, not hanging around me was sound policy, at least in greater Avenal. But I did muse briefly on the subject of Jill hanging around as long as she had. Then my thoughts and the gulls were scattered by some kids who'd discovered how much fun it was to slide in the mud. A few beers must have survived the long night after all.

Behind the stage, what had been a crowded parking area now wasn't. The motorcycle corral was completely empty, as I'd expected. The big generator truck was still there, though silent. Behind it was the blackened carcass of the vehicle I'd seen burning during the Proposition's set. Jarret's guess, which I'd been on my way to confirm when Russo had found me, had been right. The pyre was all that was left of the truck I'd driven to the concert, burned by the bikers when they hadn't found their pot inside.

Zodiac's short-bed school bus had been parked close enough to the truck to have gone up with it, but it hadn't. And it wasn't anywhere in sight. Neither were the choppers McNeal and Reber had ridden to the concert. So some or all of the film crew might have gotten clear. My money was on Riddle. He struck me as the kind of guy who'd get a seat in the lifeboat if he had to jettison his mother.

I saw someone parked near the house-trailer dressing rooms, someone who might tell me what had happened to the bus. It was a highway patrolman, leaning on his cruiser while he talked on its radio. One of the big trailers next to him looked exactly as it had when Hound and his buddies had been residents. The other had had every window broken out. The damage reminded me of the tornadoes that used to scare me under the bed back in Indiana, their crazy randomness more frightening than their winds.

The patrolman—actually a captain, I saw when I got close—didn't let me reprise my Harry James line. He let the stretched cord of his mike yank it back into the patrol car and said, "Who the hell are you?"

I cut the repartee to the bone, telling him who I was and who

I worked for. On the subject of why I was there, I used roughly the same tale McNeal had told Russo, namely that I'd tagged along to guard the floodlights and extension cords.

The captain was eyeing my gory locks, so I mentioned my disagreement with the Ninth Circle, without touching on the exact cause. That got me a sympathetic look and a proffered pack of Camels, both of which I accepted. Ella would consider a cigarette a big improvement over what I'd been smoking earlier that morning.

The cop said, "You were lucky. Those Ninth Circle thugs beat a guy to death last night. Right in front of the stage, with God and everyone else looking on. We've got no idea why."

"Have you got the guys who did it?"

"Hell, no. But we will."

I took a drag on the Camel and asked the question I'd been putting off. "How about the name of the victim?"

"Yeah, wait a minute." He retrieved his mike and stretched the cord again asking someone else the question.

The radio crackled for a moment and replied, "Maitlan, Benjamin."

TWENTY-SEVEN

I hadn't asked the captain, whose named turned out to be Widmeyer, for a seat in his car because I didn't like my chances of
standing up again once I'd sat down. But when he saw the effect Maitlan's name had on me, Widmeyer insisted. When he
had me tucked in nicely, he radioed for a replacement unit.
Then we headed out. Our first stop, which took us a while to
reach, was an emergency aid station in Avenal whose staff was
too busy to do more than give me an aspirin and a pat on the
hand. Widmeyer inquired there for Maitlan's body and was told
it had been taken to Hanford, the county seat. We set out after
it, our initial pursuit a crawl due to the outbound traffic.

After a couple of hours, we stopped at a wide spot in the
road called Lemoore. Widmeyer wanted me to eat something or
try to. While he scrounged for it, I placed a trio of calls to Los
Angeles. The first was to my home phone, to counteract
whatever news of the Avenal mess had spread that far south.
The line was busy. I didn't waste time wondering if the promised
call from Fort Ord had finally come in. I called a sweetheart
neighbor and asked her to walk a message over to Ella and
Gabby, the text of which was "I'm okay." My third call was to
Paddy. I reached his answering service, told them where I was
heading and why, and promised an update in an hour.

Widmeyer could have spent what was left of the drive pumping me, but he didn't. He told me instead about the fishing on
nearby Tulare Lake, a subject that didn't interest either one of

190

us very much but served to keep me awake. We both knew the pumping would come later.

It was late on Sunday afternoon when we finally made it to the county hospital, but Ben Maitlan had only just beaten us there. His body, still in the basket stretcher they'd used to carry it from Avenal, had gotten as far as the basement morgue. Before I confirmed the preliminary identification, which had been made on the basis of a Navy discharge found in the dead man's wallet, I asked if any of the other concert victims were females of high-school age, possibly named Miranda Combs. The man in charge said no, listened to my description of Miranda, and said no again.

Widmeyer asked who Miranda was, and when I said, "A family friend who was there last night," nodded and let it drop. Then the very bored morgue attendant pulled back the sheet covering the stretcher.

There was no doubt it was Maitlan, though the face had been worked over pretty well. The whole eggplant head had been. I recognized what was left of the face and the concave chest he'd been so proud of in his overgrown-kid way. I lifted his cold right hand and examined it. The knuckles were barked and two of the fingers looked broken. He'd gone down fighting.

I placed his hand on his chest, said "Sorry, sailor," and passed out.

I awoke the next morning to the stink and sting of disinfectant. A moon-faced nurse was dousing my head with it and looking at the rest of me like she wished she'd brought a bigger bottle. Her place was taken by a resident young enough to hold doors for me. He looked my head over, looked into my eyes as the ambulance attendant had earlier, only with a penlight, and gave me a shot.

"Your stitches look okay," he said, "but you should have gotten them a lot sooner."

"Weeks sooner," I said.

He blinked and asked, "Been hit on the head before?"

"In the same location since 1946."

He said, "Uh-huh," and yielded the floor to Widmeyer, who'd been standing in the doorway of my private room, looking antsy.

The highway patrol officer started apologetic. "Sorry, Elliott. Should have seen to your head first and the identification second. But it was a break finding you, and I wanted to make the most of it. If you feel up to talking this morning, I'd like to go through your story again."

Sometime while I'd been out, Widmeyer had acquired what Forrest Combs might have called chums, a mismatched pair of them. One was a man about my age and about the size of a cocker spaniel, which he further resembled around the eyes. The other was a stenographer, an Inger Stevens look-alike who gave me the sympathetic smile the nurse had forgotten to administer.

I kept Inger busy for a time by repeating the story I'd told Widmeyer back at the battlefield, throwing in a lot of extra details about Zodiac Productions and *Duo-Glide Rider* so they'd think the shot I'd been given was making me babble. Maybe it was, but not so much that the name Robert Sears ever passed my lips.

The spaniel, who answered to Asena and was some kind of county prosecutor, tired first. He interrupted me to ask for an explanation of the Ninth Circle's special interest in the Zodiac crew. There was plenty of special interest to explain. They'd killed a cameraman, beaten up a security operative, and burned a truck, to name the highlights. Luckily, I'd worked out an answer while listening to fish stories on the drive over from Lemoore. I'd remembered then how nervous Jarret had been about the presence of a second film crew and our lack of credentials.

"Are you telling me," the lawyer said after I'd used up several more of Inger's best notepad pages, "that this all happened because you didn't have a permit to film?"

"It happened," I said, "because some amateur concert organizers gave a lot of beer to some bikers and told them to look after things. That had always kept them quiet in the past, or so the amateurs were told. This time it bought a whole lot of trouble. Either the beer went to the bikers' heads or being connected with something that big did. Or maybe having a little power corrupted them. I've heard that's happened once or twice before."

It was a pretty good speech for a guy with a stitched-up head, even though I'd had to close my eyes about halfway through when the room had started to wobble. When I opened them again, my company was packing to go.

Widmeyer asked if I knew how to get in touch with Maitlan's family. I gave him Hedison's number, and he shook my hand. "Thanks for your help. We'll call you if we need anything else."

"We'll be calling, regardless," Asena said, not offering a paw.

The statuesque steno didn't say anything or blow me a kiss. She would have in the version I'd have worked up for Ella back in the good old days. That bit of business would have made Ella laugh or at least gotten her to forgive me faster for adding to my extensive list of injuries. But those days were gone. I had no idea how I'd hurry her forgiveness now or whether I'd get it at all.

Since Ella was on my mind, it was natural for me to think of her when the nurse came back to tell me I had a visitor. It made about as much sense to expect my wife as it had to look for Private Merritt Jackson back at the tablecloth tent. Still, I was disappointed when she didn't appear.

Not that the man who came in, Paddy Maguire, wasn't nearly as welcome or nearly as big a surprise.

"You got my message?" I asked.

"No, but I'm sure it will stand the test of time. Any chance you'll live? I've seen floaters with better color."

"Thanks. How did you know where to find me?"

Paddy was dressed for business in one of his best double-breasteds, in one hand a Homburg that had been blocked more often than Bronko Nagurski. In place of his recent muted neckwear, he wore one of his oldest, brightest ties, one he'd once claimed had been cut from Dorothy Lamour's Sunday sarong.

"We followed your trail from that field hospital in Avenal."

"We?" I looked for Ella again.

"My driver and I. He's one of Roland Hedison's youngsters, name of Jake. Roland insisted I take him and a car for him to drive. It's Roland's own, a strange little carriage built along the lines of a bedroom slipper. You'll like it."

I was sure someone had insisted on Paddy's borrowing the producer's Avanti, though who it had been was still an open question. But I stuck to the larger mystery. "How did you know to come at all?"

"Some of Roland's light brigade hit town yesterday morning. No two of them were telling the same story, but all the stories were bad. And no one knew what had happened to you. By the time Roland called me, there were news reports about the concert on the radio and even talk of ordering out the state militia. I was pretty sure it was all balloon juice till I saw Avenal. It looked like the site of an impromptu atom-bomb test.

"I don't know what this world's coming to," Paddy continued, using a familiar formula. "In my day, if we wanted music, we gathered around the parlor piano."

"And the Indians brought popcorn," I said. "Only they called it maize."

It cheered me considerably to hear Paddy talking like his old, rock-of-ages self. He even looked like the old Paddy, though he could have used one of my pillows to fill out his suit coat. The old twinkle was missing from his eyes, but I put that down to my condition.

"How do we spring me?" I asked.

"The usual way: We stroll out, ignoring good medical advice as we go. I did promise your doctor that you'd stay in bed for two days. I didn't say which two days. Me, I've always found the first weekend in January to be pretty good for that. And I said we'd get your ribs x-rayed when time permits. Remind me to send him a nice print."

We found my clothes, stiff with dried mud, hanging on a peg on the bathroom door. After I struggled into them, I got my first look at my head in the little mirror over the sink. In addition to disinfecting my head, someone had cut away a lot of my naturally wavy hair. That bothered me as much as the stitches and the mercurochrome and the ripening knot on my forehead.

"Reminds me of that haircut Tip Fasano gave you as a wedding present," Paddy said, naming a gangster who'd played at being a barber. "Don't worry, it'll grow back. Take my arm."

With Paddy's help, I made it as far as the Avanti's tiny backseat. I told a wide-eyed Jake to mind the bumps and dropped off again.

When I next came up for air, we were outside of Bakersfield, at one of those new truck stops that were popping up all over the state, the kind that were the size of a drive-in theater. This place rented showers to truckers, and I put in a reservation. It even had a camp store that sold two-dollar pipes and clothes, or what passed for clothes in the eighteen-wheel set. Paddy, who was fastidious on the subject, turned up his nose at the selection. He sent Jake into Bakersfield proper with a shopping list and a handful of his boss's money.

We sat down to wait and smoke in a canteen that was all red vinyl and checkered-flag tile. I thought that my appetite hadn't survived the concert until I smelled bacon and potatoes frying. Then I ordered the works.

The canteen was crowded with truckers and with conversations that flew back and forth between tables and counter stools. The fraternity didn't get to talk much, I decided, and took full advantage of its opportunities. Paddy and I were overdue for a talk ourselves, but he seemed content to drink coffee for the moment. I noticed that he'd left his smile back at the hospital.

I started us off by making my third report of the day, a full one this time. It didn't brighten Paddy any.

"And I pushed you into that asylum for the sake of a few more days on Hedison's payroll," he said when I'd finished.

"You didn't push me," I said. "I jumped." I made a clean breast then of my real reason for going to Avenal, my needle-in-a-haystack search for Miranda Combs, the case I'd been ordered to drop and hadn't. Well before I'd finished, I realized that Paddy already knew all about it. That and a lot more.

"I stopped by to see Ella Saturday evening," he explained. "I wanted to show her that note I'd gotten from Billy."

He paused to sip his coffee.

"I'm sorry I didn't tell you about Billy right away," I said. "I was holding out for good news."

Paddy snorted at that lie and said, "You mean, I was walking around with my head under my arm as it was. You were afraid if you told me I'd drop it altogether. Sorry for that, Scotty. Sorry for being one more person leaning on you when you needed to lean yourself. Sorry for getting old on you."

"You haven't yet."

"No? Since hearing about Billy, I've felt a hundred. But I'm not giving up hope. Not for that kid. He's the last person in the world who would give up, himself."

My breakfast arrived. My interest had waned, but I went through the motions. To encourage me, Paddy took over the conversation.

"Ella told me your theory about Sears's maybe-suicide being murder. Let me see if I've got it right. Sears's pot smuggling threatened this motorcycle picture, so the three geniuses filming it tried to tip Hedison off anonymously. It had to be anonymously because Sears knew they weren't making the movie Hedison thought they were and they couldn't take a chance on him ratting them out in return. It didn't work in any case, so they arranged for Sears to have his accident and tipped you off—also anonymously—to where the pot was hidden. Am I right so far?"

"If I am," I said.

"Let's assume you are and build on it. What happened in Avenal was all fallout from that murder scheme. Poetic justice, you might say. Instead of saving their movie by killing Sears, the three had dug a grave for it. The outlaws waiting for Sears and his pot—this Russo and company—went berserk. They stole the camera and what footage the crew had managed to shoot. While they were at it, they killed the cameraman, Maitlan. Interesting that I had to find that out from your doctor. None of the survivors thought to tell Hedison."

"They probably didn't know. The camera was snatched early on, while I was still on my feet. Maitlan wasn't killed until later, when the Roads were playing. That's what the state cop told me."

If I was remembering right. Keeping ideas in my head was like trying to carry marbles in a fishing net. They ran out every which way. At that moment, for example, I was thinking of Jill, the girl who had saved me from Maitlan's end. Had she gotten out okay or was she still wandering among the shell-shocked?

"Finish your eggs," Paddy said with something like his old decision. "We'll get you cleaned up and then brace Mr. Hedison together. We'll tell him your secret fears. He can hire us to find Sears's murderer or show us the door."

"It'll be the door, ten to one."

"Fine. Then we'll be free to find Miranda Combs together."

TWENTY-EIGHT

My rented shower was a religious experience. When they forced me out of it at gunpoint, Jake was waiting with my new outfit. To simplify things, he'd tried to duplicate my ruined one, right down to the desert boots. That was fine by me. I couldn't have broken in any tougher footwear, all the hot water having softened my bones.

We drove to Hedison's office via Oxnard, so I could rescue my car from the gas-station parking lot. To convince Paddy that it was safe for me to get behind the wheel, I sat up straight all the way down from Bakersfield, made bright comments about the scenery, and generally hid the fact that I was near to losing my breakfast the whole time.

At the Oxnard limits, Paddy doubled back to our conversation in the truck-stop café. "Maybe Maitlan was trying to rescue his camera from those hell-raisers. Maybe that's why he was killed."

From my vantage point in the backseat, I saw our driver squirm. "Got an opinion on that, Jake?" I asked.

"Not me," he said quickly.

"Come on now," Paddy said. "You're among friends."

"It's nothing I know for sure, just something I heard."

"Hearsay's admissible in this court," Paddy assured him.

Our latest red light turned green. Jake got us going again and said, "The day of Bobby Sears's accident, right after it happened, Ben was telling people that he was the guy who'd gotten

199

you called in, Mr. Elliott."

"Ben got us called in? You heard him say that?" I asked.

"Not exactly, sir. I heard it through the grapevine. You hear about everything going on at Zodiac, sooner or later. The units all share people, so news gets around."

"Is Hedison wired in?" I asked.

"God, I hope not. I'm pretty sure not."

"The day of the accident, when I was asking people about the Mexico trips, you said you hadn't been along. Is that still right?"

"Yes, Mr. Elliott, I swear. Zodiac's too cheap to send a full crew on something like that."

"But you heard what happened down there. You heard about the extra baggage that came back with them."

The playground honor system kicked in. "I didn't hear anything about any baggage," Jake said. Then he squirmed in his seat again.

"Thanks, kid," I said.

The Charger was right where I'd left it. So was the forty-five I'd locked in its trunk. I strapped it on and covered it with my stiff, new golf jacket. The weight of the gun against my sore ribs was actually steadying. It didn't keep me from looking over my shoulder for the Ninth Circle, but it changed my attitude about spotting them.

At his first sight of the gun, Jake had headed for the gas station's restroom, giving Paddy and me a chance to chat in private.

"I'll meet you at Hedison's," I said. "I've got a stop to make first."

Paddy ground an invisible cigar butt underfoot. "If you're thinking of going by your house, I'd think again. Her nibs had a bag packed and ready when I was there the other night. The minute you show up, she'll be on her way, stitches or no."

"Just to the beach house," I said, trying to make it sound like no big threat.

Paddy shrugged.

"Anyway, I'm not going home. I'm going to see Ben Maitlan's mother."

"Why?"

This time I shrugged, the holster making it a painful exercise.

Paddy didn't press me. "That'll give me a chance to soften Mr. Hedison up on the subject of you. When last we spoke, he was blaming you for everything that happened around Avenal on Saturday, including the rain. Just don't be too long. My lungs aren't what they used to be."

On the drive to the concert, Maitlan had told me all about Garden Grove, his hometown and the place where his widowed mother still lived. It was well to the east of the formal boundary of Los Angeles, but the city's penumbra of ranchless ranch houses and supermarkets was reaching out for it. A nearer threat was Anaheim and all the clutter around Disneyland. But I could still see traces of the small-town Garden Grove where Maitlan had flown kites and collected frogs.

His autobiographical ramblings hadn't included an address, but there was a Maitlan listed in the local directory, first name George. The male name didn't worry me. A widow often kept the protective cover of a dead husband's name in places like the phone book. I was more concerned over the possibility that Mrs. Maitlan didn't know what had happened to her son, since his name hadn't been given in any of the news stories about the concert we'd heard on the drive down from Hanford. Widmeyer hadn't seemed like the kind of cop who'd let grass grow under his feet, but he'd had a lot to deal with. I didn't want to be the man who broke the news to the widow, the one she'd always remember for it and maybe always hate.

The Maitlan house was a neat white bungalow awash in flower beds. An elderly black Ford was parked in the driveway. The car told me I could stop worrying about breaking Mrs. Maitlan's heart, as it had a clergyman's license plates. A couple of days earlier, when I'd seen Forrest Combs's sedan parked in my own drive, I'd mistaken it for the ride of a professional consoler. Here was the genuine article, complete with rusted rocker panels and balding tires. I thought of Ella and Gabby again, forced myself not to, and rang the bell.

The door was answered by a man with watery eyes, a bulbous nose, and pure white hair. He only glanced at me before he closed the door again—or tried to. My left foot, with its vast experience of slammed doors, had anticipated the move.

"It's okay," I said. "I'm a friend of Ben's. I was up at Avenal with him."

That only made the old man shove harder. I realized then that he'd already placed me at Avenal and on the wrong side of Ben Maitlan's last fight.

Then another face appeared in the gap my boot was holding open, a woman's face. I heard her say, "It's all right, Philip," and the pressure on my instep eased.

I'd cast Mildred Natwick or Margaret Wicherly in the part of the Widow Maitlan, which is to say I'd been picturing her as an older, almost wizened woman. The person who took the place of the front door wasn't much older than Ella. And she was so far from wizened that she was actually plump, a condition she'd tried to hide by not tucking her blouse into her shorts. That blouse was a sunflower print she probably wouldn't have chosen if she'd known how bad her day was going to be. Her face was blotchy from crying, though, at the moment, her large brown eyes were dry. They were also sad, as sad as any I'd seen.

"Who did that to you?" she asked.

"A motorcycle gang. The one that killed your son."

"Please come in."

In was a craftsman den with a lot of quartersawn oak trim. The man with the clerical plates stayed, but he kept to a window seat and never spoke. Mrs. Maitlan sat me in a leather chair whose broad oak arms were inlaid with cigarette burns, courtesy of her late husband, perhaps.

"The policeman who came said that Ben was working at the concert. Working on a film."

"That's right," I said.

"What . . . what kind of film?"

That seemed a little beside the point. I decided she was stalling, but I went along with it. "An antiwar film."

She looked impressed by that. "Is it good?"

That was hard to say about any movie-in-progress. You could screw one up as late as threading it through the projector at the premiere. Before I could answer, she reframed the question. "Is it an important film?"

"It's very important to the kids who are making it. I think it was important to Ben."

"I'm sorry," she said. "I haven't asked how you knew my son."

I told her my name and the same half-truths I'd used on Widmeyer and Asena, the story of the biker gang that had overreacted to a film crew sneaking in under the fence. Mrs. Maitlan was as skeptical as Asena had been, and she had something the prosecutor had lacked: a moral claim to the truth and the whole truth.

So when she said, "What really happened, Mr. Elliott? Tell me, please," I did.

"I think it had something to do with a load of marijuana someone on the film crew was supposed to bring to Avenal."

"Ben?"

"No. I don't think he was involved." Not with the smuggling.

His mother didn't share my conviction. "I told him. I told him to watch who he associated with. Watch what kind of work he took. He'd just smile and pat my head, like I was the child. He came back from Vietnam that way, like he was all grown up all of a sudden."

"A war can do that to a man," I said.

"I don't think so." She didn't break down, but her speech took on the breathless rhythm of sobbing. "I think that's a mistake people make about war. It ages parts of a man and not others. They come back half men and half boys. That's why so many of them don't know what to do with themselves. But the difference in Ben was bigger than that. Deeper than that. He acted sometimes like the world owed him something. He'd been to a war. He'd done his bit, as my dad used to say. Now he expected to be paid back for it. He expected to do anything he wanted to do and nothing he didn't want to do and no questions asked."

That didn't sound like the Maitlan I'd briefly known. But it was familiar. It reminded me of my own postwar philosophy as I'd summed it up for Jackie Jarret: regular Gibsons and a warm place to sleep and the world could go hang itself.

"He would have gotten over it," I said.

We sat thinking about that lost opportunity and all the others Maitlan would never have. At least, I was thinking of them. His mother was still stuck on the good advice her son hadn't taken from her.

"If you're ashamed of a job, don't do it," she said. "That's what I told him. If you can't stand up in church and talk about it proudly, don't do it."

I dropped a step behind at that point, wondering how many of the jobs I'd done for Paddy I'd be willing to talk about in a church. Or a bus terminal for that matter. When I woke up, I realized that the widow with the pieta eyes was trying to tell me something.

"What job was Ben ashamed of, Mrs. Maitlan?"

She hesitated, and I remembered the first time she'd had trouble finding words, when she'd asked me what kind of film her son had been working on when he'd died.

"Was it another movie project? Something you didn't want him to do?"

Her firm chin quivered, and I knew we were talking about more than any artistic reservations Maitlan might have had over the hackwork Zodiac turned out. But it didn't have to involve Zodiac. Maitlan the gypsy worked on other things for other producers.

"He called them nudies," Mrs. Maitlan blurted out. She glanced over at the minister, who hadn't blinked a watery eye. He was an elder in Paddy's congregation: the first church of guys who'd heard everything.

The answer hadn't surprised me either, I realized. Porn movies, hard and soft, had been a regular subject of my conversations lately. It took me a second to remember, in my battered condition, that those conversations had all been about the Miranda Combs case and not about the Zodiac business. So Maitlan's other freelance work, however embarrassing to his mother, couldn't be the reason he'd been killed.

The widow had switched to a study of the hardwood floor, but kept talking. "He laughed about it, said those movies were a quick buck and didn't hurt anybody. He didn't like to talk about them, once he knew it upset me. But I kept after him. And I was getting to him, too. He hadn't laughed about it lately. I think he was starting to see how serious it was. He wasn't laughing as much about anything."

Mrs. Maitlan raised her eyes from the hardwood. "He was worried about something this last little while. I know it. Are you sure he wasn't mixed up with this marijuana, Mr. Elliott? Don't be afraid to tell me if he was. I couldn't feel any worse than I do now."

Which got us to the subject I'd come to discuss and had managed not to. "He may have been mixed up in it, but not the smuggling part. The marijuana didn't make it to the concert because one of the kids who work for Zodiac tipped off the headman, anonymously. I think it might have been Ben. Does that sound like something he might have done?"

That was my explanation for the rumor Jake had picked up at the Zodiac watercooler, that Maitlan had claimed to be responsible for Hollywood Security being called in. Jarret and company hadn't been the anonymous source after all. Ben Maitlan had.

His mother wasn't encouraging at first. "It doesn't sound like something Ben would have done. Not lately. Not since his discharge from the Navy. The old Ben would have. He was his father's son."

That reminder of her double loss got the tears going again. The silent minister came over to comfort her, but she didn't take her flowing eyes from mine. There was something else in them. Defiance.

"I hope it was Ben who told, Mr. Elliott. I hope he stood up for something at the end."

Twenty-Nine

Before leaving Garden Grove, I asked Mrs. Maitlan for her son's Los Angeles address. She went me one better, lending me the spare key she'd kept for him. Maitlan's apartment was very near the Hollywood and Vine office where Paddy was holding the fort for me. It was in what once had been a salesman-grade hotel and was soon to be an urban-renewal project.

My intention was to look around for rough drafts of anonymous notes, but a police car was parked out front when I arrived. The caretaker at the front desk told me the cops were in the Maitlan suite, so I put off the search until a later time that never actually came.

When I reached Zodiac's busy front office, I could hear Paddy and the headman going at it through the producer's heavy front door. I didn't feel ready to wade in, so I sat down with the ladies of the bullpen, who fussed over me and my honorable wounds. When they'd settled a little, their conversation reverted to the crisis du jour, which involved the sci-fi epic Hedison had once mentioned to me in passing, *Queen of Blood.*

"Our next release," the senior aide said proudly. I was struck again by the mismatch between her thin arms and her big hands, thinking, unkindly, that she could have done semaphore without the flags. "The poster was supposed to come from the printer today." She waved a catcher's mitt at the framed prints around the room. "I don't know if it will. What a day!"

"Mondays," I said, sipping the tea that was the staff's late-morning stimulant. "Can't trust that day. *Queen of Blood* must have been in production about the time you were wrapping up *Die, Zombie, Die,*" I added, naming the current holder of the newest-release title, the picture that had landed Zodiac in the drug trade.

"Yes," the woman said. "*Queen of Blood* is really a foreign film, but we dubbed it and added some additional scenes. I believe those were being shot around the time *Zombie* was in postproduction. Let me check. Yes, that's right."

"While you're checking," I said, "could you tell me who the cameraman was on *Queen of Blood*?"

"For the new scenes?" She consulted her paperwork again. "Oh, my. It was Ben Maitlan, the boy who was killed."

"Thanks," I said, handing her my empty cup. "I think I feel up to going in now."

I'd often witnessed Paddy and a studio big shot knocking heads or heard about it afterward from the victor himself. He and Jack Warner had once had their horns locked so long they'd had to send out for sandwiches. So the tableau inside Hedison's USC shrine was a familiar one. The producer, red in the face, was leaning across his desk, his hands on its near corners like he was thinking of tossing it aside. Paddy was leaning back in a comfortable chair, blowing smoke rings at the ceiling.

The sight of my multicolored head calmed Hedison slightly. "Damn, Elliott, I'm sorry. Really. I'm glad you're on your feet. But use them to go somewhere else, will you? And take this Ancient Hibernian with you. Take him to a quiet bar and explain to him what 'you're fired' means."

"You'd better explain it to me first."

"Don't tempt me. If someone hadn't beaten me to it, I'd be playing handball with you right now. When I think of Ben Maitlan lying in a cooler—"

"You look around for someone else to blame," I said.

I was used to Hedison's bluster running out faster than a forty-eight-hour pass. A little of it left him now.

"Are you saying this is my fault?"

"Yes. You lied us all into this mess."

"Now, wait a minute—"

"You told me those notes you got were anonymous. You knew damn well who sent them."

So did I, now: Ben Maitlan. And I knew how he could have heard about the first pot shipment even though he hadn't been along on the first Mexico trip. The freelance cameraman had been working on another Zodiac picture then, *Queen of Blood,* and not off wandering Southern California in the service of some other fly-by-night producer. Meaning he could have heard about Sears's little sideline through the Zodiac grapevine Jake had told us about.

"So I knew who'd written me, so what? He wanted to be anonymous, and I respected that. I still do."

"He's dead, Hedison. That cancels all deals, real and imaginary."

"I don't agree," the producer said, getting lofty on me.

"Not even if the tips he gave you got him killed?"

That put a little of the burgundy back in Hedison's cheeks. "For Christ's sake, Elliott. His death was an accident."

"How can you call a beating death—" And then my head suddenly got a little less porous. "You're talking about Robert Sears."

"Of course I am. Who did you think I was talking about?"

The world got wobbly again. When it steadied, I had a view that went on for miles. I saw people scurrying around like ants, and I understood what all the scurrying was about. That kind of mountaintop experience can make a person giddy. It made me curt. "You stupid, lying bastard," I said.

Hedison rose to his full height, which appeared to be seven

foot two. "That's all, brother," he said and started for me.

I didn't notice Paddy slip the cosh out. The first time I saw it, he was flicking it at the producer's knee as Hedison passed his chair. The big man genuflected, and a second flick of the sap tagged him on the jaw. He crumpled onto the carpet almost noiselessly.

Paddy covered what sound there was by booming, "Let's keep our voices down, gentlemen. I'm sure we can discuss this without bothering the neighbors."

I slipped back to the office door and locked it, the Heifetz of the blackjack nodding his approval. "We'll have a few uninterrupted minutes," he said. "How do we spend them?"

"Finding those notes."

It wasn't much of a challenge. They were stuck between the pages of a dictionary Hedison had in a desk drawer. Unlike the message that had drawn us to Lancaster, these were handwritten. And they weren't anonymous. Robert Sears had signed his full name, though in the text he had asked Hedison to keep that name to himself. What the text didn't contain was the identity of the person or persons bringing the marijuana north. When Hedison had complained to me at our first meeting about the code of the school yard, he'd had good reason to.

Our host hadn't stirred. "I hope I didn't hit him too hard," Paddy said, kicking him medicinally.

"You didn't hit him hard enough. He knew Sears was the tipster. So he couldn't have really believed that his death was an accident or even a suicide. And it's worse than that."

My boss didn't need any arithmetic lessons from me. "The bales of pot we found at the Sears ranch were a plant. Hedison had to know that as soon as I told him about them. And he sat in that very chair and let me brag about the great job we'd done."

He kicked the corpse again with a little more enthusiasm and got an answering moan. I retrieved a jug of water from Hedison's credenza and emptied it on its owner's head. The seepage from a leaky tent had done wonders for me, and this little baptism had a similar effect on Hedison. He sat up, his legs spread wide for support, and said, "Who?"

"The coach is sending you in," Paddy told him. "We're down by seven, and the breaks are beating the boys." To me, he added, "I've often been told I could pass for Pat O'Brien."

"Never noticed," I said.

Hedison had stopped fumbling for his helmet by then and started rubbing his jaw. Through the strands of wet hair, the scar on his forehead was livid. "You gangsters," he said. "I'm going to have you arrested."

"Think again," Paddy said. He let Hedison see the notes from Sears before tucking them into a breast pocket. "If we get involved with the law, we'll have to turn over this vital evidence. You could end up an accessory to two murders."

"And two attempted murders," I said. "The real smuggler, the one you decided to protect, tried to kill us with Sears's shotgun."

Paddy, who'd been idly swinging his blackjack, let it brush the still-seated producer's ear. "I'd almost forgotten about that. You listened to that report of mine with nice wide eyes and never once thought to mention that the citizen who set the trap was still walking around loose, maybe getting ready to try again. Why? Why didn't you tell us Sears was just a fall guy? We were working for you, for crying out loud."

Hedison was crawling to a chair, so I answered for him.

"He'd known all along who the real smuggler was. The real smugglers were, I should say. They were the cream of his best unit. That's why he hadn't wanted an investigation, only a cover-up. Those kids were getting ready to leave him for something better, like his best people always did, but he wanted their last

211

picture finished without a scandal. After Sears was killed, he
figured out a way to keep them on his payroll forever."

That was what had turned Jackie Jarrett against Hedison on
the morning we'd driven up to the concert.

The accused man said, "Turning them in wasn't going to
help Rob."

"How about Maitlan?"

My question reminded me that I'd lost my shiny new motive
for the cameraman's murder. He hadn't been killed for informing because he hadn't informed. I'd also lost my ready explanation for the odd claim Maitlan had made. I ran that claim by
Hedison.

"Maitlan told people he was responsible for Hollywood
Security being called in."

The producer said, "If he did, he was covering for Rob. I
don't know why Ben would do that. And I don't know why he
was killed, Elliott. I swear I don't."

"Maybe the best people in your best unit do," Paddy said.

"Where are they?" I asked. "McNeal and Riddle and Jarret?"

"They took the news about Ben pretty hard. I told them to
go home and rest up. As far as I know, they're still home doing
it. Except for Jackie. She's at my house. It's not what you're
thinking, either. She said she couldn't get any rest at her place.
Noisy neighbors, I think."

"Noisy ghosts, I think," I said. "Let's have some addresses."

THIRTY

"Roland's been holding out on us nine ways from Sunday," Paddy said. "And here's the latest one: There's money in the zombie business."

That observation was prompted by our first sight of Hedison's getaway. It was in the Hollywood Hills, in a section of houses built in the late thirties by the old studios' second tier, the department heads and production-line directors and nickel squeezers, the men who'd kept the town running back when it really had run. Colonial homes had had a vogue at that time—though they looked about as natural against the local flora as a minaret—and Hedison's was one of these, a pale yellow saltbox of at least seven gables with parking for a parade on its crescent drive.

Until we added ours, the only car parked there was a vintage Plymouth Valiant with a teddy bear in its back window. The owner of the car and the bear, Jackie Jarret, must have been watching the drive. She had the heavy front door open by the time we walked up. She was still wearing her concert jeans; I recognized the dirt on them as dried Avenal. But she'd lost her macraméd top and was making do with the white T-shirt that had been visible through its many gaps. Behind her porthole glasses, her big eyes were pink. From crying for Maitlan, maybe, or smoking Jill's all-purpose pain remedy.

Or maybe crying for me. She certainly wilted when she saw me, but then just about everybody had that day.

"I'm fine," I said. When her gaze passed to Paddy, I added, "He's my nurse."

"Where's his?" Jarret shot back, raising a deep laugh from the injured party. Then she asked, "And Ben?" in a hopeful way.

The hope made no sense for a beat and then it did. If I'd risen from the grave, maybe the reports about Maitlan had been exaggerated, too.

"Still dead," I said.

Jarret broke down at that, sobbing so hard her skeletal frame shook in my arms, where she'd thrown herself. I walked her inside, Paddy following us. I noticed he'd drawn his gun.

We made our way to the kitchen, where Paddy checked the contents of a percolator and then plugged it in. A minute later it was bubbling away. By that time I had Jarret seated at a breakfast-nook table, and her sobbing had settled down to the emotive equivalent of the dry heaves, spasms that were as painful to watch as they were unproductive.

"How'd you get away?" I asked when I thought she could manage the answer.

"After I talked to you," she began, her breathing keeping pace with the climaxing percolator, "I wandered around. I don't know how long. It was getting dark when Matt and Sol found me. They said we had to get away right then. The Roads were just arriving, and everybody was going nuts. That would give us our chance.

"Mike was waiting at the bus. He'd backed it clear when the truck was torched. And that actress chick Hayden was with him. He was trying to hit on her, but she was too hysterical to notice. I guess the bikers almost had her on the ground at one point. When they took our film. When I ran away and found you."

She was leading me in a circle, intentionally or otherwise. I nudged her out of the orbit.

"Did that other actor, Reber, catch the bus?"

"No. No one saw him after the Ninth Circle broke us up. He called while we were talking to Roland yesterday. He'd gotten away on one of our bikes but gone north by mistake. He ended up in San Jose."

"That leaves Maitlan and me," I said.

"Leaves you is right," Paddy said from his place behind the counter. "Smack in the frying pan."

I would have thrown a pan at him if I'd had one handy. But Jarret didn't seem to have heard him.

"I told them I'd talked to you," she mumbled. "They said we couldn't wait."

"What about Maitlan?"

"Matt said he'd talked to Ben, tried to get him to leave. He wouldn't. He said he had business there."

"Rescuing his camera," Paddy said, backing his own horse.

"I don't know. Matt didn't say. I don't think he would have sent Ben back alone to get the camera. He would have gone with him."

Wearing shining armor, perhaps. All the same, something about her hero's behavior under fire seemed to worry her. And I thought I knew what it was.

"It wasn't just the Roads arriving that got you clear, was it?" I said. "McNeal had given your business partner, Russo, someone else to blame. When we first showed up that day, he told Russo who I was. That bought you a little time, but not enough. Russo found out you hadn't brought the pot you'd promised him—you, McNeal, and Riddle. He took it out on your truck and on me and finally on Maitlan. And that sequence was no coincidence. McNeal fingered Maitlan for Russo, just like he'd fingered me. He told Russo what Maitlan had admitted out loud, that he was the real reason the smuggling scheme had fallen apart."

There were a lot of accusations in that monologue. Jarret didn't deny any of them. Instead, she solved the mystery of how her eyes had gotten pink. She fumbled in her pocket and produced a joint so big it looked like a baby cigar in a paper diaper. I took it from her and passed her the cup of coffee my boss had passed me.

"None of that matters now, Elliott," she said. She looked at the kitchen wall clock, which had the profile of a teapot.

"Why not?"

Still looking at the clock, she said, "Because nothing does."

"If that's true," I said, "you won't mind telling us about the marijuana. Whose idea was it to bring that back?"

I thought she might prefer any other topic to that, including why she found the teapot clock so fascinating. Instead, she dove in headfirst.

"Sol thought of it, though he convinced Matt that it was Matt's idea. Sol's a master at putting his schemes in other people's heads."

"What was Sol after?"

Paddy rephrased my question. "What was the dream?"

"Independence. We figured Roland would release *Rider* even if he hated it, just to get his money back. But there was always a chance he'd tell us to burn it. If he did, we wanted to have the money ready to buy the negative from him. Everything's been for the movie."

She looked up at the clock again.

"Including killing Sears?" I asked. Jarret didn't dive into that one, so I said, "How did he find out about the pot?"

"Are you kidding? Loading the trucks was part of his job."

"So he was in on it?"

"No. We offered to cut him in, but he wouldn't take any money. That would have violated the moral principles he'd brought back from 'Nam. We thought he was cool with it, though."

"When did you find out he wasn't?"

"When Roland spread the word that someone—he wouldn't say who—had told him about the pot. We knew it was that peckerwood Sears."

"Then why did you take him to Mexico with you a second time?"

"Because he had more than the pot on us. You got that part right the other day in Matt's trailer. Sears knew *Rider* wasn't the picture Roland ordered."

"He didn't mention that in his notes to Hedison."

"It didn't violate his code. Not the way smuggling pot did. And holding that back gave him something he could use on us if we tried to get him canned. A little job security."

"Kids grow up so fast these days," Paddy said musingly.

I said, "So you had plenty of reasons to kill him, especially after he'd informed on you a second time. Hedison let you know he was hiring us. He wanted you to have time to cover your tracks. You used that time to plan a murder."

"That was Sol's idea, too."

"He's some salesman," I said. "Did he convince McNeal that it was his idea all along?"

"No. He presented it to us as a plot problem. How would we work out the murder if we were writing it in a script? It was almost like a game."

"Your solution was to monkey with some pins and then cook up a fight between Sears and me so you could substitute them while no one was looking. By that time, I'd become another plot problem, one with a wife and kids. So you sent me out to Lancaster to eat some buckshot."

"You're in a bad business, Elliott. You should have thought of that before you had the wife and kids."

I'd never get ahead trading barbs with a writer. "Where did Russo come in?"

"We needed somebody to buy the pot. Sol approached the guy he bought from, but he was just a small-time pusher. He offered to put us in touch with his supplier, the Ninth Circle. I knew from the beginning they were out of our league. Sol thought he could handle them." Again, she checked the time. "He thinks he's smarter than Cal Tech."

"How smart was showing up at Avenal empty-handed?"

"We had to go. We couldn't finish the picture if we didn't. We counted on the concert security to keep us safe. We didn't know the Ninth Circle would be the security. Nobody could have known that."

"How did that get set up to begin with? Wasn't going up there Hedison's idea?"

"He thinks it was. Sol planted that one, too. It started out to be about the movie, not about the pot. It was the big sequence we needed to make the story work. Then Russo came up to Port Dume to arrange the pickup of the second shipment. When he heard we were going to be at Avenal, he decided it would be safer for us to bring the stuff in ourselves. And to break the bales down into bags for him first. And to shut up and like it."

"So when you gave up the pot, you were doing more than framing a dead stuntman and maybe getting rid of me. You were trying to get out from under Russo."

"We couldn't give him what we didn't have. Only he wouldn't listen to excuses. He still won't. We'll never be rid of him. And we'll never get away from Zodiac. Roland's figured everything out. He thinks he owns us, too. He and Russo will be fighting over our bones. We blew it, Elliott. We really blew it."

She started crying again, softly this time.

THIRTY-ONE

Paddy cleared his throat. "Do we roll up the other two ourselves or send the police?"

"The police won't find them," I said. "Neither will we without help." I shook Jarret by the shoulder. "How overdue are they?"

"How did you—" She shot the teapot clock an angry look. "They were supposed to call an hour ago."

"Where did they go? They were meeting Russo, weren't they?" The man who was supposed to be halfway to Canada.

"They're trying to get back the footage we shot at the concert, what there is of it. They still think there's a chance to finish the movie. They still think they can talk their way out of anything."

"Boys after my own heart," Paddy said as he reached for his hat.

"Where was the meeting, Jackie?"

"The airport where we killed Robby."

Paddy had gotten as far as the kitchen entry. "We can't leave her here alone."

"Nobody knows where I am, except Roland and you. All I gave Matt and Sol was the phone number."

"Give it to me," I said.

My restorative tea had worn off. It was hell getting off that breakfast-nook bench and a long hike to the front door. Jarret, who I'd all but carried in, stayed by my elbow, ready to catch me. That kept her within range of my third degree.

"Why would Maitlan claim to be the one who'd gotten me hired?"

"I don't know."

"Was he trying to impress somebody? Some girl?"

"He has a steady girl, I think. Had one. Anyway, he wasn't bragging when he said it. He was blaming himself for it."

"You actually heard him?"

"Yes."

"Did McNeal?"

"No."

"But you trusted him with the information. Just like you trusted him with what I'd told you about my boy being in 'Nam. McNeal passed that on to Russo, too."

"Get one thing straight, Elliott. I'd trust Matt with my life."

Those brave words were still bouncing around inside the Charger when we reached the head of the drive and I got a last glimpse of Jarret. She'd retrieved her stuffed bear from the Valiant and was squeezing it to her chest.

Our run to Torrance, mostly along a boulevard named Crenshaw, was all red lights. Paddy kept me from boiling over by telling me a story or two I'd almost forgotten and by mentioning names I hadn't thought of in years. He was so nostalgic, so like his old breezy self, that I started to worry. Mary Jordan, the woman who now commanded Paddy's office, fretted about him wanting to make one last financial score. I was more worried just then about him wanting to go out in a blaze of glory, something the boys would talk about for years.

"I intend to be home for dinner," I said to him when we finally spotted the sign for Whitman West. "For years yet."

He laughed easily. "If that's an invitation, count me in. If you're worried about me trying to cheat the retirement home, don't be. Funny thing, though, I was just thinking about death wishes myself."

"McNeal and Riddle don't have a death wish. They're just too cocky for their own good."

"I was thinking more of Miss Jarret. Oh well, there's the airfield."

The gate was open, as it had been the last time I'd visited, but the dangling chain and padlock that had decorated the gate post then were now missing altogether. I drove us in along the road McNeal had used when he'd accepted the flower from the little girl. The only sign of the unit's late encampment was a brown stretch in the grass.

The road ended at the Quonset-hut office where Maitlan had called for the ambulance. The pay phone he'd used was hanging on one of the flat ends of the building. I parked the Charger beneath a sign whose red lettering Paddy read aloud as we climbed out: "Have you closed your flight plan?"

I'd seen similar signs often at airports, once at a little strip north of LA where a starlet and her producer had closed both their flight plan and their obituaries. The memory made me more uneasy, if that was possible.

Beyond the office was a single hangar whose gray concrete walls were breaking out in blotches of powdery white. Sitting beside it was a vehicle I'd last seen in Point Dume, a Willys station wagon. There were no motorcycles to keep it company.

"They could have them parked inside," Paddy said. "But they'd have left someone on guard."

I tried to talk him into taking that job himself, but he was preoccupied with the unwrapping of a fresh cigar, which he stuck in one corner of his mouth but didn't light.

We crossed the tarmac and entered the hangar though a side door near the station wagon. It was easy to do, as someone had gone to the trouble of kicking the door's frame into kindling. The dim interior still smelled of oil and aviation gas from the lost squadrons that had passed through. There was another odor, too, something more acrid and recent. When my eyes got accustomed to the light, I saw all there was to see in the vast space: two shapes in the very center of the greasy concrete floor. From a distance, they looked like two piles of old clothes with a pair of shoes tossed on each, their soles facing us.

"Ah me," Paddy said.

The pile containing Riddle was relatively tidy if you overlooked the bullet hole in the back of his head. McNeal's corpse, though fresher than the one I'd identified in Hanford, bore the marks of a similar beating.

"Tried to get something out of him, do you think?" Paddy asked. "And, if so, what?"

"Jarret's hiding place. The Ninth Circle is cleaning house. What were you thinking just now about her and a death wish?"

"Only that the line she handed us, about these two not knowing her current whereabouts, sounded thin."

"She told me she trusted McNeal with her life. She'd made up her mind to stick to that if it killed her."

"Her mistake was trusting this character." He indicated Riddle with a wave of the match he'd finally used to light his cigar. "It doesn't look like he put up much of a fight on her behalf. Come on, we'll try the pay phone."

Russo hadn't bothered cutting the phone line. I put that down to overconfidence until I dialed the number Jarret had given me. I heard the click of the other phone being picked up, but no one spoke. I said, "Jackie?" and heard a smothered giggle.

"That you, bastard man?"

"It's me," I said.

"You don't die easy. Not like some people I know. Where are you, buddy?"

"What have you done with Jackie?"

"Ruined her life, I think. Told her what happened to her

boyfriend. But you know all about that. She sent you to save him, didn't she? How's that coming?"

I was holding the phone sideways to my ear so Paddy could hear both ends of the conversation. When I drew a breath to answer Russo, my boss put a hand on my arm. It took almost a minute of silence, but the biker finally blinked.

"You there, Elliott? You asked about pretty Jackie. You could still help her out. My boys and me need a little traveling money. We can't tap our gang brothers. They're too pissed at us for bringing the pigs down on their heads. And my ex-business partners didn't have forty bucks between them. So I got to thinking about their boss, this Mr. Zodiac guy. When you called, I was hoping it was him, but you're even better. You still listening?"

"I'm here. How much do you want?"

"Ten grand. From the looks of this place, that won't dent him too bad. I thought we might even find it lying around, but so far, no luck."

"Let me talk to Jackie."

"Fuck you, buddy, we aren't playing cops and robbers. Here's the deal. You get the money and meet us. Alone. And you get Jackie."

Along with a brand-new hole in my head. From somewhere in that head came the glimmer of a plan, based on something Jackie had told me about the last meeting the trio had had with Russo before the concert. For my idea to work, I'd have to get ahead of the Ninth Circle for once, which meant finessing their giggling leader.

"The meeting place has to be public," I said. "Manhattan Beach, say."

"Say again, buddy. That's too public."

I jumped us north along the coast. "Topanga Beach is smaller," I said and held my breath.

Russo could hardly control his laughter. "Tell you what. A good pal of mine has a place just past there. At Point Dume. Just follow the signs for the bird sanctuary. Hector will meet you on the road."

I hesitated for a moment, wondering if I should admit having been to the trailer in case he knew it and was testing me. I decided on an equivocal answer that was in character for the part I was playing: "Too private."

"Too bad. You want to listen to a black girl scream while you change your mind?"

"You win. But it'll take me a couple hours to get up there. That's if Hedison can raise the money."

"He'll raise it. Just don't be too long about it. There's five of us and only one of Jackie. You don't want she should be all wore out."

THIRTY-TWO

I asked Paddy to check McNeal for keys and fed the phone again. I dialed the number I'd been dying to dial all day. Gabby answered.

"Dad," she said, "are you really okay?"

She was close to breaking down, and suddenly I was, too. I steadied myself against the warm metal of the hut's wall.

"I'm still on my feet," I said. "How about you?"

"Still here. Still waiting for news."

"How's your mom?"

"The same. She's out on the front porch. She's been out there a lot since you left. Should I get her?"

"No." I'd have to explain too much to Ella. "I need you to do something for me right away. Grab your mom and get out of there. The house isn't safe just now, thanks to Hollywood Security. Go to Winnie Mannero's and wait to hear from me."

Russo and his gang were already on the move; I was sure of that. They couldn't afford to stay at Hedison's. For all they knew, I had the police on the way. If Russo should make a side trip in search of spare hostages, I wanted Ella and Gabby long gone. We'd never been listed in the phone book, but McNeal and company had had days to check up on me. And whatever they'd found out, Russo now knew.

"In ten minutes, I want you ten blocks away from there."

"Right, Chief. And Dad, I love you. I forgot to tell you that before you left."

225

"No, you didn't."

Paddy was rocking on his heels beside the hangar when I skidded up in the Dodge. He handed me a well-packed key case.

"Found it under the front seat of the wagon. Do we have time to call this in?"

"Not now."

He let me concentrate on my driving until we were on the San Diego Freeway and doing eighty. Then he said, "You remembered Miss Jarret saying that Russo had visited Point Dume to make final arrangements for the concert. So you nudged him along the coast until he had the bright idea of luring you there. So our play is to get there first and turn down the sheets for him and his pals."

"Right."

"Our old drinking buddy Tory Beaumont pulled this gag in one of his pictures. Convinced the bad guy he was phoning from some hick town when he was actually hiding in the very house he knew the bad guy would use for a trap. Worked like a charm for him, as I recall. What are our chances?"

"I don't know. There's a lot of city between Russo and the nearest freeway. And he doesn't think there's a reason for him to hurry, I hope. So he may keep off the main roads altogether, to avoid the highway patrol."

We picked up the Santa Monica Freeway and rode it down to the coast highway. Once we were on that, Paddy gave me some advice on my driving.

"Slow down a little. We'll make better time if we don't stop every mile or two to chat with a constable."

"Speaking of constables," I said, "we're going to need as many as we can get. We can't call them from the trailer. There's no phone." No phone, no neighbors, no distractions. "There's a roadside joint in Topanga Beach." One of the two or three hundred places where I'd passed around Miranda Combs's picture in a earlier life. "It's right on the highway."

"Renaldo's," said Paddy, who could give tours to the tour guides.

"Right. One of us should be there to call the cops after the gang passes by."

"Assuming they haven't passed already. But why wait? Why not call right now?"

"We don't want them pulled over while they have Jarret to use as a shield."

"Some shield," Paddy said. "I've seen more meat in a boarding-house stew. But we'll play it your way. Maybe I can tag along after the gang, catch them in a squeeze play."

I didn't like the sound of that, but getting Paddy to agree to stay behind was no small victory. In Renaldo's sloping lot, he got less cooperative, leaning back in through the open window of the car door he'd just shut and acting like a guy who had no place special to be.

"I'll need those directions I read you over the phone," he said.

The envelope I'd scribbled them on was still on the dashboard. I handed it over. "Anything else?"

"Yes," he said. "Don't forget you intend to be home for dinner. For years yet."

"I won't."

"You know, this highway isn't the only road to Point Dume. There's two or three goat tracks through the canyons they might take, if there's a local boy in the group."

"Cheer me up later," I said. "Right now, I'm in a hurry."

Even so, I took time to look back from the next crest in the road. Paddy was seated at a roadside table, fanning himself with his hat. Or waving good-bye with it. I almost waved back. I felt a similar pang when I passed the sign for Malibu. I hadn't suggested the beach house as Ella and Gabby's hiding place because I'd told McNeal and the others about it. And because I didn't want my family on the same road as the killers, maybe at the same moment, even though there was a lot of traffic to hide in on that road and no way for Russo to pick one car out of it.

The road to the bird sanctuary had no traffic to hide in. Not that I was worried about an ambush. Not on the road, at least. If Russo had gotten there first, the guide he'd promised me would be my tip-off. I made it to the turn for the trailer without seeing anyone.

The trailer's little parking area was empty. I left it that way, taking the Dodge as far as the next bend in the road and hiding it as well as I could in the thin pines. Back at the sandy lot, I came across motorcycle tracks. I told myself they were the ones I'd seen on my last visit, the ones I'd mistakenly thought had been left by Robert Sears. Despite that pep talk, I got a lot less confident. As I circled the dunes that hid the trailer, I saw leather jackets behind every tree.

When I reached the top of the dune behind the clearing, I lay on my bruised ribs for a time, sweating into the sand while flies buzzed around my disinfected hair. Then I started down, the holes I left on the steep wall of sand refilling themselves as I went. The trailer's late owner hadn't believed in closing his blinds. I checked all three back windows and knew I'd won the race.

At the front door, my fatigue or my age caught up with me. I couldn't find a key that fit the toy lock, couldn't even hit the keyhole every time I tried. Finally, I got the door open and climbed inside. I closed the blinds on the front door's window, but bent back one end of the bottommost slat.

The only thing I'd brought with me from my car besides an extra box of shells was my truck-stop pipe. I decided that smoking it would be too big a risk, so I sat chewing its stem in a dark corner that commanded a view of front and back windows.

Though my life and Jarret's depended on my staying alert, I fell into thinking about Maitlan and his unexplained place of honor at the center of things. Jarret had described Maitlan as unhappy about that honor. His mother had noticed the same mood, but she'd had an explanation that didn't involve marijuana or Hollywood Security. Her son had simply begun to see that his pickup work in the blue-movie industry wasn't as innocent as he'd thought.

I'd been quick to dismiss Maitlan's little sideline as a distraction, since it had nothing to do with Zodiac and Avenal. Now, I wondered if I'd been too quick. I'd no sooner had that doubt than an answer came to me, a way to explain Maitlan's claim of responsibility for me and why he'd been ashamed of it. At least, I thought it might explain it. To be sure, I had to ask Roland Hedison a question I should have asked the day I met him.

I looked around for the phone McNeal had never put in. Then I heard a faint popping sound high in the trees. It was the reflected noise of motorcycles coming my way.

THIRTY-THREE

I moved to the front door and crouched there, my eyes just above the sill of the tiny window, level with the peephole I'd made in the blind. Five of them came into the clearing, Jarret and Russo and three others, the guy who'd broken a pool cue over my head and two I didn't recognize. Russo was keeping Jarret close, but he was being possessive, not cautious. None of them was looking around or making any effort to be quiet. The two dress extras carried six-packs in each hand. My old friend the pool pro was swinging a big revolver. It looked like a three-fifty-seven magnum, the gun movie cops were making way too popular.

I ducked out of sight and braced myself against the wall near the door's flimsy hardware. One part of the setup was exactly as advertised. The fifth man—Hector, probably—was back in the road, waiting for me. But there was a spoiler, too, the drawn gun. I couldn't hope to get the drop on four of them, not when one had his gun out and ready. So I switched to Plan B or maybe Plan J or K; I'd run through so many.

By then I could make out the dialogue. They were arguing over who got Jarret's company second. First dibs belonged to the man who was walking with his arm around her neck. I could hear his nasal singsong above the deeper rumbling of the others.

"Matt coulda done better than this dump. That's what the Riddler told me. He said Matt's old man owned most of Santa

230

Barbara. He said Matt coulda made one phone call and gotten all the bread he needed to make things right with me. But he wouldn't do it. He was one stiff-necked son of a bitch was Matt. You got a key or does Burt have to shoot the lock off?"

That got me on the balls of my feet. The lock was six inches from my head, and a stray shot from the three-fifty-seven would go right through the trailer's wall.

"I've got a key," Jarret said. From the sound of her voice, she was almost on the front steps.

"Course you do. Ol' Massa Matt didn't deprive himself of all the luxuries, not him."

Jarret's hands were steadier than mine. She got her key in the lock on the first try. I stood up as the door banged against the back wall.

"Lucy, I'm home!" Russo called out.

Jarret came stumbling up the steps. She was too off balance to notice me or keep her feet. The giggling man who'd pushed her stepped into the threshold next. He saw or sensed me right away and dodged the descending arc of my gun barrel. I still managed to land a glancing blow that sent him sprawling onto Jarret.

I took his place in the doorway, my gun hand moving in search of the man holding the magnum. He was already raising it, the barrel looking like a naval gun at that range. He was biting his lower lip with a big front tooth. I remembered as I pulled the trigger that he'd bitten the same lip while swinging his pool cue at me. His gun went off when mine did. He and his shot both hit the sand.

The one on the left was already backpedaling, so I fired at the one on the right, and he dropped his beer and ran. His buddy got off one wild shot, shattering a window.

Behind me, Jarret was screaming. I swung the door shut and turned to help. She was struggling with Russo, who had one hand on a gun of his own, a frontier Colt. I cracked him on his scarred ear with my World War II model and collected his.

Jarret was trying to scramble to her feet. I pushed her back down and joined her there, tipping over the little dining-room table for extra cover.

"Think you could make it out through the bedroom window?" I asked when we'd caught our breath.

"No way I'm leaving you, Elliott." She made it sound like I'd be lost without her, while all the time squeezing the blood out of my arm.

I freed myself to crawl to a front window to check on our guests. The two beer carriers had taken up positions behind a little breastwork of sand, about half the distance to the nearest full-size dune. They were well within pistol range, I was sorry to see. Burt, the man I'd shot, was still frozen in the act of making a sand angel.

The sight of him kept me too long at the shattered window. The survivors spotted me and loosed off a few rounds, breaking another window and knocking a framed photograph from the wall. The long roll of shattering glass reminded me of the death knell of Robert Sears, the client I never knew I had. And it brought the moaning Russo fully awake.

I was back behind the table by then. When another chorus of shots inspired Russo to crawl our way, I planted a heel on the top of his head.

"Stop firing, goddamnit!" he shouted at the nearest window. "Stop firing and wait for Hector!"

Once the shooting had stopped, he snarled at Jarret and me. "You wait, too. He'll be here any minute. Let's see what you do against three guns and a brain."

"I've met Hector," I reminded him.

Jarret was pressing against me again, her lips at my ear. "What *do* we do, Elliott?"

She was more herself now than she'd been at Hedison's house. Still scared, but stony sober.

"Think of it as a plot problem," I said. "How would you work it out?"

"I'd have John Wayne ride in with the cavalry, like he does in *Rio Grande.*"

Just then the Duke Wayne picture that came to my mind was *The Alamo,* but I said, "I'll see what I can do."

She gave me some space while I changed the clip in my gun. Then she pressed in again.

"Listen, Elliott. What that scumbag said about Matt's father being rich, it isn't true."

It also wasn't important, but we had to pass the time some way. "Hedison told me McNeal spit silver spoons."

"That's what Matt told everybody. He didn't want people to know how poor his folks were. He should have been proud of working himself out of that, but he kept it his big secret. I wanted you to know, none of this happened because Matt was too stubborn to ask for money."

I squeezed her hand, but we weren't done. In fact, we were just getting to her point.

"That scumbag said it was Matt who told him where I was."

The scumbag giggled.

I said, "I've been wanting to try out this hog leg," and unlimbered the old Colt. "What do you say we shoot at his toes until he tells us the truth?"

Russo didn't even make me draw the hammer back. "It was Riddle, the fat pig. He told me where you were. But McNeal told me about the other one, the guy who fucked up the whole deal, the dude with the camera."

"The dude you killed," I said.

"Not me, buddy. It was Burt. Burt killed them all."

That was encouraging. Russo wouldn't have been lining up

fall guys if he still liked his prospects.

"Burt killed Maitlan because he'd gotten me called in?"

"Not just for that. That's why we hunted him down. When we found him, one of my boys recognized him. He said Maitlan was one of two who'd snuck you off while I was down. Him and some hippie chick. He wouldn't tell us where you were. We—I mean Burt—asked him too hard."

He distracted me from a follow-up by muttering, "Where the hell is Hector?"

I risked a quick look out the back window, in case the answer to that question was sneaking up behind us. It wasn't. I ducked back down, expecting any second to hear the crack of a pistol. What came was deeper and duller, like a distant sonic boom. Before the dunes had finished playing catch with the sound, a ball of black smoke rolled upward from the parking area.

"The bikes," Russo said.

He started to scramble toward the door. This time I did cock the revolver's hammer. Then another gas tank went up, followed by two more almost on top of one another.

"Who the fuck?" Russo said.

"John Wayne," I said and made for the window. The two gunmen were running for the towers of black smoke. They were weaving as they ran and were already too far away for me to hit, but I fired anyway, to warn whoever was beyond the dunes.

Russo was still in shock. "What happened to Hector?"

"He sold you out," Jarret sneered at him. "He didn't want to go down with a psychopath. He brought the cops!"

I told them both to shut up. I was straining to hear the sound of gunfire. Nothing came.

"Now what?" Jarret asked, taking the words out of my mouth.

A figure appeared at the head of the path, a broad-shouldered man in a double-breasted suit and a board chairman's hat, ap-

234

parently out for a Sunday stroll. Once in the clearing, he paused to light his cigar. Then he waved the hat over his head.

THIRTY-FOUR

I left Paddy and his latest pupil to deal with the mop-up at Point Dume. The pupil's name was Cooper, and he was a sheriff's deputy who'd happened to be passing Renaldo's when Paddy's call for help hit the airwaves. Together, they'd tailed the gang, disarmed Hector, torched the Harleys, and taken the two bikers who'd had Jarret and me pinned down, all without firing a shot. When I'd thanked him, the deputy had seemed a little puzzled as to how the miracle had been worked, but I knew it would come to him eventually. In later tellings he might leave Paddy out altogether.

There'd be hell to pay over my leaving, what with Burt lying dead in the sand, but Paddy had waved it off, saying, "If you know where the Combs girl is, go get her. We're clearing up four murders for the police, counting Sears. That'll occupy their minds for days at least."

I barely made it to the highway before the reinforcements came charging up like the cavalry I'd promised Jarret. I drove past them slowly and carefully, and not just because I didn't want to be pulled over with a warm gun in my holster. The steering wheel of the Dodge was shaking like the one in the Zodiac panel truck, only this time the problem wasn't a bent rim. It was me. Somehow I made it to Hollywood and Vine without killing anyone else and found a parking space near the Zodiac Building. On my way in I nodded to the effigies of Gilbert and Shearer. I was pretty sure Norma nodded back.

Like me, the front office was running on empty. The secretarial staff was still present—they probably kept longer hours than Norad—but instead of answering phones and shuffling paper, they were engaged in redecorating. The overdue poster for *Queen of Blood* had finally arrived. All the other posters in the room were being shifted one place to the left, so the oldest could be rotated out and the new one added. *Die, Zombie, Die* had lost the place of honor by the front door. As I watched, its former spot beneath the electric sign identifying the company's newest release was taken by a lurid rendering of bikini-clad women with a green tint to their skin and blood on their fangs. Its best people were dead or bound for jail, but Zodiac marched on.

Hedison might have been touchy on the subject of marching just then. When I entered his office, he was sitting with his leg propped up on a chair, an ice bag on the knee Paddy had knighted. A little surplus ice was cooling a glass of general anesthetic on his desk.

"Did you hand them over to the cops?" he asked as soon as the door shut behind me.

"In a manner of speaking." I'd already decided to let Paddy deliver our official report. Few of our past clients had deserved the royal treatment more than Hedison.

"How about *Duo-Glide Rider*?"

"Don't order a frame for the poster," I said. "And think twice about the poster."

The big man moved the ice bag to his forehead. "Why on earth did I hire you guys?"

"Let's talk about that. You said someone recommended us. Who?"

"Are you going to make trouble for him?"

"He won't get off with a sore knee." Not if I was finally seeing things as they were.

"Good. It was Ted LeRoy, the nosy bum."

I wasn't surprised, but I tried to act it. "LeRoy the nudie guy? How do you know him?"

"All the local small-fry know each other. We use a lot of the same freelancers, borrow each other's equipment, cry on each other's shoulders. We've talked about giving a name to our group—the Microorganisms of Hollywood, Ted wanted—but we've never done it."

"When did he put in the plug for us?"

"About ten minutes before I first called your boss. I don't know how he'd heard I was having problems. He's got a nose for other people's troubles. He sees them as opportunities, I think."

"I think so, too," I said. "When I turned you down, did you call him to complain?"

"No, he called me, to see how things had gone. I told him you weren't interested, and he said to give it time. Sure enough, you came around. So, Elliott, if the police show up here—"

"If? You should put on a pot of coffee right now."

"Okay. But what do I tell them?"

"Whatever Paddy tells you to tell them. In the meantime, don't warn LeRoy that we're coming his way. If you do, your current troubles will seem like the good old days at USC."

In the outer office, the secretaries were arguing over whether the *Queen of Blood* poster was hanging straight, which naturally drew my eyes to the Rembrandt. After a time, my gaze wandered from the aliens' D-cups to the printing at the bottom of the poster. I scanned the cast list from old habit and saw a name I knew. That wasn't an odd thing in itself, given where I lived and worked, but this name got me out of low gear. It was the last one I'd expected to see sharing a frame with space vampires: Forrest Combs.

Forrest Stick-up-his-ass Combs, it might have read, the man

so jealous of his good name it was the first thing he thought of when his only child tried for a career in skin flicks. The man who preferred genteel poverty to getting his hands dirty. The man I'd been kicking myself for letting down.

That name was yet another piece clicking into place, and the click was so loud it changed my plans. I borrowed a phone and called the vice squad. My friend Lieutenant Sharpe was still hard at it. And still inclined to forgive the world for its many shortcomings. When I told him that Ted LeRoy was the man behind the underground porno films, I could almost hear him turning the other cheek.

"Can't be him, Scotty. LeRoy's been around longer than Lawrence Welk. And he's at least as harmless. They'll be showing his stuff on the late show before we're much older."

"What better front man could the mob have found? I'll explain it all to you later. For now, put some men on his studio. Make sure they have that picture I left with you. Search any car going in or out for the girl, especially the ones going out. I'll be there in an hour."

Combs's brown Matador was baking its paint in the front drive of his ranch. Otherwise, I might not have knocked on the home's front door as long as I did, which was so long the swelling around my knuckles came back. When the actor finally showed up, I understood the delay. He was a good half bottle into the day's drinking, though the sight of me sobered him a little.

"Scotty, my God! What happened to you? It was that awful concert, wasn't it? It's been all over the television. Did something happen to Miranda up there? Tell me, Scotty, please."

I pushed him backward into the shuttered living room, but gently. "I didn't find Miranda in Avenal. As far as I know, she was never there."

"But who did this to you?"

I had him to the sofa by then. He sat down with a thump as soon as the backs of his knees touched it.

"That's more story than we have time for now. I came to ask you a few questions. The last ones."

"Anything, Scotty, of course." He looked around vaguely.

I retrieved his drink from the coffee table for him, ignoring the reproving look his late wife was giving me from her altar-piece.

"I just came from Roland Hedison's office. I took on a job for him as a way of getting to the concert. I didn't think his problems had anything to do with yours. Now I'm not so sure."

I was more than unsure. I was seeing both cases as strands of a single web. Combs seemed to be feeling the same way. He was pushing himself back into the sofa like he hoped he'd slip between the cushions.

"I don't understand," he said.

"Let's figure it out together. What made you go to work for Zodiac?"

He started to deny he'd ever heard of the place. Then he said, "Money, of course. Why else would one do something one's ashamed of? Miranda's nearly college age. I want to send her away somewhere, somewhere with a good reputation. To give her an education that would make up for all of this."

The sweeping gesture with his now-empty glass took in the whole San Fernando Valley.

"I told my agent I'd consider absolutely any offers, and he called my bluff. He came back with Hedison's project, *Queen of Blood*. It was a foreign film he'd bought for pennies, made in Czechoslovakia of all places. He planned to dub it, of course, but he also wanted to add new scenes. That's where I came in.

"I played a scientist named Eisenstein. Get it? I was the head of a UN science organization. I wore a lab coat to prove it. I contacted the space vampires by radio and, all unknowing, guided them to earth. We shot my scenes in an awful rented studio. I have no idea how well they fit in with the rest of the story. I hope I never know."

He was overplaying, even given his drinking and his natural tendency to chew the scenery. I said, "It's not that bad. You didn't stick up a bank."

"What I did was worse. Don't you see, Scotty? It's what drove Miranda away. If I was going to sell out, sell my good name, my almighty good name, why shouldn't she? I was selling myself. Why shouldn't she sell her body in some basement studio? Or on the street outside?"

He'd worked himself up to a bout of sobbing, which I countered with a fresh drink and a Parliament. I lit another of his cigarettes for myself and settled a little heavily on the coffee table.

Everything hung together for Combs. He had his connection between Hedison's epic and Miranda's disappearance: His act of selling out had driven Miranda away. But that wasn't the link I was after.

"Do you remember who you worked with at Zodiac?" I asked, getting methodical now that it was too late to buy me much.

"Roland himself, of course. The ex-footballer."

"Who else?"

"The director, an Italian youngster named Coppolini. He and I wrote my scenes together. If they'd been ready to go, we could have finished in a day. You can't imagine what it was like, Scotty. It was an overheated little room with a desk. On it was a cardboard box with dials that was supposed to be an interstellar radio. That was the whole set. The only people there besides myself and Mr. Coppolini were a young man who arranged the lights and ran the camera and a sound man older than the other two put together. He was quite an interesting old duffer. Told me he once recorded Garbo. He—"

"Do you happen to remember the cameraman's name?"

As I asked that question, I could almost hear the crackle of a police cruiser's radio.

"Maitlan," Combs said. "Ben Maitlan. A nice young chap."

That confirmed the information I'd brought with me. Now I went after something only Combs could tell me. "How did Miranda find out about *Queen of Blood*?"

"I told her about it. Not right away. But as the release date approached, I thought it better that she hear about it from me. I tried to make light of it, and she seemed to take it well. But she must not have done. After a week or two that now seem idyllic, she disappeared."

"When you told her, did you mention Maitlan's name?"

"Yes. Meeting him was almost the one bright spot of the whole business for me. As I said, he's a nice young chap, the kind I hope Miranda meets someday."

THIRTY-FIVE

I wasn't far from Ted LeRoy's and my promised rendezvous with the vice squad, but I didn't head that way. I drove a couple of blocks to the home of Glenn Starkey, Miranda's first fan. He was seated on the curb in front of his house between two younger kids, the bookends making Starkey seem an even odder match for a would-be porn star.

I didn't bother getting out of the Charger since my agenda for the meeting consisted of exactly one item. It was another question I should have asked days back and hadn't. Starkey ambled over when I waved to him, did the usual double take when he got a good look at me, and took a step back. If it hadn't been for the peanut gallery on the curb, he might have cut and run.

"You should see the other guy," I said, though that might have scarred him for life.

Starkey collected himself and asked a question that made me like him. "Is Miranda okay?"

"Not yet." A woman came out onto the front porch, wiping her hands on her skirt. "I need to know about the music she listened to. Was she a fan of a group called the Proposition?"

"Those mother—" Starkey blushed. "Sorry. No, she didn't listen to those creeps. She liked the Strawberry Alarm Clock and Jefferson Airplane."

I usually found those kind of jokey names irritating, but just then they sounded great. I thanked Starkey, tipped the hat I wasn't wearing to the woman on the porch, and drove off.

Again, not to LeRoy's. I headed west down the valley, content for once with the unhurried pace of the traffic on Ventura Boulevard. To pass the drive, I told myself a story.

Once upon a time, a girl whose mother had been a burlesque queen decided to take up where Momma left off. She found her way to the studios of Ted LeRoy, where, during the course of a phony screen test, she met a freelance cameraman named Ben Maitlan. She was smitten with Maitlan, eggplant head and all, so smitten that she'd carried a torch for him, one that had kept her from finding a boyfriend her own age.

That part wasn't hard to sell myself. Miranda seemed to like them underfed, and Maitlan had had an easygoing charm. He was an older man to boot and worldly, at least compared with the boys at Reseda High. Even the character flaw Maitlan's mother had fretted over, a certain amorality where getting his was concerned, might have been attractive to a girl Miranda's age.

They didn't have much time together; LeRoy handed her back to her father on the very day they met. But later, when Combs mentioned meeting Maitlan, it was enough to send Miranda off again in search of her prince. They didn't live happily ever after. The prince's boss was involved with some pretty shady stuff by then, stuff he hadn't been involved with when he'd tossed her back to her dad. Not harmless nudies but hard-core porn, financed by the mob. The prince or his boss decided that Miranda was just what their new customers in Thailand wanted to see. End of fairy tale.

Not that they'd grabbed her right away. There had to have been a time when she was sneaking out to see Maitlan behind her father's back, the week or two Combs was now remembering as idyllic. It had to have been that way, because she'd seen Topanga Canyon and raved about it to Glenn Starkey. And he'd told me. My showing up there had been the catalyst for everything that happened afterward. When I'd come by his studio, LeRoy had handled me without breaking a sweat. But when I'd found my way to the Infinite Pad, he'd gotten worried. He'd decided to distract Hollywood Security with a paying job, which he happened to know we needed. He'd heard about the marijuana smuggling plaguing Zodiac. Ben Maitlan had picked up the rumor at the Zodiac watercooler and passed it along to the gossip-loving LeRoy. LeRoy had contacted Hedison and suggested that he employ us. When I'd played hard to get, LeRoy had had one of his people call me to tell me about the Proposition and the big concert where they'd be playing and where their groupie Miranda was sure to be. That had set the hook but good.

The Zodiac business might have kept me away from LeRoy forever—it was that messy all by itself—if it hadn't been for Maitlan. The human shuttlecock was back on the Zodiac side of the net by then and incautiously telling people that he was the guy who'd gotten me hired, which was indirectly true, given that he'd told LeRoy about the pot. He'd been blaming himself when he made that admission, according to Jarret, and that was easy to understand, since by then LeRoy's little diversion had gotten Sears killed.

All of which meant that I probably had Sharpe's men watching an empty rabbit hole. It wasn't likely that Miranda was at LeRoy's legitimate studio. But it never hurt to be safe. And this arrangement gave me a chance to pay off a debt.

Maitlan had tried to tell me what was really going on more than once. That fit his mother's fond belief that he was ready to turn his back on the sordid business he'd gotten tangled up in. Being his mother, she naturally gave him the benefit of the doubt. And I owed Maitlan the same break. Owed him that and more, the man who'd saved my life at the cost of his own.

At Woodland Hills, I picked up Topanga Canyon Boulevard and headed south. It was almost evening by then and quiet, once I was up in the hills. Near the ridgeline, it was also cool. When I started down the other side, I did it slowly, almost crawling into the horseshoe bend that held the boxcar and caboose and the Infinite Pad.

The old house turned head shop was once again the hub of local activity, such as it was. Two figures were coming down its rickety steps, two women, a lady wrestler and the woman she was supporting. A Volkswagen Beetle was parked in the Pad's gravel lot.

I floored the Dodge and then slammed on the brakes. It slid to a stop at the edge of the gravel, blocking the Volkswagen in. I was out of the car before the woman doing the heavy lifting had a chance to move. It was Myrna, the bargain-size brunette who'd looked on in silence while I'd tackled the two teenage robbers. She proved that she'd been paying attention that day by using the same tactic that had worked so well against me then. Without a warm-up, she threw the other woman my way like she was tossing a beach ball.

I made a catch Hedison's old coaches would have smiled on and still managed to draw my gun and align the sights on Myrna's broad back as she ran for the trees. She didn't turn on me and paw the ground, so I let her go.

The woman I'd fielded was a teenager with golden blonde hair and lots of it. She was barefoot in jeans and a sweatshirt, and her face was puffy and pale, except around her eyes, where the skin was dark. Despite the wear and tear, I would have known her even if I hadn't taken to carrying her picture around in my wallet. She was the breathing image of her dead mother, Betty Ann.

Miranda Combs, at long last.

"Judge Crater, I presume," I said and hugged her.

She didn't respond, not to the nonsense dialogue or the hug or to being shaken gently. I checked her pulse. It was slow but steady, which gave me the nerve to leave her, though that was hard after all I'd gone through to find her. I carried her to the Charger first, got her comfortable in its backseat, and locked her in.

The inside of the Infinite Pad looked like Avenal on D-day plus one. I found Jill sitting up in a heap of secondhand clothes, rubbing one eye and sobbing as she had back at our tent. As far as I knew, she'd never stopped.

I searched the rest of the house, looking for other lost daughters and not finding any. I did find a makeshift movie studio in one of the bedrooms, but I left that for Ed Sharpe and his boys to pick over. Back downstairs, I got Jill on her feet and checked her eye. She'd have a shiner in the morning but wasn't hurt otherwise.

"Myrna's taken her," she said. "I tried to stop her. LeRoy called. He said the police were watching his place."

"Miranda's fine," I told her. To reassure us both, I took her out front where she could see the sleeping beauty hard at it.

"What did Myrna give her?"

"Just the usual sleeping pills. She'll be okay in a couple of hours."

I'd feel better when I'd gotten a second opinion on that. But there was a final bit of business to attend to first.

"Do you want to hightail it from here or from somewhere down in the valley? That's where I'm heading."

"You're letting me go?" Her surprise squeezed her eyes dry.

If she'd been there, Ella could have given her transference theory another workout. I wasn't able to save Jackie Jarret from the police, she might have said, so I was saving Jill, sending her back to Minnesota sadder but wiser. My actual motive was much simpler.

"I owe you. And Ben. He was the one who helped you get me away from the Ninth Circle."

"I helped him," Jill said.

Her finding me just when I'd needed her hadn't been the million-to-one miracle I'd taken it for. She'd rendezvoused with her boyfriend Maitlan by then, which had put her ringside for my bout with the Ninth Circle. Together, they'd gotten me away while the gang had tended to Russo. Then Maitlan had died without trying to bargain my hiding place for his life. He couldn't, not without endangering the flower child he'd left to watch over me. He'd died to save her. The least I could do for him was finish the job.

"What's it going to be?"

"Will you be able to get LeRoy without me?"

"I don't know. Miranda can testify. Maybe Myrna, when they catch her."

"The girl doesn't know that part of it. And Myrna will spit in the cops' eyes. No, I'm sticking." She pulled on the locked door of the Charger. "Let's go."

"This won't be any parking ticket. Ben wouldn't want you in prison."

"You'll get me a deal, flatfoot. If you don't, I'll tell them you smoked pot."

"You'll need something on the judge, not me."

"I don't care. Ben paid for what he did. Now it's my turn."

"How did Ben explain you to Miranda?"

"I was his sister. She believed anything he told her."

And look where it had gotten her, I thought. Or maybe said. Jill certainly reacted as though I'd spoken aloud.

"Ben meant to get her home. I know he did. Now I want to see it done."

THIRTY-SIX

We took Miranda to a medical center in Woodland Hills. While they were pumping her stomach, I borrowed a phone from a sympathetic nurse. I called Forrest Combs and then Ed Sharpe to tell him to reel in LeRoy. Then I phoned a lawyer pal of Paddy's who specialized in deals with the police. He was there patting Jill's hand when Sharpe came for her. Long before that, Combs had arrived, driven by Glenn Starkey, so I was free to slip away.

I drove to Winnie Mannero's pink house in Beverly Hills, where my hospital haircut scared first a busload of evening-shift tourists, then Winnie, then Gabrielle. My daughter ended up in my arms, crying, finally, like she'd been saving it up for years. She was the third crying woman I'd held that day. This time, I joined in.

Our hostess left us to it for as long as she could. The thing that forced Winnie to interrupt finally was the need to pass on bad news. Ella had taken off an hour earlier, heading for the beach house.

So Gabby and I started for Malibu. Our part of it was called "the other Malibu" by the better-heeled locals. When we'd bought our place in the fifties, it had been one of a string of old rental cottages on a dead-end street that ran between the highway and the beach. Most of those places had been razed and replaced, and the few that remained, like ours, had been seriously remodeled.

Ours still had its original board-and-batten siding, though, over which the wind and I had fought a long tug of war. Every summer I added paint, and every winter the elements sanded it away. Lately, I'd had an ally in the fight: Billy. I thought of him when I saw the place, and not just because of the siding. His surfboard was still leaning casually in the carport. Beside it was Ella's car.

She'd left the front door unlocked. The inside of the cottage was dark and musty. And empty. We walked through to the back, where the rooms had a reddish cast courtesy of the sunset taking place outside. We went out through the screen door and spotted Ella. She was standing at the surf line, a small figure with crossed arms, facing the setting sun.

It was quite a show just then, the sun a dark-red ball right above the horizon, its color picked up by a spray of clouds, by a million crimson peaks in the darkening blue of the sea, and by the bloody foam at Ella's feet.

I was pretty sure she wasn't seeing any of that. I started down to her, but her poet daughter, who had me by the hand, tugged me to a halt. We sat down together, on a dune already cool and damp, to wait.

ABOUT THE AUTHOR

Terence Faherty is the author of eleven novels and three novellas, including five titles in the Shamus-winning Scott Elliott private-eye series set in the golden age of Hollywood. His other books are from his Macavity-winning and Edgar-nominated Owen Keane series, which follows the adventures of a failed seminarian turned amateur detective. Faherty's short stories have appeared in *Ellery Queen Mystery Magazine, Alfred Hitchcock Mystery Magazine, Strand Magazine,* and in anthologies published in the United States and the United Kingdom. His novels have been reissued in Italy, Germany, and Japan. Faherty, a former technical writer who lectures on the films of Basil Rathbone, lives in Indianapolis with his wife Jan.